"Hold me, Kelly." It was a gentle, undemanding entreaty, Jonathan's voice soft against her mouth. Kelly heard the sounds he made deep in his throat as her fingers explored his rib cage, drifting in slow motion over the high bone of his hip, across the tautness of his stomach, into the crease of his thigh.

The sharp intake of Jonathan's breath parted her moist lips and her body pressed closer as his kiss became more demanding, his hands insistent in their probing, seeking, taking, giving. Jonathan loved her the way she had known his love would be, bringing to reality Kelly's dreams of being held the way he was holding her tonight. It had taken months to fulfill the sweetest of her dreams, but it was all there as he claimed her for his own. . . .

Dear Reader,

It is our pleasure to bring you a new experience in reading that goes beyond category writing. The settings of **Harlequin American Romance** give a sense of place and culture that is uniquely American, and the characters are warm and believable. The stories are of "today" and have been chosen to give variety within the vast scope of romance fiction.

The importance of seeing-eye dogs trained to work with small children is the subject of articles written by the heroine, Kelly O'Neil, in Zelma Orr's *In the Eyes of Love*. This writer takes you on a strange and compelling journey where reality is not always what it seems.

From the early days of Harlequin, our primary concern has been to bring you novels of the highest quality. **Harlequin American Romance** is no exception. Enjoy!

Vivian Stephens

Vivian Stephens
Editorial Director
Harlequin American Romance
919 Third Avenue,
New York, N.Y. 10022

In the Eyes of Love

ZELMA ORR

Harlequin Books

TORONTO • NEW YORK • LONDON
AMSTERDAM • PARIS • SYDNEY • HAMBURG
STOCKHOLM • ATHENS • TOKYO • MILAN

Published August 1983

First printing June 1983

ISBN 0-373-16018-6

Printed in Canada

Chapter One

The gentle breeze stirred mixed fragrances past Kelly's nose, and her steps were springy as she started the four blocks to the library. Late spring in Utah was a beautiful time of year when temperatures were mild, neither hot nor cold, and flowers rioted, spraying perfume for her to inhale. Short tendrils from the cap of red-gold hair brushed her cheek. She stopped, listening to the birds mix their melodies in a lilting choral rendition of their spring symphony. Shifting the books to her left arm, she started on, catching the sound of occasional traffic on the street, relatively quiet at this time of day. Her next step hit wrong and she stumbled forward, her ankle turning, and books went flying as a horn gave an angry blast. There was a squeal of tires as her wrist came down hard on the bumper of a car.

The slam of the car door, hurried steps, and muffled swearing came all at once. "Can't you see something as big as a car and look before you step into the street?" an angry voice blasted her. "Where the hell is your mind?"

When she didn't say anything, the voice changed to ask brusquely, "Are you all right?"

She wasn't. Her heart hammered in her chest and she leaned against the warm hood of the car, her voice quavering as she said, "I think so."

A deep indrawn breath was followed by another accusation. "You young kids run around like you own the world, your head in the clouds, expecting everyone else to look out for you. For two cents, I'd put you over my knee and spank you."

Kelly stood still, waiting for the tirade to cease, not moving an inch. An impatient sound was followed by a cool, "If you'll move, I'll be on my way. If you don't think that's asking too much." The sarcasm wasn't lost on Kelly and she straightened.

"Can you hand me my books? Then I'll get out of your way," she said, wincing at the explosion.

"What? You want me to pick up your books and point you in the right direction with my blessings, is that it?" The voice was deeper now, anger building with each breath.

"Yes, please."

There was a long silence, but she could sense the hostility, the urge to shake her that was evident in the charged air. Through clenched teeth the male voice told her, "Get your books yourself, young lady, and be glad I don't turn you over to the police for jaywalking." His footsteps moved away.

She had scared him out of his wits and she didn't blame him for his anger. "Please," she said. "Don't leave me here. I'm sorry I stepped in front of you, but I was enjoying the pretty morning and I guess I miscounted."

"Miscounted?" The voice came back toward her. "Miscounted? Are you also trying not to step on the cracks in the sidewalk? Of all the juvenile—" The voice choked.

"I can't see," she said quietly. "I count steps on each block, but I stopped back there and forgot how many more steps it was to the curb." She could almost feel the snap of his head as he looked at her, feel his disbelieving glance cover the slender figure in front of him, paying attention to the eyes that were wide open, not exactly looking straight at him.

The silence grew and she spoke urgently. "Please, just hand me the books and my cane too. Even if it's broken, I can still use it."

There were no words spoken but she heard movement, then the books were in her outstretched hand.

"The cane isn't broken. Which hand holds it?" the now subdued voice asked.

"My left, please." As her fingers closed over the head of the white cane, she said, "Just turn me to the curb and I'll be all right." A hand on her arm guided her and the voice said, "Take two steps, then up," which she did.

Drawing in her breath, she said, "Thank you, and I'm really sorry. I usually pay more attention, but this morning—" She shrugged and smiled toward the breathing she could hear. When he had handed her the cane, she had smelled after-shave lotion that reminded her of tangerines at Christmas, light and tangy, with pleasant memories attached. His hand on her arm now was firm, and she could tell he was a tall man from the angle at which his voice reached her.

"Where are you going?" he asked.

"The library on the next corner," she told him.

"How do you know it's on the next corner?"

"I've already walked three blocks, so I have one more to go, cross that street, turn left sixty-five steps, then there are fifteen steps up to a landing, six more to the next five steps that go up, and sixteen across to the door." She grinned. "So, you see, I have to concentrate or I'll never make it. Spring fever got to me today and I am sorry."

"I'm the one who's sorry. I'll drive you to the library."

She shook her head. "No, thanks, I'll be all right."

"My name is Jonathan Heath, if you're worried about who's picking you up."

The name meant nothing to Kelly but she said, "It

isn't that, Mr. Heath. I have to depend on myself and
there's no need for you to be troubled. Thanks, anyway." She moved back from the curb, careful now to
count her steps.

She felt him hesitate. "Why are you going to the library? Does someone get the books for you and read
them?"

She laughed. "Of course not. The books are in
Braille, see?" She extended the books toward his
voice. "I've been there so much everyone knows me
and I know where all the books are that I can use.
When they get new ones, Mrs. Linton, the librarian,
saves them for me."

"I see." She could feel his eyes on her, taking in
everything probably. "Are you sure I can't drop you
there?"

"Yes, thank you, Mr. Heath." She heard him walk
away, the car door close, and the soft purr of the car
engine. She listened to the sound recede, then, taking
a deep breath, finished her interrupted trip to the library.

After seating herself at a table near the front of the
library, Kelly thumbed through two new books Mrs.
Linton had brought her. One was on the schools where
Braille was taught and another on how to acquire a
seeing-eye dog. She had attended one school for
Braille and quickly adapted to the use of it. She was
more interested in the dogs, knowing how much they
could mean to a nonseeing person. If she had had one
this morning, she would never have miscounted her
steps and ended up almost under a car. She drew a
sharp breath. Just a careless moment when she had
stopped to savor the lovely spring morning. What most
people took for granted twenty-four hours a day, three
hundred sixty-five days of the year, had almost cost her
life.

Mr. Heath was justifiably upset, she knew, but he

had seemed appeased once he realized she couldn't see him nor his car. He thought her a child and she wouldn't have blamed him if she could have seen herself—dressed in jeans, a light blue T-shirt, and tennis shoes, her short hair windblown in a shining mass over her forehead, thick dark brown lashes over eyes not quite opaque, but the color of doeskin. She was five foot five inches tall, weighing 110 pounds, not petite at all, but the facial expression was much younger-looking than her twenty-six years.

Kelly thumbed through the book on the seeing-eye dogs, thinking of her chances to get one. If she did, then loneliness was something else the dog would help. Friends weren't available at all times, no matter how attentive they were; they did have lives of their own, and she didn't want anyone around all the time, anyway. Dogs were costly and organizations who worked with them were frequently limited in funds with too many needy people waiting, but she had hope.

Even without a dog, Kelly was rather independent. She worked for the local paper, doing very well at her job as roving reporter with the help of tape recorders, was an excellent typist, depending on no one but herself, much to Fred Tate's chagrin at times. Fred worked on the paper with her, but he would have liked for her to be more dependent on him for some things.

She checked out the two new books and started home. After the noon hour now, traffic had picked up, so she paid attention to her steps, reaching her small ground-floor apartment without mishap. Her building was one of the lovely old homes converted into four apartments: two downstairs, two upstairs. Kelly's was a one-bedroom, a sitting room-kitchenette combination plus a bath with dressing area, which she was proud of, simply because it boasted lots of shelves where, by feeling and smelling, she separated clothing into sets. From time to time Cora, the woman from upstairs, stopped to check on colors for her, but she made out quite well alone.

She fitted her key into the lock, felt to the left to her mailbox, but she either didn't have any mail or it was too early. Usually Mr. Shields would knock on Saturdays when she was home and hand her the mail. She had left a window up and could still smell the fragrance that had caused her distraction and almost catastrophe. Her movements in the apartment were automatic and without counting, she seldom miscalculated. Hanging the cane on a chair, she placed the books on the table nearby where they'd be handy when she got ready for them.

Excitement must have tired her, for she felt ready for a nap, kicked off her shoes, and lay across the bed. Fingers on her Braille watch face said two thirty. *I can eat after I have a nap,* she thought, her face turned toward the breeze coming in the window.

Kelly stretched, slowly letting consciousness bring her awake, and sat up as she heard a knock at the door. Maybe the mailman, she thought, fingers checking the time. *Gracious, almost five. I was really tired to sleep so long.*

"Just a minute," she called, hurrying toward the door and bumping a chair in the process of moving too fast.

"Who is it?" she asked, hand on the doorknob. She seldom had callers unless Cora or Fred came by, but Fred was on an assignment and shouldn't be back before late Sunday, and Cora worked Saturdays.

A deep, well-remembered voice answered, "It's Jonathan Heath."

Oh, Lord, she thought, *maybe I damaged his car.* Pulling the door open, she smiled. "Yes, Mr. Heath?"

"May I come in?" She could tell he too was smiling.

"Yes, of course." She unhooked the screen and

stood back for him to enter, catching the tangy fragrance of his after-shave as he walked past her. Leaning against the door, she waited for him to speak.

"Did I wake you?" he asked.

Her head lifted. "Why do you ask?"

"Your face is flushed and your cheek has the imprint of your hand on it."

"Oh." She was flustered, thinking how she must look. "Yes. I slept longer than I intended. Please sit down." As she heard him at the big chair, she moved to the small couch. "Did I damage your car?"

"What?" Surprise was in his voice, then he laughed. "No. No, of course not. I was in such a hurry this morning, I was afraid you may have been hurt and I came to check on you, and to apologize for being so rude."

"No need for that," she assured him. "I'm quite all right, but how did you find me?"

"Mrs. Linton, at the library, although I had to give references all the way back to kindergarten before she'd give me your name and address." The deep voice was dry.

Kelly laughed. "I'll bet you did, knowing Mrs. Linton. What finally convinced her?"

"My fatal charm, of course, which I'm hoping will also convince you to have dinner with me tonight."

"Yes, but she can see you," she teased back.

"Perhaps that's why she doubted my honorable intentions," he said. "It's a little early to eat, but if you'll agree, I'll pick you up at seven."

"Mr. Heath, I don't think—"

"Please. I'm alone in the big city and surely you can take pity so I don't have to eat alone."

She still hesitated, wondering who this man was. *If I could see....*

"Would you like me to call my mother and let her vouch for me, Kelly?"

She laughed. "No, that won't be necessary. All right. I'll be ready at seven. Informal, I hope."

"Yes." He stood, but didn't move toward the door, and after a moment, he said, "You aren't a teen-ager."

"No, I'm not." She smiled toward him.

"May I ask how close to being a teen-ager you are? I'm afraid people may think I'm robbing the cradle."

"I'm twenty-six, Mr. Heath, hardly qualifying me for the cradle. Are you old enough to be my father?" she queried, her voice light.

"Not quite. I'm thirty-five and unmarried, if that's your next question."

Smiling, she stood up. "I'll be ready at seven, and thanks for the invitation."

"Who helps you dress?" he asked.

"Why, no one," she answered, then grinned. "If you don't like my color combinations when you see me, just tell me so."

"All right," he said. The door opened, and she walked toward it. "I'll pick you up at seven, Kelly."

She heard his steps go down the sidewalk to the street, heard a car door open and close, then a motor came to life and moved out of hearing. Bemused by the unexpected visit and invitation, she went to get a glass of milk to satisfy her till dinner, since she had missed lunch by sleeping through it.

She'd make up for it at Mr. Heath's expense, she decided. *Thirty-five and unmarried, huh? Could be interesting, but I can't see him. Damn!*

She didn't dwell on that aspect of it, but went to the separate section of her closet where her dresses hung. She pushed aside hangers till her fingers touched the dress she liked, then slipped it from the hanger and chose underclothes and finally high, thin-heeled shoes and a small bag.

No time for a shampoo, she thought, spraying light

cologne over her hair and brushing it till it lay in a burnished cap over her forehead, barely curling over the lobes of her ears. Sensitive fingers selected tiny toadstool earrings to punch into her ears, and a thin gold chain to circle her throat. She couldn't see the apple-green knit dress clinging to her slim figure in just the right places, darker green pumps and bag for contrast. She was ready when the knock sounded at exactly seven.

"Who is it?" she asked.

"Jonathan."

She opened the door, smiling, and explained, "I always ask before I unlock it," she said, "since the peephole is little use to me."

"I understand," he told her. "I should have identified myself." She waited, knowing his eyes were going over her.

"You do an excellent job of coordinating. Do you know the color of the dress you have on?" Curiosity was evident in his voice.

"It's pale green, with darker shoes, but you'd better check them. I once went to a dance wearing one wine and one bright red shoe."

His laugh rang out. "You didn't!"

"Yes, I did, but, fortunately, I wore a long dress and no one noticed, till I came home and kicked off my shoes." She remembered the incident, her cheeks flushing.

"Who told you about it?" he asked, the smile still in his voice.

"My date, whom I didn't know very well at the time. And to be honest, he's rather stuffy."

"What was his reaction?"

Kelly's head tilted to one side as she mimicked Fred's rather snobbish tone. "'Well, Kelly, it looks as though we'd better get married so you'll have someone to dress you correctly.'"

"And your reply to that?" The question was very soft and he was no longer laughing.

"I asked why he couldn't dress me without being married." She laughed. "Before you ask if he choked on that, it took him two weeks to ask for another date."

His laughter showed he could imagine things like that. "Kelly O'Neil. I like that name and I don't think I'd change it to whatever his name is," Jonathan told her. "The temperature dropped. Do you have a light wrap?"

"Yes. In the closet behind you there's a lacy sweater that matches this, if you would."

A moment later he slipped the sweater around her shoulders and asked, "Ready?"

"Yes," she answered, reaching to check the lock and preceding him out the door, where he took her arm and guided her to the car.

As she sank into the luxurious seat, she took a deep breath and ran questioning fingers over the upholstery. "It smells new."

"I've had it a year but I don't use it much. The Cherokee, a four-wheel drive vehicle, is more serviceable where I live." He was concentrating on his driving and made no further comment till he told her, "I don't know much about Salt Lake City and I've been to only a few restaurants. Do you trust me?"

"Of course."

When the car stopped, she asked, "Marcellano's?" Before he could ask the question, she wrinkled her nose. "I can smell their veal parmigiana."

He touched her arm enough to guide her inside, past the tables, for which she gave him a grateful smile.

"Have you eaten here?" he asked.

"A long time ago but I remember it was excellent."

The waiter was nearby and Jonathan asked, "Would you like me to order?"

"Please." As the waiter moved away, Kelly asked, "Are you new in our neighborhood, Mr. Heath?"

"Since I'm not too old," he said, emphasizing the words. "Call me Jonathan. I'm visiting here from Santa Fe."

"I was there once," she said. "It's beautiful."

"Beautiful?" he asked. "How would you know that?"

"I could see up until a year ago," Kelly told him. "We were there in late fall and they had a very early snow that we got caught in." She smiled, remembering, and he wondered at the slow fading of that smile.

"If you could see till a year ago, what happened?"

She sat back in her chair, the unseeing amber-colored eyes looking at him. "It's something I've always had, but it was undetected until I woke one morning and couldn't see. No one knows why." Her hands moved on the tablecloth, then dropped to her lap, her glance following the movement.

"What are the chances that you'll see again?" he asked.

"That's an unknown factor."

"Who's your doctor? Do you have a specialist?" He was leaning toward her from the sound of his voice coming closer.

She smiled. "Why?"

"Because you should have the best in a case such as this."

"Right now I'm more interested in getting a seeing-eye dog, since the doctors don't know what they're looking for and I need help now rather than later."

"What's the problem in getting a dog?"

She spread her hands. "Money and availability." She warmed to her subject. "Then, should I succeed in getting a dog, I'd have to move, since dogs aren't allowed in my building. Besides the initial cost, of course, they're expensive to feed and care for."

"I thought dogs for blind people were allowed everywhere," he persisted.

"You can go anywhere with them but there are ordinances against animals in some areas for any purpose."

"All right. Suppose you moved where one is allowed?"

The waiter came with their orders and she drew in an appreciative breath. "Smells good and I'm starved." She smiled across at him. "I slept through lunch."

"There are several salad dressings. Do you have a preference?"

"Thousand Island."

"I don't mean to be a pest but can you manage all right?" Jonathan's voice was hesitant.

"Yes, really, I can, thank you. If I make a faux pas, make believe you don't know me."

He laughed at her. "Just let me know if you need anything," he said.

The meal was excellent and as they concentrated on eating, he went back to his question. "If you moved?"

"I don't want to move. I know my area, the bus that takes me to work, the corner grocer." She flashed him a grin. "And if I keep my mind on it, I can even find my way to the library without getting killed."

He grunted. "I came so close to you, it isn't funny to me yet. Maybe six months from now I can laugh about it."

"Six months from now you'll be in Sante Fe and have trouble remembering you were ever in Salt Lake City."

"Not likely," he denied, then continued. "Aren't there any buildings in your immediate vicinity that will allow a seeing-eye dog?"

"I don't know about anything nearby. If I can ever get enough money for one, enough money to train me and the dog, and think I won't let both of us starve in the meantime, then I'll think about a different apartment."

"Do you have family here?"

"I have a married sister in Albuquerque."

"There must be many organizations that work on your type of problem, the Lions Club for one."

"Yes, but I'm new at this by comparison and they have long lists of people who have waited years." Her fork lay still on her plate. "Especially children. Can you imagine not ever having seen the colors of flowers, houses, clothes, stars, or the blue sky? You don't know what's meant by 'blue sky' because you've never seen blue."

He spoke into the silence. "No, I can't imagine it."

"I'm lucky. I saw all that for twenty-five years, but I didn't pay attention because I thought it was there forever."

"You don't sound bitter."

She lifted her head, looking at him with the clear eyes he couldn't imagine not seeing. "Oh, I cry sometimes, usually over the silliest things." Her soft lips curved in a smile.

"Like what?" he asked.

"Well, I'd love to know what color your eyes and hair are." As he started to speak, she held up her hand. "Oh, I know you can tell me but I want to be sure you're truthful. You could tell me your eyes are green but actually, one is blue and one is blue and green." She sobered. "If you can see out of them, it doesn't matter." She picked up her bread, reached for her knife, and Jonathan quietly moved the butter near her hand. "The last time I cried was last week when it rained. I could hear and feel it, but I love to jump the puddles and watch the dimples when the big drops hit and the ducks swimming in the pond, tucking their heads under their wings to keep from getting wet." She laughed. "If I keep this up, you'll think I'm maudlin, if not bitter."

He changed the subject then and they went on talking and laughing. He offered dessert, which she refused.

Later, when they had left the restaurant and Jonathan was opening the door of the car, he said, "Tell me what you and your date might do since you can't see movies or plays or television. It's dark, but I could drive around and describe everything I can see." He got in beside her, started the engine, and pulled out slowly into the light nighttime traffic.

"What would you describe? The lights twinkling all over downtown Salt Lake City? The mountains tiered like dark ghosts around the hole they surround?" Her head tilted as though listening.

"How do you know what Salt Lake City looks like?"

He saw her teeth white in the dimness of the car interior. "The library abounds with books on this area, most of them in Braille as well as regular print." She was turned fully to face him as she went on. "I have tapes and a radio and have been known to sit through poetry readings."

"Fred?" he asked.

"Yes. He's quite good at it, although I do sleep sometimes."

He chuckled. "Fred doesn't catch you?"

"Well, you see—" She hesitated, about to confess that her idea of poetry was the soft, sentimental kind that rhymed and Fred's taste ran to more sophisticated prose-poetry that didn't make much sense to her.

"Go on."

"Nothing. I also skate if I have someone who doesn't mind staying close to me, but Fred doesn't skate," she finished.

"It's been years since I tried to skate."

"Are you dressed for it?"

"Why not? A business suit sounds like a sensible outfit to skate in, don't you think? Is there a rink?"

She sat up against the seat belt. "If we're on Andalusia, turn left at Cranston, go four blocks, and you can see the arena."

She felt the car turn and later as he stopped for a light he asked, "How did you know we were on Andalusia?"

"I didn't really, except I unconsciously count and arrange streets and I was guessing we had gone that far," she told him. "When I started to work on the paper, the Lions Club furnished me with a Braille map of the city and I've depended on it so much that I've almost memorized it."

He didn't say anything as the car moved, then he asked, "Is the arena the big stadium-looking building on the left?"

"Yes."

The parking gate clicked and she heard him take the ticket out. A moment later, he pulled into a parking spot.

"Doesn't look too crowded," Jonathan said.

"There are local ball games this weekend and the Rolling Stones are at the university, so it should be quiet."

Inside he rented their skates and, having removed his jacket and rolled his shirt-sleeves, checked their things, putting hers in the basket with his. She had her skates on but let him fasten them and check to make sure the hangover strap wasn't enough to trip her.

He helped her to her feet and for a moment, she was close to him, both his hands holding her upper arms. Her left hand went to his chin, fingers moving quickly across a wide mouth with firm lips parted in surprise at her touch. Fingers retreated to his right ear to the cheek, to the high peaked, thick-bristled brows, down the bridge of his nose, skimming his mouth once more, then dropping to catch his shirt collar.

"What was that for?" he asked.

She was looking straight up into his eyes and for an instant, he thought she could see him, then she grinned. "If I lose you, I want to be able to describe you."

"My hair is blond and my eyes are light blue."

She continued to look up at him. "Really?"

"Yes."

She shook her head. "I would have guessed your hair dark brown with eyes to match."

"Why?"

She shrugged. "The hair on your arms is thick and wiry and your eyebrows are too. Blondes aren't usually that wiry."

"Does being blind automatically make you psychic?"

"Psychic? No, it makes you aware of everything and you compensate for not seeing by touch."

After a moment he said, "Shall we?"

"Okay."

Music from the Broadway show *Oklahoma* played a smooth tempo and he held her arm lightly, catching her around the waist once to pull her out of someone's path. When the song ended, Jonathan guided her to the side and they leaned against the rail, both breathing hard.

"You're all right for having had no practice recently," Kelly said.

"I'd forgotten how much fun it is. Ready?" he asked as the music started again. When the haunting strains of the "Blue Danube Waltz" reached them, Jonathan's arms pulled her closer, swinging her until their thighs came together and they waltzed in smooth rhythm. As the last notes died away, they glided to a stop, and caught in the mood, she stayed in the circle of his arms, hands resting on his waist. Sighing, she lifted her head and said, "That was beautiful. Thank you."

His arms were still around her and one hand had moved up to touch her lips. "I can see them but I want to know if they are as soft as they look." His fingers drifted to her chin. "They feel soft but this should be an even better test." His breath was warm on her cheek an instant, then the lips she had touched earlier were on hers, gently questioning, easing hers apart. She stood still, fingers curling into his shirt, feeling her mouth come alive beneath his.

He lifted his head. "Yes, I was right. They are soft." Steadying her upright, he said, "The bench is just behind to your right."

She bent her knees, going down to the bench, aware of warm blood coursing through her. He knelt in front of her, big hands gentle on her ankles, removing her skates, putting her shoes on her feet before he moved away to replace his skates and gather their things.

"Ready?" His hand caught hers and they walked to the car, swinging their hands between them. They didn't talk on the way to her apartment till they reached her door. He asked, "May I come in, Kelly?"

"Yes." She walked into the room, then sensing he wasn't by her side, said "Jonathan?"

"Where's the light switch?" he asked from near the door.

"Oh, I'm sorry." An instant later the table lamp flicked on. "There aren't any ceiling lights and, believe it or not, I don't need them." She laughed lightly.

"Do you always make use of the advantages that being blind offers you, Kelly?" he asked, watching her sure movements through the room.

She stood still, remembering a small boy with fingers confidently tucked into hers and stared at the sound of his voice. "There aren't any advantages, Jonathan. It's lonely, and the dark stretches forever." She made an impatient gesture with her left hand and her voice changed. "Would you like a glass of wine?"

"Yes. Let me get it."

She shook her head, moving to a glass cabinet then to the refrigerator, fumbling less than he would have, and presented him with a small crystal glass and a napkin with the picture of a small dog sitting up to beg for food. As he waited for her to be seated, she turned back to reach for a small plate of cheese, which she placed on the table by the big chair, then, kicking off her shoes, she sat on the floor by the chair, her glass near his.

His glance went quickly around the small apartment back to the woman at his feet and he asked, "What do you do with yourself all day besides read and walk?"

"Work."

"Work?" he asked, not bothering to hide his surprise.

"Sure." She grinned up at him. "I have to eat, you know."

She couldn't see his head going from side to side in a negative movement. "How can you work? And at what?"

"I'm a newspaper columnist who does quite well at her job of reporting," she assured him, taking a sip from her glass and replacing it just a tiny bit closer to his than it had been. Leaning toward him, she said, "I know I have to live in the dark, but you and other people who take your sight for granted should learn that we are not helpless, merely different."

"But try to understand our side, Kelly," he told her. "We try to imagine ourselves blind and find it difficult to know how we'd manage."

She sat back, laughing a little. "I'm sorry. I do have a tendency to preach sometimes." She reached for her glass but took his instead. His hand stopped hers before she could take a sip.

"You may drink it if you like but this one's mine," he said, his voice light.

Color lit her face as she shook her head. "I seem to always be apologizing to you for something, but I must have moved my glass too much."

"Just a bit. Here." He placed her glass in her left hand and removed his. "Back to your job. Out of plain curiosity, tell me how you report news you can't see."

"Using a tape recorder for interviews, even telephone interviews, and all my copy is edited just like everyone else's."

"Who do you work for?"

"Hap Alston of the *Sentinel* and he's the greatest." Her voice was enthusiastic.

"Yes, I've heard of him. Gets some good shots at the unions through his editorials."

"Yes, and everyone else whom he thinks doesn't measure up," she said. "He gave me my chance on his paper but if I hadn't been able to do it to his satisfaction, I'd be gone." Her hand reached for her glass, but hesitated a second, and she felt his fingers guiding her. Smiling, she said, "And what do you do, Jonathan?"

"I have a ranch just a little southwest of Santa Fe."

"I remember mostly mountains. How do you ranch in mountains?"

"There's a lot of rolling hill country and high plains up there that makes good cattle country."

"Are you a real, honest-to-goodness cowboy?" she asked, her face alive with interest.

He laughed. "I work on the ranch, wear a hat, boots, and jeans, if that makes me a cowboy."

She continued to look up at him, then shook her head.

"Now what?" he asked.

"You don't sound like a blonde," she said. "Especially a blond cowboy."

"What kind of logic is that? I don't sound like a blonde? How can anyone sound blond or brunette or redhead?" He was laughing at her.

She stood up, moving to the side of his chair opposite their wineglasses, and sat on the arm of his chair. Her left hand went to his hair going from his forehead back, feeling the thick roughness that indicated waves. He sat still as her right hand moved down the side of his face, touching a deep groove she had missed before and she hesitated, fingers busy, then went on over the almost square chin with just a trace of beard since he had shaved, to his throat. Moving past the smoothly knotted tie, she unbuttoned two buttons of his shirt and slipped her hand into the opening to rest against the curly thickness of chest hair that her plundering revealed. Her fingers moved a little and she said, "If you're blond, this should be silkier, not so thick."

His voice was low as he asked, "Do you examine all your male friends this way?"

Wide eyes stared at him, unblinking. "I've never been curious before." She removed her hand, standing quickly to move away from him, but he caught her, pulling her down into his lap.

"I want to do some examining of my own," he said, his lips touching hers lightly, one hand supporting her head, the other caressing her breast, sliding over her hip, firm beneath the smooth knit material, trailing over her thigh, hesitating to return to her flat stomach. He pressed gently, his palm moving in a small circle. Her lips parted, stirring beneath his and her hand went back inside his shirt, fingers working into the thick hair. The pressure of his lips increased as the tip of his tongue trespassed inside her mouth, questioning, holding.

His arms folded her close a long moment, then his mouth left hers and he stood, letting her down from his lap. He steadied her on her feet, his hands resting under her elbows. She waited, wondering if it was only her heart that made all the noise. She felt his lips on her hair and he held her away from him.

"You're right, Kelly. I'm very dark, my hair is almost black and I have brown eyes."

"But why would you tell me otherwise? Surely—"

"I didn't really believe you could tell so much about a person by listening and touching," he told her. "I should have known better than to doubt you." He laughed, releasing her. "You are an education for people like me, Kelly. When Alston gives you a vacation, come to Santa Fe and I'll show you around my ranch." He stopped, taking a deep breath, and amended, "I've been there long enough that I'll be able to describe it to you so you can appreciate it."

"You're leaving Salt Lake already?" she asked, wondering at the letdown feeling she had.

"Yes, I leave early in the morning. It's a long drive and I have to be home Monday." He took her hands again. "I'll try to remember what you said about not being helpless but looking at you, it's hard to do." His lips touched hers and he said, "I'm sorry I almost ran you down but it was almost worth heart failure to meet you. Good-bye, Kelly, take care."

She heard the door close and his quick steps down the walk to his car. The car door slammed, accentuating the loneliness of the small room he had left.

Chapter Two

She wondered at the care she took in dressing for bed, wondered too at the intense wish that she could see her mouth where Jonathan had kissed her. It would look the same as when Fred kissed her, of course, but it had never crossed her mind to think about the shape of her lips where Fred touched her. Frowning, she tried to remember her response to Fred's kiss and could not. Couldn't even remember if she had ever felt a thrill from his dry, restrained lovemaking. It was just something he did because he thought she expected it of him. She remembered her hands tracing Jonathan's features, his hair, going underneath his shirt to tangle her fingers in thick chest hair, and the electric current that zinged through her when she did. He sat still for her curiosity, letting her examine all she wanted of him. She didn't know what the investigation did to him, but it stirred her to her very toes. What was the groove on his cheek? A long dimple that sliced his face? A scar? Was he ugly? No. Rugged, yes, but never ugly. His mouth was wide, belonging with the squared chin and deep-set eyes. He said he was dark but how dark? Santa Fe had a large Indian population—he could be part Indian or all. Heath could be an English surname but she knew little about name origins and less about who had settled in the Santa Fe area.

What would Fred do if she took him apart as she did Jonathan? she wondered. She thought of the result and laughed aloud. *He'd make me go take a cold shower before he kissed me good night,* she concluded.

As if on cue, Fred telephoned. He was back from his assignment and called to say he was tired and would see her on their regular Friday night date, which was standard procedure for Fred. Kelly wondered, if she were Jonathan Heath's girl and he had been out of town for a week, would she have to wait till he rested to see him? Not a chance, she decided, but actually she didn't mind at all if Fred delayed their dates a couple of days.

She sighed, thinking of her reason for meeting Fred in the first place—her job at the *Sentinel.* Aside from him, none of the other employees paid Kelly special attention, despite their first curiosity about a blind reporter. She seldom needed help in getting her job done, and if someone moved a chair out of the way once in a while, she gave them a quick grin of thanks and went on her way.

Kelly's work on the small privately owned paper was mostly routine, except for the special report for which she had been hired. Although her inquiries to organizations affiliated with blindness were met with polite interest, they were stymied by red tape and shortages of funds, personnel, and dogs. She wanted in the worst way to be able to ferret out a clear-cut path to acquiring a dog, to learning how to care for and feed one, but so far she hadn't found the right person willing to put forth the effort she needed.

She had come to Hap Alston, editor-in-chief of the *Sentinel,* with her story, her reasons, and her request, and he had listened, dumbfounded at the plan and her audacity to approach a newspaper editor with her idea. She had been to school to learn Braille and had found her slender fingers sensitive and quick at the process. Hap Alston was nobody's fool, and he put her through tests that would have sent a less determined person scurrying for cover. He had found no such fright in the slender girl with hair that shone like gold with fire built into it, her light brown eyes the only part of her that didn't sparkle.

Hap gave his talk in front of all the paper's 220 employees. "Kelly will be working with us until she proves she can or cannot do the job. You will give her courtesy and help if she's stuck in a situation where she needs physical help. She is to be left alone to do her job, sink or swim. That's the way it's to be."

Kelly felt all 219 pairs of eyes on her during that speech and wondered if she was not already over her head. But she had memories that drove her to accomplish things that no one else would give a first thought to, much less a second. That was a long eight months ago, and Hap had given her a year to do the job she outlined to him. The four upcoming months would prove even longer if Kelly couldn't get more information than she had in the past.

With that on her mind she slept fitfully.

It could have been a dream.

It was Saturday, two weeks since her run-in with Jonathan Heath, and Kelly was dusting furniture, her fingers touching and lingering on the table where she had switched wineglasses with him. She smiled, remembering that he had offered her his wine if she wanted it. Few of her mistakes embarrassed her, but somehow, knowing she would have to put her lips to his glass was an intensely intimate feeling, and she had blushed.

The doorbell interrupted her memory and she turned, making sure she backed away from the table before she took a step so as not to trip.

"It's Hap Alston, Kelly," a voice called.

She stopped short, alarm quickening her breath, then hastened to the door. "Mr. Alston. Come in." As he walked past her, she stood by the door. "What brings you here?" It must be bad for a private visit early on Saturday morning.

"Well, Kelly, your guardian angel seems to like working on weekends. This came to my house by air express at seven this morning."

"This?"

She heard him move, a sound like a soft command, then Hap said, "Put out your hand."

She hesitated, then obeyed, and instantly a huge furry paw filled her hand. She caught her breath as her other hand went over the silky mass of fur, over short pointed ears, down strong forelegs.

"Oh," she said. "Oh." Her hands came back to the massive head, going over the face and big snout, and her arms went around the slim, but strong neck. A wide smile shot across her face as she hugged the animal, who stood still, allowing her explorations without protest. "But where . . . who . . . ?"

"To answer your questions, she was delivered by air express to me to be given to one Kelly O'Neil, donator anonymous. An account has been opened at the Starnes Bank to feed her and train her, and I have an address of a place in your neighborhood where you're allowed to keep a seeing-eye dog. Oh, yes, her name is Ebony, and she's a two-year-old black German shepherd."

Kelly sat on the floor staring at the voice of her boss, unable to comprehend that what she had hoped and dreamed for had happened. "I don't understand. She's mine? But why?"

She heard his laugh. "I've told you all I know, Kelly, and I'm as curious as you are. Here you've been trying to find out how to get a dog, how to train and feed one, and one drops in your lap. Maybe you have a fairy godmother who waved her magic wand.''

Or godfather. The thought came unbidden—Jonathan Heath. But ranchers couldn't wave magic wands and accomplish in two weeks what months hadn't done for her. An account opened and an apartment? It made no sense but for the moment she gave up trying to figure it out.

"You know, one of your articles could have struck a chord somewhere, Kelly, but whatever, you're the recipient, papers all made out to Kelly O'Neil, so we won't argue about it. And, oh, yes, starting Monday, you'll have an instructor coming here to work with you and Ebony. Name of Chuck Benson. He's coming to the office first for me to meet him, then I'll bring him out here and we'll check the apartment while we're at it. You'll be allowed to stay in this apartment until we can move you to the new place. You won't work at the office at all next week, but do your regular column at home and someone will pick it up." Hap rose to go. "I have some food in the car, a leash, and a dish. She came well prepared."

Ebony didn't move, but waited quietly as Kelly tried to take in what was happening. "Where did you come from, you gorgeous thing?" she asked, and got a quick wet kiss on her mouth.

She heard Hap reenter the room and go to the kitchen. "The dish and leash are on your counter and the food's on the floor. Okay?"

"Yes, Mr. Alston, thank you." She stood, her hand still on Ebony's head. "I guess there wasn't any information on Chuck Benson that would help, either."

"No, nothing, but perhaps he can fill us in Monday. It would be nice, anyway. I'll call before we come out. See you then, Kelly."

After Hap left, Kelly sat on the floor, having Ebony

sit, walk forward, halt. She wouldn't need much training and Kelly guessed most of the training would be hers. Her thoughts returned to Jonathan Heath time and again, but she came up against a dead end, knowing too little about him to come to any decision. But why, after all this time with no results of her inquiries, did she suddenly get a dog, an apartment, support, and training from an anonymous benefactor just after a visit from an out-of-town stranger?

Don't question it, Kelly, take it and be happy, she admonished herself.

For once, she was glad Fred was out of town two weekends straight. She spent her time getting acquainted with Ebony, walking miles, her heart and mind engrossed in learning from the dog.

She was up Monday waiting for Hap's call and it was early, not even nine o'clock. She opened the door a few minutes later.

"Kelly, this is Chuck Benson, and I hate to tell you he knows as little as we do. He received a wire from his national headquarters and here he is."

Kelly's hand was swallowed by a strong clasp and she looked up to the sound of his voice. "Thank you for coming, Chuck. Ebony is such a love, she doesn't need much training."

"We'll see." Chuck's voice was a deep southern drawl, and she listened as he talked to Ebony. Hap left them alone, saying he'd call later in the day to see how they were doing.

Chuck gave them what he called his classroom theory for four hours, then they stopped for lunch. Kelly fixed them sandwiches and Cokes and they relaxed with Ebony close by.

"She's already accepted you, which, believe it or not, does not happen often," Chuck told her. "It's not unusual to have to try two or more dogs before either the person or the animal will accept." She could feel his glance coming her way. "For someone who hasn't been blind very long, you've adjusted well."

Kelly turned to him. "I haven't adjusted to being blind, Chuck. I went to classes, read all the books I could find in Braille, and talked to others. If I have to stay in a dark world, I have to know any angles I might work."

He was quiet, probably looking her over, she thought. "Would you like to walk over to the building where the new apartment is? Mr. Alston took me by this morning to show me and we can practice our theory on Ebony."

"I'd like that," she told him. She let Ebony lead the way, finding it easy to follow her without hesitation, trusting the dog completely.

"Where do you work from, Chuck?" she asked after a bit.

"I'm in the Atlanta Field Office now," he said. "I had been in the downtown office, but they needed someone free to travel and I'm it."

"Your family doesn't mind?"

"My parents live in Charleston, South Carolina, and I go home every few months, so they don't miss me anymore this way." He sounded as though he was grinning.

Kelly stopped as she felt Ebony hesitate and Chuck said, "We're at Fifth and Saratoga. We make a left turn, go two blocks, and it's the building on the corner."

"Is it like the one I'm in now? I mean converted to apartments?"

"Yes, but there are only two apartments. You have the first floor, and a couple lives upstairs. It's on a direct bus route right to your office."

"Good. How big it it?"

"I don't know, but we'll get the key from Mr. Alston and go in tomorrow if you like."

"Yes, I would like."

They finished their walk, returning to her apartment by a different route, with Chuck issuing one word commands to Ebony. He left Kelly with the assurance he'd be back at nine the next morning.

The following day Kelly could hardly wait till lunch break to visit the new apartment after Chuck told her he had remembered to get the key, and she stood on tiptoe as he unlocked, then opened the door.

"It's furnished, Kelly, and nicely at that. The walls have wallpaper coordinated with a multicolored carpet, mostly gold and brown." He took her through the two bedrooms, kitchen, and bath, describing in detail the colors, kinds of furniture, and placement.

Kelly sat on the couch, wondering at her luck, but she only shook her head and grinned in Chuck's direction. "It's much bigger than my apartment, now. I guess Ebony deserves her own bedroom."

Chuck laughed. "Of course, but if I can judge by her attention to you, she'll share yours at bedtime."

Kelly's fingers scratched a pointed ear. "Ready to go, girl?" Immediately Ebony stood, waiting for her next order.

Each day, Kelly was becoming more aware of Ebony's sensitive guidance. Through Ebony's own confidence and Chuck's simple instructions, she learned to trust herself and the dog, so that when Friday came and Chuck had to leave, Kelly was sure she and Ebony would work well together.

But Fred wasn't as enthusiastic about Ebony. It seems he disliked dogs, having at one time been allergic to them and gone through all the shots. So when he came over for their usual Friday night date, he didn't stay long.

"Well, Ebony," she told the dog. "If I have to choose between the two of you, guess who goes?"

She spent the weekend walking between the two

apartments and writing her story on acquiring a seeing-eye dog when she had almost given up, emphasizing the boost to her morale and the feeling of total trust in the animal. Pure human interest, she thought.

By late Sunday afternoon, she finished her column for Monday's paper, and Jessie Cain, their feature editor, picked it up, telling her he might have to shave a few words, to which she agreed. She was standing at the sink, her face turned toward the open window where a fragrant breeze played with the curtains, when the phone rang.

"Kelly here," she said.

"Hello, Kelly," a quiet voice said.

Her heart skipped. "Jonathan," she exclaimed. "Where are you?"

"At the Holiday Inn downtown."

"Downtown where?"

"Salt Lake City," he told her, laughing.

She held her breath, then let it go. "Will I get to see you? I have so much to tell you. How long will you be here?"

"Till tomorrow," he said. "You want to see me, Kelly? *See* me?"

"Oh," she laughed. "Can you come by?"

"Yes, I'll be there in half an hour if that's all right."

"Yes." As soon as he hung up, she went to the closet, slipped the white piqué dress from the hanger, made sure the brown and white belt was attached, found her brown and white sandals. When his knock sounded, she hoped she was altogether.

"It's Jonathan, Kelly," he called just as she reached the door.

"Hello, Jonathan." She smiled at him, stepping aside to let him in. He didn't walk in, but turned, caught her hand, and pulled her to him. His hands on her arms held her there, then as she tilted her head, his mouth found hers, shaping her lips to the curve of his.

He took a deep breath as his mouth freed hers and said, "What's this?"

"You mean Ebony?" she asked, her breath a little short. "Isn't she a beauty?" She stood looking toward Jonathan. "I thought maybe you could tell me."

"I don't understand," he said, shutting the door and leading her toward the couch.

She explained and added, "You were the only one I could think of who might go to all that trouble," she faltered. "It's expensive, I know, and I wondered who else would do it."

His fingers touched her lips lightly. "You flatter me, Kelly. I wouldn't have any idea how to do things like that."

She sighed. "I just thought—" She broke off. "Now I don't know what to think."

"Don't question. Just enjoy," he told her.

"Okay. So what are you doing in Salt Lake?" she asked.

"A stopover. Do you have plans for dinner?"

"No."

They ate Chinese food, but it wouldn't have mattered to Kelly, as she was full of her good fortune, telling him, "Chuck said the apartment is very nice, and there are two bedrooms. It's only a few blocks away."

"Chuck?" he asked.

"Chuck Benson came with Ebony and the training. He was here a week with us." She launched into detail of her instructions, unable to see Jonathan's study of her animated features.

"You liked him? He was a good instructor?"

"Oh, yes." Grinning, she imitated his southern drawl. "Y'all go through the commands lack you've done 'em all yo' life."

"A southerner?" he asked, grinning at her accent.

"From Atlanta, no less, originally from Charleston," she informed him.

When they arrived back at the apartment, Ebony loped to the door to meet her, glad to have them back after so brief an absence. "She's already spoiled," Jonathan said. "Doesn't want you out of her sight."

"Do you like dogs?" she asked.

"Yes," he said. "I have several of my own."

She sighed with relief. "Fred's allergic to them."

He sympathized, glad she couldn't see his face. "That's too bad," he said.

She moved to sit in the armchair but he said, "Sit here with me on the couch." She did as was requested.

"I'd like to have you come up to the ranch for a week. Will you be off on July fourth?"

She looked straight at him and blinked. "I don't know. Since I haven't taken any time off, I might, but I'd have to ask Mr. Alston. It'll depend on what he has lined up for everyone."

"I leave early tomorrow. Suppose I call you Tuesday night after you talk to Alston? Will you come if you can get off?"

"Yes. I'd love to." She hoped the paper paid vacation bonuses in advance or she knew she'd have to borrow. She winced, wondering if there would ever be a time when she didn't have to pinch pennies. She didn't just pinch; sometimes she squeezed so hard she was sure Lincoln groaned.

As Jonathan prepared to leave, she stood, trying to keep her face clear of what she was feeling inside. She didn't want him to go, it was that simple. He turned her to him and her hands went to his face, tracing his chin, down the groove in his left cheek, to his mouth, dropping to his shoulders, denying the impulse to unbutton his shirt and explore the broad expanse of chest.

"Is that as far as you're going?" he asked.

"Yes," she whispered.

His hands on her waist pulled her upward and against him, his lips on her temple, across her closed eyes, the tip of her nose, to settle on her lips, gently at first, then with increasing pressure that brought Kelly up on her toes, her parted lips seeking the deepness of his kiss. His hands moved upward, thumbs beneath her breasts, caressing. Her hands left his shoulders, going behind his head to hold his kiss to her.

Jonathan lifted his head, lips barely releasing hers. "Kelly?"

She sighed, withdrawing from the warm arms and warmer mouth, light brown eyes staring into darker ones. "I shouldn't do things like that, but the feelings make up for any guilt I might have for it," she said.

"Why would you feel guilty about a kiss, Kelly?" he asked, still holding her hands.

"Do you feel sorry for me?" Her question was unexpected and he frowned, waiting a second before answering.

"I seldom kiss women because I feel sorry for them," he said evenly. "You're no exception and I enjoyed it very much."

She was silent, her eyes looking straight into his, rather disconcerting even though they saw nothing. A smile touched her mouth. "Thanks for stopping to see me, and thanks for dinner."

"I'll call you Tuesday evening, Kelly," he promised as he left.

There wasn't much time to think about what could happen if she was to talk to Hap about leave, get moved into the new apartment by the first, and get reservations, which might be at a premium for the fourth.

She talked to Hap first thing on Monday. "Tell you what, Kelly," he said. "We'll all pitch in and move you on Tuesday night, since you go in your new place the first and the fourth's on Saturday. If you can get reservations out of here on Saturday, fine. You may have to wait till after the weekend what with vacationers all turned loose for the long weekend."

"Oh, thanks, Mr. Alston."

"You'd better draw your pay from finance and check those reservations now. How about a column on your first plane ride with a seeing-eye dog?"

"You got it," she promised, and felt Ebony's gentle presence at her knee. She breathed a sigh of relief when he mentioned pay. Saved, by a wonderful boss.

Back at her desk, she dialed the 800 number for airline reservations to Santa Fe. Her heart sank as the woman said, "I'm sorry, we are booked solid for Saturday and Sunday, July fourth and fifth. Would you care to leave your name and number for a standby flight? Or I can give you a seat on the noon flight to Sante Fe on Monday, July sixth."

"Yes," Kelly told her. "Make the reservation for July sixth, please, returning Sunday, July twelfth, and confirm that for me. And, oh, yes, I have a seeing-eye dog. Can she travel with me?"

"Yes, seeing-eye dogs are allowed to travel with the passengers and stay with them at all times. When they announce boarding time for people who have special requirements, that's you."

"Fine. My name is Kelly O'Neil."

"One moment, please." The voice left the line and Kelly closed her eyes in disappointment. Well, Monday was better than nothing, she decided.

"Hello, Miss O'Neil," the operator said.

"Yes."

"There is a reservation for a Miss Kelly O'Neil on the noon flight July fourth to Santa Fe, also traveling with a seeing-eye dog, with return July twelfth. Do you think it's possible there could be two of you? This reservation was made by a Mr. Jonathan Heath and the tickets have been mailed to Apartment A, 1001 Appleton."

Stunned, she swallowed, then said, "No, no. I'm the only one. I just didn't know he had time to do all that."

The operator laughed. "Mr. Heath evidently knows how to use his time. You already have your reservations, Miss O'Neil, and thank you for traveling with us."

Jonathan Heath, she thought, *you are something.*

Chapter Three

True to his word, Hap Alston and the employees who were off on Tuesday morning moved her few belongings into the new apartment, explaining in detail the layout for her.

"It's so roomy," she said, pleased at the extra space. "I can't believe the rent is only five dollars more than the old place."

"It's nicer than the other one," Fred told her. She was glad he got over his dislike of Ebony enough to help move her but he didn't mention seeing her again and she didn't ask him to come back.

Everyone but Cora had gone and they were sharing iced tea before going back to the old apartment to wait for Jonathan's call. "Can you help me pack, Cora? I'll take one small suitcase for underthings, bathing suit, and shoes, and the larger one for clothing. I guess jeans and shorts, mostly. When Jonathan calls, I'll ask about dressy stuff."

Cora was curious. "Who is this Jonathan Heath?"

Kelly laughed. "I wish I knew but since the day he almost ran me over, he keeps turning up like a shiny new penny."

"Don't you mean 'bad penny'?"

"Nope, nothing bad yet. Now, if he takes me up to his ranch in the wilds of New Mexico and propositions me, then maybe I won't think he's so shiny."

"What if he does?" Cora asked.

"Does what?"

"Propositions you and you're all alone out there with him and no one around for protection?"

Kelly's voice was dry as she told her. "He sees me as a helpless, young creature who needs looking after." She thought for a moment of her feelings as he kissed her, and shrugged. "He mentioned once that his mother lives in Taos, which isn't far from Santa Fe, and she'll probably be elected to baby-sit."

Cora laughed, taking their glasses to rinse them, and asked, "What time is he gonna call?"

"Any time now, I guess, so we'd better get back to the phone. I'll be glad when I'm completely moved and have everything together again so I can find what I need."

The humidity had increased with darkness and they walked slowly the few blocks back to Kelly's old apartment and had only sat down when the phone rang.

Before Kelly picked up the receiver, Cora said, "I'll be back in a while to walk back to the other place with you, okay?"

Kelly mouthed "Thanks" as she said into the phone, "Kelly here."

"Kelly," Jonathan said, "I'm sorry to be so late calling but we had a storm last night and had to rescue some cattle. How are you?"

"Tired but in my new apartment," she told him.

"Same telephone number?"

She laughed. "No. Cora came back here with me to wait for your call. I won't get my phone in the new place till Thursday." She drew in her breath. "I got my vacation time and went to make reservations when, much to my surprise, I already had reservations and my tickets have arrived."

"I was a little afraid if I waited there wouldn't be any space left since it's a holiday weekend. I hope you won't think I'm too pushy."

"No, of course not. I'm glad, but—" She didn't know how to approach him to mention repayment of the money.

"Good. I'll pick you up Saturday and I'm looking forward to it, Kelly."

"Wait, Jonathan. What about clothes? What kind, I mean?"

"We're informal most of the time here, Kelly, so jeans, shorts, pantsuits. However, we do change for dinner, so if you can, squeeze in a dress or two. Don't overpack; we'll make do with whatever you bring. Okay?"

"Yes. Good night, Jonathan." Kelly sat by the phone, pulling on her bottom lip, frowning. *I don't think I'm any match for that man,* she thought. *Not because of him but because of me. I've never felt so—so animated inside with any man I can remember and that could mean big trouble brewing.* She shrugged. *As long as he thinks I'm a sweet, helpless child, he won't get me into trouble—maybe.*

Thursday night Cora came to help her pack. "I'm packing the long green voile dress and the yellow dotted swiss, Kelly. They both fold up small. Your black sundress, gray pantsuit with gray print blouse, and the navy and white blouse, matching shoes. Two pairs of jeans with various and sundry shirts, two shorts sets, and two bathing suits."

"Sounds like I plan to stay a month." Kelly grinned at her. "Just don't put anything red or pink in there with this hair of mine."

Cora looked toward her as Kelly ran fingers forward through the short russet-gold hair that lay close to her head never seeming to need brushing. It framed a face of translucent skin with freckles marching across the small, straight nose. Instead of blistering, the skin had taken on a light tan after a few days of walking in the summer sun.

"Your eyes should either be blue or bright green, Kelly," Cora told her.

Startled, Kelly raised her head. "Why do you say that?"

"Whoever heard of a strawberry blonde with brown eyes?" Cora countered.

Kelly's look was relieved as she laughed at the other girl. "You know how mongrels are. They turn up with the oddest features." She felt better when Cora changed the subject and, a few minutes later, wished Kelly a wonderful vacation and left.

Even though all her preparations were completed, Kelly still could not relax. The anticipation continued throughout the restless night and on into Friday at the paper. At lunchtime Hap stopped by her desk, interrupting her thoughts of Jonathan and the ranch.

"You got a way to the airport, Kelly?"

"I'll take a cab, Mr. Alston. Most everyone has plans for the weekend."

"I don't. I'll pick you up, say ten thirty?"

"You don't have to do that," she began.

"But I am. Be ready." She heard him move away.

She was ready by ten with all of Ebony's papers on shots and registration, and the tickets Jonathan sent her. She had never flown and had what she imagined were nervous butterflies in her stomach, since she'd never had those either. Hap loaded her bags, opened the door for Ebony to get in the back, and helped Kelly into his car, reversing the procedure at the passenger-unloading zone at the airport.

"This is Kelly O'Neil," he told someone nearby. "She'll need assistance on and off the plane."

"Yes, sir," a polite voice responded. "Come with me, Miss O'Neil."

"Have a good time, Kelly, and don't forget the story," Hap said, touching her arm.

"Bye, Mr. Alston. Thanks." Swallowing past her uneasiness, Kelly let the unknown attendant direct her steps. She was the first passenger on the plane. A stewardess came down the aisle to assist her.

"The first seat, Miss O'Neil, and Ebony is next to you. Would you like a pillow?"

"No, thank you." She kept her hand on Ebony, wondering what the dog's reaction to flying would be.

The hustle and bustle continued, takeoff was announced, and Kelly breathed easier as they became airborne. Ebony sat through it as though she had done it many times before. Lunch was served and it seemed only a short time till they were in Santa Fe.

The flight attendant's voice came over the intercom. "The captain asks that you please remain seated until certain passengers are safely off the plane. It will only take a few extra minutes."

Ebony's big nose found Kelly's hand and Kelly caressed her face, then wrapped the leash around her wrist and stood to walk unassisted down the steps with Ebony guiding her. She could feel the plane holding its collective breath and she bent to hug Ebony as they reached the last step.

Jonathan was waiting right there to meet her.

"Hello, Kelly," he said, his lips touching hers very lightly, his large hand reaching out to take her free one. They walked through the terminal to retrieve her luggage, never letting go.

Jonathan talked easily on the drive to the ranch, describing in an offhand manner the mountains or a stretch of flat land, the river that wound through the countryside. The car slowed, making a sharp right turn, and a few minutes later slid to a quiet stop.

"Here we are, Kelly." He opened the back door first, letting Ebony out, and Kelly heard the click of the leash as he removed it. As he helped her out, he said, "Run stretch some, Ebony, I'll take care of Kelly for you. Beowulf can give you a tour of the place."

"Beowulf?" Kelly questioned.

Jonathan laughed. "My friend. He and Ebony could be from the same litter." His hand on her arm guiding her, he said, "Three steps up, Kelly, then across a wide veranda. All the house is on one floor, so you won't have to negotiate stairs." A screen opened, and they stepped into a carpeted hallway. A light floral scent reached Kelly and she heard another set of footsteps nearby.

"Selena, this is Kelly O'Neil. She may get lost occasionally, but just turn her toward me and she'll be all right."

"Kelly," a soft voice with only a slight accent spoke. "Welcome to Heath Cliffs."

"Thank you, Selena."

"Haskins put her bags in the last bedroom on the west side, Jonathan."

"That's fine." Then to Kelly, "Did you have lunch on the plane?"

"Yes, and I'm not the least hungry. Are you going to show me around?"

He laughed. "Of course. Change to jeans and we'll go horseback riding." He hesitated. "Do you ride?"

"After a fashion," she told him. "I haven't been on a horse in more than a year."

As Jonathan's hand guided her into the bedroom, he described it to her, even down to the wide three-width bay window. "The sunsets from here are fabulous, Kelly. I wish you could see them."

"So do I," she said, listening to him open her suitcase. "Heath Cliffs?" she asked, remembering Selena's welcome.

He laughed. "My mother said if she had to live here, the place would certainly have a name she could refer to. Her favorite novel about then was *Wuthering Heights,* as you might guess. Now, Kelly, what do you want from your suitcase?"

"Give me the long-sleeved blue-checked shirt with the jeans, and the boots from the smaller case."

He did as he was told. She felt him turn toward her, and she took a step forward as he touched her hand, his voice teasing. "Want me to stay to make sure you get the right colors?"

She shook her head. "Even I can't get into much trouble with jeans. I can manage, thank you."

"Pick you up in twenty minutes. I'll check on Ebony, and saddle the horses. You can ride Goldie. She's a gentle quarter horse and not too big."

She listened to his receding footsteps and dressed quickly in the clothes he had left where she could reach them easily. She flipped her hair with a small brush from her purse and was ready when he knocked on the door.

As they walked outside, bounding four-legged footsteps heralded Ebony's approach and Kelly patted the sleek head. "You can walk with us, but you don't need to see for me." It seemed Ebony understood, and once Kelly was mounted on Goldie, she could hear the dog walking nearby.

"We'd better not ride too far if you haven't ridden for a while," Jonathan said after they'd ridden a time. "Let's sit here a few minutes." They dismounted and he led her a few steps and told her, "There's a log, just sit down." He sat beside her, his arm casually around her waist, as he talked. "The Jemez Mountains are to our south just past Los Alamos. We're about seven thousand feet elevation and the ranch borders national parks on the north and west. At the risk of sounding like a travel agent, the scenery is spectacular."

"I remember," she said. "It's a lot cooler than Salt Lake City."

"Yes. This time of year is pleasant here. It doesn't get extremely hot. However, it does get very cold in the winter."

She leaned against him, propping her elbow on his knee alongside her own leg, turning her face to him. "Do you live alone?"

"Yes, why?" His voice sounded amused.

"The house seems awfully big for just one person."

He went still, saying nothing more for a moment, then he pulled his arm from around her, not disturbing her elbow. "I've been married, Kelly. There's only me now, but, yes, the house is big for just one."

"Oh, I'm sorry, I didn't—" She stopped, flustered.

"It's all right. No tragedy involved, just a normal, everyday divorce." She wasn't sure if there was bitterness in his voice, but he seemed to be stiff there beside her. She didn't ask what a normal, everyday divorce consisted of as opposed to some other kind.

They rode back and as he put the horses in the stable, he said, "Mother lives in Taos and she has opera tickets for us tonight if you'd like to go. The Santa Fe Summer Opera is well known for quality productions."

"I've heard of it, Jonathan, but those tickets may be wasted on me, since I know little about operatic programs."

"Would you like to go?"

"Yes, if you'll look at the two dresses I have to see if one is suitable."

They walked arm in arm into the house and Jonathan went to check her dresses as she sat on the edge of the bed.

"Either dress will do," he said after a moment. "Wear the green one."

"All right. What time?"

"We should leave here around eight. Since we have reserved seats and a reserved parking place, we don't have to rush. The program starts at nine." He sat beside her on the bed and one arm went around her, easing her against the pillows. "Tired?" he asked.

"No."

"Rest, anyway, and let's have a light snack before the opera, then dinner later."

"Okay." Her hands went to his face, farther from her than she had thought, so she pulled him down, her fingers exploring the rugged features, coming to rest on his mouth. His breath was warm against her fingers and she smiled straight up into his face.

"Kelly." His voice roughened and his hands were tight on her shoulders. His mouth came down hard on hers as his fingers moved to tangle in her shining hair. She moaned but he cut off her breath, so turning her body, she moved closer, pushing into him, hands searching.

His kiss drained any will of her own and she held him to her, fingers digging into his back, feeling the sweetness wash over and through her, and when he released her, she gasped, "Jonathan."

"This has gone far enough." He took her arms from around him, kissed both hands, put them crossed on her chest, and stood up. "Ebony's here with you, take a nap, and I'll see you later." He was gone.

She lay there, taking deep breaths to quiet her pulse. What would she do if he propositioned her as she and Cora had speculated? He may not be the type to ask, but take what he wanted. He was certainly capable of doing just that. Rolling over, she buried her face in her pillow. *I may be in big trouble if I allow myself to fall in love with him.*

The thought haunted her till she gave way to sleep.

Opening her eyes, she wondered what had awakened her and for a moment forgot where she was. Her fingers felt the face of her watch. Six o'clock.

"Kelly?"

"I'm awake. Come in."

Jonathan spoke from the door. "If you want a bite to eat, we'd better start."

"Be right with you." As the door closed, Kelly found the bathroom to wash her face then went to meet Jonathan.

Selena served them a small buffet of salad and sliced chicken with fruit and they ate on an enclosed patio, so Jonathan told her.

"Can you manage dressing?" Jonathan asked as they finished eating, adding, "Oh, yes, I know you can do all right but just make sure your shoes match." They laughed together and he walked back to her room with her and said, "I'll be back for you in thirty minutes."

She slipped the green dress Jonathan had selected over her head, zipped it up, and found her silver sandals, identifying them by the brocade design. Using a small brush, she guided it over her short hair with one hand, using her fingers to smooth it down to frame her face. Running her fingers across the bottles in her makeup kit, she found cologne and sprayed it lightly on her throat and wrists. When Jonathan knocked, she was ready.

"You've never been to the summer opera here, Kelly?" Jonathan asked as he took her hand and led her to the car.

"No. One year we came sight-seeing but it was after the close of the summer season. It's sort of open-air, isn't it? Some friends were telling me about their visit up here."

"Yes. The stage and portions of the seating are in the open area. Very pleasant, usually, even in hot weather." When they arrived a few minutes later, he said, "Well, they certainly have a good turnout, if the parking lot is any indication."

She waited for him to open her door, guiding her

steps away from the car, and as they walked toward the entrance to the opera house, Kelly's fingers tightened on his arm.

"All of royalty must be attending," she whispered.

"Why?" he whispered back.

"It smells like the perfume factories from France, Italy, and England all combined."

"You smell quite heady yourself, did you know?"

She shook her head. "I don't know how you can tell around here."

"I rode in the car with you, remember?"

She turned toward him, lips parting in dismay. "I'm sorry. I didn't realize I used that much."

He squeezed her hand. "Just enough to tantalize and make me want to get closer."

Her hand on his arm tightened and she lifted her head to him. Before she could find the words she wanted to say, Jonathan said, "Hello, Mother," and gentle pressure on her arm stopped Kelly. "Mother, Kelly O'Neil."

"Kelly," a strong voice said. "How nice to see you and I'm glad you talked Jonathan into using the tickets for the opera. He'll never sit still with me that long."

"Hello, Mrs. Heath." Kelly felt her hand taken in firm, long fingers that went well with the voice.

"Are you with Rena, Mother?" Jonathan asked.

"Yes, she's here, somewhere." Kelly could feel her turning to look around the crowded lobby they had entered.

"Would you two like to join us for dinner later?"

"Yes, thank you, Jonathan. I'd better find her and we'll see you afterward." Her voice came more directly to Kelly. "Enjoy the program, Kelly. This is a particularly talented cast tonight."

"Thank you." The older woman touched her hand, then moved away.

"Is she pretty?" Kelly asked.

"Very attractive, as a matter of fact," Jonathan told her, his voice sounding amused.

"Then you must take after her since you're so handsome."

His arm was around her, guiding her through the crowd, and he didn't answer, but when he said, "Step up," his hands held her to him an instant and his mouth touched her hair.

When they were seated, Kelly tilted her head, listening to all the sounds, realizing when the lights were dimmed by the hushed voices. Jonathan leaned toward her. "If you can't follow the sequence through hearing, I'll give you an outline."

"I'll just listen to the music, Jonathan. I read this opera not long ago and haven't forgotten that much. Thanks."

"When did you read it?"

"It was one of the books I was carrying the morning we met," she said, smiling at him. "I'm not likely to forget it for a while."

His fingers tightened on hers and she liked the feeling. She became engrossed in the music but her fingers stayed alive to the pressure of his. He didn't release her hand to applaud so she couldn't either, but she sighed with satisfaction when the performance ended and Jonathan pulled her to her feet.

"There you are," Mrs. Heath said. "Rena, Kelly O'Neil."

Introductions over, Jonathan said, "We'll go in my car, Mother, and meet you at the restaurant. That way you and Rena can go straight home and won't have to backtrack for us."

At the dinner table, Kelly listened to the conversation around her, deciding that Jonathan and his mother were friends as well as mother and son.

"Jean and Rena have a ladies apparel shop in Taos, Kelly. They work very hard, I'm told, except for March and April when they go on buying trips to New York and Paris.''

Jean laughed. ''We deserve those trips, Kelly. And enjoy them too,'' she added.

Evidently, it was a job they both loved and Kelly decided necessity was not the reason they worked but enjoyment was.

''Bring Kelly for dinner Friday night, Jonathan,'' Mrs. Heath invited as they parted. ''And we'll try out the lobster at the Lodge.''

''Would you like that, Kelly?'' he asked.

''Yes, I'd love it.''

They rode back to the ranch in almost total silence, broken only when Jonathan said, ''I wish you could see the moon, Kelly. It's so bright it makes shadows from the mountains and you can almost reach the stars.''

''Get me a handful, Jonathan,'' she said, her voice full of sleep.

She felt him turn to look at her and she was looking straight at him, eyes wide and luminous from the car dash lights. One hand left the wheel and found hers to gather it to him, spreading her fingers against his chest under his tuxedo jacket. She didn't remove it till they arrived home and Jonathan helped her from the car. His strong arms pulled her against the length of him, and they stood there, not kissing, just holding each other close.

Finally he opened the side door to the house, and led her through what she guessed was the hallway, into another room. Ebony met them, touching Kelly's hand to alert her mistress she was there.

''How about a drink?'' he asked.

''Like what? Something pretty and cool?''

''Why does it have to be pretty?''

''It tastes better that way,'' she told him.

''Now, that's woman's logic if ever I heard it. I can tell you it's pretty, and you'll never know the difference.''

"You wouldn't," she protested.

He laughed. "No, you'd probably guess it was mud-colored instead of sunshine gold and waste good rum. Okay. Pretty and cool coming up."

Listening to his movements, Kelly tried to imagine how Jonathan looked. He was tall and well-built, from what she had found exploring his body with her hands. Her cheeks warmed as she remembered her fingers moving through his curly chest hair and his question: Is that as far as you're going? The wide mouth fascinated her, the feeling it drew from her at the slightest pressure, and the tips of her fingers ached to follow that deep groove in his cheek to see just how far it went. Dark brown eyes, he admitted finally, were deep set, high cheekbones emphasized a slim face, thick but neatly trimmed sideburns stretched to the bottom of his earlobes, and when he needed a shave, it was easy to tell he would have a thick beard should he care to let it grow.

Sensing him in front of her, she raised her head but he spoke before she could say anything. "I believe you do need something cool to drink," he said as he placed a tall, frosted glass in her hand. "Your cheeks are flushed. Do you feel all right?"

"Yes," she said, wondering what he would say if he knew what had made her blush. She smiled. "I was bending over a little too far, I guess, reaching for Ebony. I thought she was on this side of me."

"No, she wandered over to me, maybe thinking I had food. Could she be hungry?"

"Scavenging. She's a fake because I fed her just after we ate what Selena fixed us." She put the glass to her mouth, tasting the tangy iced drink. "Mmm. It's good and I won't even be nosy and ask the color or contents."

He laughed. "Good girl." His body settled comfortably close to her. "Aren't you tired? This has been a long day for you."

"Yes, but it's a nice, relaxed tired that a few hours sleep will take care of. If I fall asleep here, just stretch me out and I'll see you in the morning." She thought about what day it was. "Don't they have fireworks or anything around here to celebrate the fourth?"

"They have a supervised display at the stadium on the east side of Santa Fe. We can't hear it out here, although you can usually see some of the flashes."

"That wouldn't help me much, I guess," she said, sipping more of her drink, then placed the glass on the table at her side.

"No, it wouldn't." His arm slid along her shoulders on the back of the couch and she relaxed against him, turning her face to burrow into his neck where he had unbuttoned the high collar and two more buttons down the front of his shirt. Her ever-busy hand probed past the unbuttoned portion of the shirt, tugging almost absently at the white T-shirt underneath.

"What are you doing?" he asked after a moment.

Her head moved back so that he could see her face and the tiny smile playing around her mouth. "I want to touch you," she said.

Kelly could feel his face lower to hers, saw in her mind's eye how the wide mouth looked just before cool lips, flavored by his drink, touched hers. Her fingers found the bare skin at his narrow waist. There wasn't an ounce of fat there and all she could do was dig her fingers under his belt, caressing the firm flesh.

His hand released its hold on her waist and he slipped it behind her knees, lifted her, and with swift strides carried her to the bedroom down the hall. He held her a moment longer before bending to place her on the bed.

"Do you need me to find a nightgown?" he asked, his voice quiet.

Wide eyes gazed up at him. "Are you angry with me?"

"No, but if we keep this up, you'd most assuredly be angry with me." He took a deep breath. "Where are your night things?"

"The small case." She lay still, knowing she should tell him she could manage very well without him. But she said nothing, just listened to the sounds he made searching for her nightgown.

"The orchid?" he asked.

"Yes."

"It's a lovely color for you," he told her.

She knew he was close by, then felt him sit on the edge of the bed. His hand smoothed the hair back from her cheek, two fingers caressing her lips as he brought the hand back. She was startled when he covered her eyes with his hands, and blinked as he removed them almost at once.

"Can you see any light at all?"

"Sometimes I see shadows, but I'm never sure if they're outside or inside of my eyes."

"When do you see a doctor?"

"The last part of August."

"Why so long?"

"Tests were run in June and nothing can be done till all the results are back and evaluated."

"I'm not sure they're doing everything that should be done, and I don't think you should wait two months for something as important as a chance for sight." He sounded impatient. "I've been checking on an eye specialist from the clinic at Johns Hopkins in Baltimore and I understand he's the best in the States."

"Jonathan," she said, touching his arm, "I have a hard enough time paying for what I've had done and someone at Johns Hopkins is out of my reach at any time. The insurance has run out and I can't afford more tests."

"Doesn't the paper have insurance coverage for you?"

"Yes, a very good coverage; however, there's a clause that says any chronic or recurring illness contracted before the policy went into effect is not covered. You can't blame them for that; this is certainly not their fault."

"No, but there must be some other way you can get help," he insisted, unsatisfied with her answer.

"It's only two months, Jonathan, then we'll see."

She could feel his gaze going over her face, and from the warmth in her cheeks, she suspected he was also giving her slender body the once over. Only someone with hair and complexion like hers could blush from what she only supposed was happening.

He drew in a deep breath. "After August, what? If they say they still don't know, what then?" He was beginning to sound angry.

"I don't know, Jonathan. I'll have to wait; there's no other choice."

The silence lengthened and she grew uneasy, unable to tell what he was thinking, how much investigation he might insist on. Her hand still lay on his arm and he picked it up, rubbing his fingers across the back of it. She felt his lips on her palm and he closed her fingers over the kiss and stood up.

"Sleep well, Kelly. No hurry about getting up tomorrow. I'll be out for a little while in the morning, but if you can wait for a late breakfast, I should be in by ten. Good night." A brief touch of his lips on hers and she heard the door close behind him, heard Ebony's sigh as she relaxed by the bed.

Her fingers found the filmy material of the gown he placed on the bed and a few moments later, she fumbled for the lamp switch. He had left it on for her because the bulb was hot and he would never think of leaving her in the dark.

Lying still in the middle of the big bed, she tried to figure a course of action that wouldn't irritate Jonathan, but wouldn't jeopardize her program, either. If he insisted on a specialist, she had no idea what she would do. Could she confide in him and expect him to understand? Would he be impatient and unsympathetic after she had misled him so completely? She twisted, sifting her troubled thoughts. Surely, it didn't matter if he approved of her ideas or not, but suppose he was responsible for getting Ebony and the apartment for her, plus the account for upkeep. She still had strong suspicions of that, even though he had denied any knowledge of it.

Her thoughts went back to the reference he made to his divorce. Who was she, this woman who had left Jonathan Heath, a man who had been nothing but kind to her after he learned she couldn't see? But he had a temper, she thought, remembering his attack on her when she stepped in front of his car. She didn't want him really mad at her. Jonathan wouldn't be easily appeased—especially if he thought he'd been deliberately deceived.

Chapter Four

She slept without dreaming till the bright light of the morning sun came through the window. Ebony was waiting for her and a wet kiss welcomed her to Sunday.

"All right," she said, "I know I'm lazy and should have been up hours ago, but don't rush me. I'm on vacation." Kelly showered and dressed in jeans and T-shirt, then followed Ebony's lead to the kitchen.

"Good morning, Kelly," Selena said. "Jonathan said he'd be back by ten. Will you wait for him?"

"Yes, Selena." She reached for the chair Ebony had stopped beside, when she was hit by a small bundle of fur, body twisting happily, and cold nose bouncing off her chin.

"Tish, be shamed," Selena scolded. "That's Mrs. Heath's little poodle, Kelly. She leaves her here mostly because she goes out a lot and my Maria takes care of her."

Kelly laughed, her hand moving to catch and scoop the small dog into her lap. "You're adorable and you certainly want your share of attention, don't you?"

"She does that. Her hair is almost the color of yours, but they call it apricot."

Kelly laughed. "Close enough, I guess." She put one hand on Ebony's huge black head, the other scratching behind Tish's curly ears. "What do you think of this, Ebony?" Ebony's big nose came to inspect the small dog and Tish responded with a typical poodle kiss all over her big face. Kelly was laughing at their antics when she heard Jonathan's step.

"I see everyone is wide awake this morning, thanks to Tish," he said.

"She's so cute. Is she the only small dog you have?"

"Yes. Beowulf is a German shepherd, as you know. Boris and Caesar are Belgian sheepdogs, but they stay out on the range most of the time. Those are all that I claim, but you'll find others around that belong to various people." His hand caressed her shoulder as he walked behind her to take the seat next to hers.

After breakfast, he led her outside where she could tell they were on the covered patio, probably facing mountain ranges in the distance. She voiced that question.

"Yes," Jonathan told her. "Almost any direction you look, there's a range of mountains. Since there are so many people in town for the weekend," he went on, "let's swim today and decide later what we'll do tomorrow."

Her lazy voice agreed. "Sounds heavenly. Do you get to loaf very often? I would imagine there's always something to do on a ranch this big."

"How big?" he questioned.

She thought for a long moment. "If we drove about twenty minutes from Santa Fe and most of it was your property, plus we rode horses several miles almost directly opposite the road from Santa Fe, still on your property, it stands to reason that's big."

He laughed. "Kelly, were you a computer in another life? You can mark things without paper better than anyone I know and remember directions that you've never even seen. I don't understand and I'm watching you the entire time."

"You only have to pay attention," she said. "Anyone can do it."

"Not just anyone, Kelly," he told her, an odd tense-ness in his voice. Then changing the subject, "The pool's at the back of the fenced area. Can you swim well?"

"All right. Why?"

"It's an Olympic-sized pool, twelve feet deep at the deepest point, to three feet at the shallow end. All the ranch hands and their families use it with the teen-agers acting as lifeguards. They never swim alone."

"Will they be here today?"

"No. Most of them have gone camping or fishing for the weekend." He slipped an arm around her waist, turning back toward the house. "By the time you get your swimsuit, it'll be long enough after eating to swim." He released her at the door of her room. "Need any help?"

"No, thanks," she told him, following Ebony into the room. As she pushed the door behind her, a small wiry body hurled itself into her arms. Delighted, she hugged the small, squirming poodle, then dropped her on the bed.

"Behave, pest," she said. "I have to get my bathing suit." She found the one-piece blue bathing suit Cora had packed, knowing it was blue by the buckle on the side, the only one she had made like that. No cap was in the case, but it didn't matter because her hair was short enough to dry quickly and she could shampoo in a hurry if need be. Scooping up Tish in her arms and receiving a kiss for her trouble, she followed Ebony to the poolside.

"Tish loves to swim if you want to put up with her," Jonathan said close beside her.

"I might lose her in the water," Kelly told him.

"I'll watch," he told her. "The yellow suit looks good on you."

She grinned, wrinkling her nose at him. "Color blind, aren't you?"

Feet feeling for the edge of the pool, Kelly poised a moment, then went in, Tish held lightly to her chest. She let go of her as soon as they came up and laughed as she heard the small splashes move away from her. She heard Jonathan follow her in and a hand on her arm turned her to him. She rested both hands on his wet shoulders, using their strength for support in the deep water.

"Kelly." Just her name, nothing more.

She tilted her head, smiling up at him, and felt his cool, damp mouth on hers. His hands on her waist pulled her closer and she straightened her legs along his, pressing her flat stomach against his, feeling the stirrings in her body that only Jonathan could arouse. Tingling awareness parted her lips beneath his and her tongue moved questioningly against his teeth into the opening he gave her between them. He bit gently into her tongue, then suddenly, his hands tightened, his mouth crushing hers, moving back and forth until her breath was cut off and she whimpered. She was free just as quickly, but he held on to her, preventing her from going under the water.

"You okay?" he asked, his voice harsh with his heavy breathing.

"I—I'm not sure."

"Swim straight ahead three yards and I'll help you out."

When she did as he instructed, he pulled her up and gave her a towel. A moment later his hand guided her to a lounge chair and she sat down, still able to hear his breathing.

Neither of them spoke and she grew uneasy under his appraisal, as sure of it as if she could see him. "What is it?" she asked, finally, unable to wait for him to speak.

His voice was quiet when he answered her. "How frustrating it would be, Kelly, not to be able to see the expression on your face when I kiss you. Not to be able to see your look of wide-eyed wonder, your lips that trust mine to give and take." He drew a deep breath. "How do you cope with the unknown, Kelly?"

"By believing that it's only temporary," she said and knew she had said the wrong thing.

"What if it's permanent? Miracles of modern medicine notwithstanding, say, it's a fact that you'll be permanently blind." He waited, and when she said nothing, he went on, "You do accept the fact that this could be true, don't you, Kelly?"

"Yes," she whispered, hands wrapped tightly around her knees.

"Then what?"

"At least I have Ebony. She's more than most blind people will ever have."

The silence went on and this time she made no attempt to break it. The probing was getting very close, very personal. One of them would have to give one way or another, and soon.

The touch of his cool hand on her arm caused Kelly to jump and draw in her breath as the lounge chair moved with his added weight. He pushed her backward and his bare skin on hers started a trembling deep inside her. The hair on his leg against her smooth thigh caressed as much as his fingers playing along her arm to her shoulder to curve around her throat, his thumb crossing her chin.

"Kelly." Her name was whispered on her lips and his mouth remained there until she lifted her head for more pressure, begging for the kiss to be completed. He made her wait, his long fingers tangled in her hair, before he kissed her fully, then slowly released the bright head, his hand going down her back, bringing her up to him. Her hands on his shoulders moved to circle under his arms and her fingers dug into the hard muscles of his back. Her senses became Jonathan's to fondle as much as the mouth he explored with the fullness of his lips, his teeth raking a gentle path, the tip of his tongue probing the corner of her mouth, finding a soft, moist opening. Her breath came quickly and unevenly, bringing the same response from him as his body pressed downward onto hers and she moved to get closer to him.

He released her mouth grudgingly to move over her chin, nipping the curve as his lips trailed flames down her throat, lingering in the hollow for an instant before following the slight cleft ending at the clinging material of the bathing suit covering her breasts.

"Jonathan?"

He raised his head to see Kelly's eyes closed against the brightness of the sun and his long indrawn breath steadied him as he said, "Yes, Kelly?"

"Yes, what, Jonathan?" she asked, her voice soft and puzzled. Puzzled at her feelings for this man she had never seen, wondering at the response her body gave him just for the asking.

He laughed a little as he answered her question. "Right now, I'd say yes to anything you wanted, Kelly." He stood, leaving her feeling alone, and one hand went out to him. He took it and pulled her up from the lounge.

"Does the sun bother your eyes?"

"Some. I have dark glasses but I haven't been outdoors this much lately and I forgot about them."

"Let's go inside. You'll probably be sorry you've stayed this long with that skin and your eyes."

He held her in front of him and she smiled up at him, her lips soft and full from his kisses. They finally turned toward the house and walked arm in arm.

"Where's Tish?" she asked, remembering the small dog in the pool.

"Swinging on Ebony's tail. She's found a new toy."

Kelly laughed, able to picture the small poodle hanging onto Ebony's bushy tail.

"How about a drink?" he asked, leading her through the cool entrance hall, turning her into the room she recalled as the den.

"Pretty and cool?" she teased.

"I wouldn't think of giving you any other kind, Kelly," he said. "About thirty minutes."

Kelly showered, shampooed her hair, and took the long yellow dress from the hanger where Selena had hung it. After toweling her hair, she ran a comb through the short curls and fluffed them. By the time she applied what little makeup she wore and zipped her dress, her hair was barely damp. She sprayed light cologne over her hair and shoulders, and felt through the small case for the gold sandals. They weren't there and she sat on the floor, frowning, sure Cora had put them in with the others.

"Phooey," she said aloud.

"Something wrong?" Jonathan asked from the door.

"I can't find the slippers to go with this dress," she complained.

"Perhaps these I rescued from one little rogue poodle would be yours."

"Tish," she laughed. "How did she get them?"

"Fastest thief on the ranch," he said, slipping her sandals on and fastening them. He caught her hands to pull her to her feet, then held her close. "Mmm, you smell good."

They took their drinks outside, sitting in the coolness of the late afternoon. "Jonathan?"

She felt him turn toward her. "Yes, Kelly?"

"Would you like to drive down to Albuquerque one day and meet my sister, Ann, and her husband, Gary?"

She could have imagined the hesitation but he said, "Sure. Does she look like you?"

"We're the same size but she has black hair and blue eyes."

"You're teasing me."

"No. We had two parents, you know. My dad was the redhead," she told him.

"You aren't redheaded, Kelly, not that I know what color you'd call it. Is that what is generally referred to as strawberry blond?"

She laughed. "Selena said it was the same color as Tish, and she's apricot."

"Close enough. No wonder Tish fell so hard for you. She thinks you're her mother," he teased. "Would you like to go tomorrow? Will they be home?"

"Yes, to both questions. They have a small ranch but they both work. Ann's a nurse and Gary's an aircraft mechanic."

"When does he ranch?" he asked.

"I told you it was small; nothing like yours."

"Maybe you should call Ann and warn her. We could go out to dinner so she won't have to worry about cooking."

"Yes, I'd like to call, and it will be a treat for them to go out." Kelly stopped, feeling his eyes on her.

"How long since you've been to see them?"

"Last Christmas," she said and clenched her fingers around the glass, waiting.

"You haven't seen her since Christmas and you by-passed Albuquerque to come to Santa Fe? I take it you don't see each other often."

"Usually, we do. It's been difficult this year with my job in Salt Lake City." It would be hard to explain why neither had made the effort to see each other, why there was no money when it was apparent all three had decent-paying jobs. Kelly swallowed past the lump in her throat, reluctant to tell Jonathan their problems.

Sensing her discomfort, Jonathan was silent and she heard his deep breath before he finally said, "Perhaps you should rest some before dinner, Kelly."

He took her hand and held it as they went into the

cool house and stopped at the door to her room. "The dogs are exploring outside so you have your room to yourself." He kissed the top of her head. "Dinner about seven?"

She nodded and, as he walked away, slid her hand along the door to her room, turning slightly right to reach the bed. She sat there, thinking about Jonathan Heath. After a few minutes, she sighed, kicked off her sandals, and lay back across the bed.

The next thing she knew, Jonathan said, "You gonna sleep your vacation away?"

He sat beside her and pulled her to a sitting position. "I didn't intend to sleep," she said.

"You did well without intentions," he said, laughing. "It's time for dinner."

"Oh." Dismay was evident in her voice.

"It's all right," he said, his voice gentle. "You're on vacation. I'll wait while you get ready."

She washed her face and ran the brush over her hair and returned to the room, going to the bed to reach for her sandals. Jonathan had them in his hand, ready to slip on her feet and fasten them. He took her hand as she stood and they strolled through the hallway toward the dining room.

Selena had prepared another delicious meal and Kelly relaxed, letting the tightness in her throat lessen. In the living room afterward, Jonathan put on tapes, adjusting speakers and sound till it was the same as an orchestra, then took her hands and pulled her into his arms. She followed his lead, giving herself up to the music and his expert guidance, wanting to cuddle closer to him, yet afraid of the consequences. She did it anyway, letting her right arm go around him, her left move back and forth over the thin material of his shirt. He kept his distance, but she felt his breath quicken and his lips on her hair.

When the song ended, he pulled away to look down at her. "You'd better call Ann before it gets too late."

"All right."

"I'll dial for you if you'll call the numbers to me."

She repeated Ann's telephone number and a moment later, the receiver was placed in her hand. On the third ring Gary answered. "Hello, Gary, it's Kelly."

"Kelly, how are you? There's nothing wrong?" She heard the pleasure in his voice, hesitant because she didn't call, but wrote instead. It was much cheaper. They should know she was in Santa Fe because she had sent a card as soon as she had known for sure she'd be there.

"Nothing's wrong, Gary. Did you get my card?"

"Yes, just today as a matter of fact. You know the mail and the holidays. Are you actually in Santa Fe?"

"Yes. And I wanted to know if Jonathan and I could come down tomorrow."

"Kelly." Gary's voice was warm. "Let me get Ann. Hang on."

In a second her sister was on the phone. "Kelly, are you okay?"

"Certainly. And only seventy-five miles away from you, dying to visit."

"When? When?" Ann could be jumping up and down from the sounds.

"Tomorrow, if you'll be home. Jonathan will be with me. What shift are you working?"

"Seven till three. Perfect. Be here when I get home, Kelly."

"All right, Ann. See you." Jonathan took the phone from her hand, as she sat lost in thought.

"Well?" Jonathan asked.

"They'll be glad to see us." She raised her head to look toward him. "They seem happy."

"Any reason they shouldn't be?" he asked.

"They had a four-year-old son who died eighteen months ago," she blurted.

Jonathan was still for a moment, then he took her hands in his and waited for her to go on. When she didn't, he asked, "What happened, Kelly?"

She shivered, unable to tell him all that had gone on in her little family. "Meningitis." She sat stiff, remembering the horrible times they had lived through, but she breathed deeply and continued, "They're doing fine now, but it was bad for a long time."

"Yes, I'm sure it was." He sat beside her. "What time should we leave tomorrow?"

"Ann gets home around three thirty and Gary about five. She wants us there then." She smiled. "Can we take Ebony? They'll love her. There's a place to leave her if we go out."

"Of course."

Kelly's thoughts kept returning to Ann and Gary as they talked. From Ann, she would learn what Jonathan Heath looked like, and a quiet thrill slid across the bottom of her stomach.

"Why are you smiling?" he asked.

"Thinking. I'm looking forward to tomorrow."

"In that case maybe you'd better get to bed and get ready for it."

He walked her to the bedroom door, kissed the top of her head, said good night, and left. She fell asleep quickly, warm thoughts of Jonathan's embraces and the anticipation of tomorrow's visit with Ann failing to keep her awake. She was glad when Ebony roused her in the morning.

Kelly removed the gray crepe pantsuit from the hanger, found the matching short-sleeved print blouse and black sandals that she could wear with one of Ann's dresses if she needed something different to wear to dinner.

Taking a small bottle of drops from her bag, she lay

across the bed to put them in her eyes and was still there when Jonathan knocked.

"Come in," she called, not moving till she felt the drops soothing her irritated eyes.

"What's wrong?" he asked anxiously, standing by the bed.

"Nothing. I use these occasionally when my eyes get sore." She held up the small bottle.

He made a sound that she couldn't understand and she sat up. "What?"

"How do you know you have the right bottle, Kelly?" he demanded, concern clearly in his voice.

"I only have one and it's marked in Braille," she told him.

He muttered something else and she heard his indrawn breath. "Ready for a very late breakfast?"

"Yes."

Over another of Selena's delicious breakfasts they discussed their plans for the day. "It will probably hurt Tish's feelings to be left behind," Jonathan said, "but Maria will take care of her, so let's just take Ebony."

Later, as she walked beside Ebony to the car, the fresh breeze coming off the mountains felt damp on her face. "Is it supposed to rain today?"

"Scattered showers are forecast for tonight, but it's humid. There's fog still lying around the ranges to the southeast of us but our route should be clear," Jonathan explained, shutting the passenger door behind Kelly and getting in on his side. The car moved quietly, then gathered speed as they entered the main highway. "Which side of the city is their ranch on?"

"West. Turn right on I-Forty to the first farm road and turn left a couple miles. It's not far from the interstate."

The radio was playing and they talked little. She listened to the poignant words of a song. "The sweetest thing I've ever known is loving you." *The sweetest feel-*

*ing I've ever known is love for a man I've never seen,
neither do I know him,* she thought, turning her head
away from Jonathan to gaze through the window as
though she could see the rugged countryside. Could he
read her thoughts? He had asked, "Suppose I couldn't
see your expression, the wide-eyed wonder, your
lips?" That meant he could tell some of her feelings, so
she warned herself to be careful what she let show
through from then on.

"Is the farm road number fifteen-oh-six?" he asked.

"Yes. Turn left."

The car turned and she said, "Perhaps a mile to their
gate. It's RAG Ranch."

"RAG Ranch?" he repeated.

"Yes, Robbie, Ann, and Gary. They bought it while
Ann was pregnant with Robbie." She smiled a little.
"Had it been a girl, she would have been Robin."

She felt his quick glance in her direction, but she
concentrated on finding the keys in her bag, and had
selected the one she wanted when the car pulled into
the circular drive in front of the small brick ranch
house. Jonathan let Ebony out and as he opened the
door for her, she gave him the key.

"You're sure it's the right key?" he asked.

She smiled up at him, wrinkling her nose. "Yes,
Jonathan." She reached to his hand, turned the key
over, and touched the engraved letters RAG. He said
nothing more and walked beside her to the front door,
opening it with the first turn of the key. Ebony moved
just in front of Kelly, realizing they were in a strange
place, thinking that Kelly would need guidance. Arm in
arm she and Jonathan made a tour of the house Kelly
knew by heart. They heard a car pull into the driveway
and Kelly said, "That's Ann. I'd recognize my Mustang anywhere."

Jonathan started to ask a question, but a whirlwind
with short black hair and blue eyes burst in and swept

Kelly to her, hugging her tight. When they finally let go of each other, the woman turned, and said, "Hello, Jonathan. I'm Ann. I'd know you anywhere. I'm so glad you came." Her arm around Kelly, she moved to sit down, motioning Jonathan to the bigger chair.

"And how would you know me, Ann?" he asked. "Don't tell me you and Kelly transmit thought waves." His voice was questioning and the girl's eyes went back to his face.

"As a matter of fact, Kelly described you very well," she told him.

"I don't doubt it," he said. "She drives me to distraction pinpointing things people with eyes don't see."

Kelly's face was turned toward Ann, concentrating on the expression in her voice. "How's Gary keeping up with both jobs, Ann?"

"Things are looking up, Kelly. He got a big raise and we paid off some—some—" She hesitated. "Paid off one of our mortgages. That helps the morale." Her eyes went from her sister back to Jonathan. "Want some iced tea? Gary said he'd leave early if he could and he should get here shortly."

As they moved to the kitchen Ann watched Kelly walk with Ebony. "She's beautiful. You still don't know where she came from, Kelly?"

"No, but wherever or whoever, she's the best thing that's happened to me. I don't understand," she started, hesitated, then went on. "I wish Ebonys were available to every person who can't see. I don't know how I managed without her."

"Almost got yourself killed, that's how you managed," Jonathan said.

She smiled across at him. "Yes, but in the process I met you."

They heard another car drive in and Gary came through the back door, still in his mechanic's coveralls. He was a big man, well over six feet and close to two hundred pounds, mostly muscle, and when his arms went around Kelly, he picked her off the floor and hugged her close, then put her down away from him to stare into her face.

"How are you, Kelly?"

"Fine. You, Gary?" Her voice was soft, showing any who cared to see that she loved her brother-in-law.

As he let her go, he saw Ebony, shoulders braced, waiting for a wrong move toward Kelly.

Gary turned to shake hands with Jonathan at Kelly's introduction. Then he glanced toward the dog. "So this is Ebony? You're right. She's a beauty." He got himself a glass of tea, dropping a kiss on Ann's head in passing. "Just give me time to shower and dress."

"Am I all right dressed like this?" Kelly asked.

"The Barbecue Shack is anything but a shack, but that pantsuit's fine. Is the Shack all right with you, Jonathan?" Ann asked.

"Sure. I haven't been there in years, but it was very good the last time I visited."

"Still is," Gary assured him.

Kelly followed Ann into the bedroom. "What does he look like, Ann?"

"Do you know of an accident he was in?"

Kelly's head came up quickly. "No. Why?"

"From one side he's a very handsome man, Kelly, but the left side of his face is scarred, maybe from a burn. The scar starts at his eye, pulling the skin down, and it goes all the way to his mouth, pulling his lip upward. Dark brown, almost black, eyes that miss nothing. One side of his mouth is beautiful, sensuous if you will, and a chin that's all but square."

"I know," Kelly said, thinking of her curious fingers covering his features

"You know?"

"I touch him whenever I can," she told her.

"Kelly, are you sure this is right?" Ann was hesitant.

"It's almost over, less than two months, Ann, and I have to finish it. Mr. Alston has put me in for an award, and if I get it, we can pay everything. How much do we still owe?"

"Not 'we,' Kelly," Ann said. "It might take much longer, but Gary and I can do it now. You've pulled us along till we can make it on our own when we thought we'd never be able to do it."

"Sure, you can handle it, Ann, but it's not just the debts now. If this works, it will help other kids like Robbie before it's too late."

Ann was quiet, then she said, "Yes, I know, Kelly, but I can't stand the thought of—"

"Then don't think about it," Kelly broke in. "We've gotten this far and we could get everything we wanted this way."

"A year is a long time out of your life, Kelly."

"I've learned a lot, Ann, more about life than I would have had I been seeing all this time. I wouldn't change it for anything."

"What about Jonathan?"

"I don't know what about him except he's divorced, has a huge ranch, a very nice mother, and has been wonderful to me."

"Are you in love with him?"

"Yes, I'm afraid so."

"And Jonathan?"

"Feels sorry for me."

"You know the old adage, Kelly. 'Pity is akin to love.'"

"Not for Jonathan. He thinks I need caring for like a six-year-old, not a twenty-six-year-old."

There was a knock on the door. "We're starving," Gary called. "You girls about ready?"

At dinner Kelly listened to the talk around her, satisfied that Ann was much happier, and if not over Robbie's death, at least had accepted it. Gary and

Jonathan talked like old friends, on ranching, aviation, weather. She heard Jonathan speak on aviation, wondering how he knew so much about it if he didn't work with it. There was a lot she didn't know about him, she admitted to herself. The scar on his face she knew was there but had avoided in her tactile forays. But Ann's description—how bad a scar was it, and from what?

She was tired when they said good-bye, and she fought tears as Ann hugged her. "Will we see you in September, Kelly?" Gary asked.

"Oh, yes, you will. Could be mid-September, but I'll try to make it earlier."

"Good. Hurry back. You too, Jonathan. Any time."

Ebony sighed in the back and stretched out for the hour-and-a-half drive back to Jonathan's ranch. Jonathan drove, not attempting to make conversation when Kelly put her head back against the seat and closed her eyes. Her head was turned on the seat so that her face was toward Jonathan. He glanced at her; her dark brown lashes lay against her fair skin, shadows from the dash lights hiding the stray freckles across her nose.

Jonathan's hand left the wheel to touch her cheek, then he picked up her left hand lying relaxed on her thigh. She didn't move, instead her breathing deepened, so he kept it beneath his between them on the seat. As he turned into the drive to the garage, the scattered showers forecast for the evening hit full force.

He opened the door from the garage to the hallway, let Ebony out, and opened the door to help Kelly. She was still sleeping, so he gathered her up in his arms and walked into the house, stopping only when he reached her room.

As he laid her down, she stirred, but turned on her side and slept on. Tish sat on the pillow watching as he removed Kelly's shoes, let Ebony in, and closed the door behind him.

Thunder rumbled through the canyons to the west and Jonathan stood at the window in his bedroom, watching the play of lightning for several minutes. They could certainly use the rain. Undressed, he pulled on a pair of pajama bottoms and, restless, went to the bar in the den to pour an ounce of whiskey into a glass with two cubes of ice. The storm moved closer and thunder no longer rumbled but crackled in ear-splitting crashes, continuous lightning kept the outside like day, and rain came in sweeping torrents.

He returned to his bedroom and as he watched from the window, the sky split in a jagged flame. The crash shook the big house and the lights went out. He thought it must have wakened Kelly, though he heard nothing but the storm. He took a flashlight from the drawer of his nightstand and moved quickly down the hallway to her bedroom. Flashes of lightning played through the room and Kelly was sitting on the side of the bed, eyes wide with alarm, holding a trembling Tish, her hand on Ebony's head. He was by her side in two strides.

"Jonathan." She let Tish go and turned her face against his chest, holding tight.

"It's all right. Someone will get our generator going and we'll have lights." He didn't stop to think that the lights meant nothing to Kelly, that it was the deafening noise that frightened her. As his arms folded her close, he realized she had undressed and wore a gown of soft, gauzy material that let his hands feel her body without actually touching the skin. His long fingers moved over her, bunching the fabric against her outline as he pulled her down to the pillows with him, turning her face to his throat. The supple slimness of her trembling body molded itself to him, arms tight and clinging, as the storm raged in untamed fury outside the solid walls of the house. He murmured her name, lips on her hair, hands following the curves so close in his arms. She moved her face from his throat down to his bare chest, rubbing her cheek against the roughness of the hair, one leg sliding on the cotton material of his pajamas.

Realizing her position, she stiffened, and her head went back on the pillow as she whispered, "Please?"

He didn't know what the "Please" was for, but his mouth found hers, soft lips parted invitingly, and he held her completely as he never had, knowing the shape of her as it hadn't been revealed in a dress, not even her bathing suit. The thin material of the gown was somehow more intimate than bare skin and her wide-eyed fright caused by the vicious storm made her an appealing armful. He wrapped her in his arms, releasing her lips to pull her ever closer, whispering reassurances as the thunder rolled and crashed. Unaware of when the storm eased, they slept.

Chapter Five

The kisses that woke Kelly were not the ones that quieted her the night before, but were moist and demanding ones from Tish. Her arm, outflung across the bed, moved to find the empty pillow, causing her to wonder when Jonathan left her. She had no recollection of anything beyond the storm and his arms holding her, protecting her, until she slept once more. Her watch said a little past eight o'clock.

The steady sound of rain falling was all she heard as she sat up, swinging her legs over the edge of the bed, feeling Ebony's head on her hand. She found her robe and went barefoot down the hallway, making the two turns she counted to the kitchen.

"Selena?" she called.

"Yes, Kelly" came the soft answer.

"Is everything all right?"

"The storm caused a lot of damage, and Jonathan is out with the crew checking and repairing as they go. He's been gone since before five and I thought he might soon come for breakfast. We have power, but the telephone is out." Her footsteps came closer to Kelly. "Let's go ahead and eat and I'll fix something for whoever comes in later."

It was after breakfast when Kelly said, "Let me help you with the cleaning, Selena. I can do the bathrooms and make beds."

"Could you, Kelly? I do have several things I could do if you can manage that."

Kelly had no trouble with beds and Selena put cleaning products out for her, indicating which was which, and although she was slow, it wasn't difficult for her and it helped pass the time as they waited for Jonathan to return. As the day went on and the rain continued, she worried, although Selena told her it wasn't unusual for him to remain away from the house when they had trouble such as the storm had caused.

They ate a light meal as it grew dark and Kelly went to her room with Ebony and Tish. Lying across the bed, her thoughts went to Ann and Gary, so much better now than a year ago when Ann had a breakdown after Robbie's death. She had given up for a while, but when she realized what Kelly was doing, she started improving until she was able to return to work after a short time. Unbelievable doctor bills stared them in the face and Kelly dealt herself in to help repay them despite Ann and Gary's protests. But her stubbornness and determination paid off royally, and if Hap's award nomination for her went through, they could pay off the remaining medical bills, plus establish a fund for research on children like Robbie.

Somewhere a door slammed and Kelly sat up, listening as footsteps sounded through the entrance hall and another door closed. Ebony led her to the kitchen where she could hear Selena moving around.

"Yes, he's here, Kelly, but was soaking wet and covered with mud. Would you set him a place please? The plates are on the table with the silver. Are you hungry?"

"No, I'm still full from our dinner." She got a plate, cup, and silverware from the end of the table, set butter and cream out of the refrigerator. He would need some of Selina's good coffee to wake him up if he had worked since five this morning and it was now close to seven o'clock.

She turned as footsteps paused in the doorway and smiled. "Jonathan?"

"Hello, Kelly." His voice was tired. "Not much weather for vacation, is it?" He talked quietly about the flooding, moving cattle to higher ground, dragging uprooted trees from roads and trails, replacing windows in some of the ranch homes of the workers.

"Our place here suffered little damage, lost a few shingles here and there. How are your nerves after the extremely noisy night?" His voice teased her as he reminded her of their closeness and she felt her face redden.

"All right. I think Tish is the one who needed a tranquilizer and Ebony wasn't exactly happy over it."

"Yes, I noticed," he said.

Selena placed his dinner on the table, touching Kelly's hand as she set a cup of coffee in front of her.

"How about a roll, Kelly?" Jonathan asked.

She shook her head. "We ate long ago."

He tried to tempt her again. "Sure? The rolls are still warm."

She smiled at him without answering and tried to imagine the way he looked as he used his knife and fork. Was he left-handed? She could ask, of course, but she didn't.

"Did Selena tell you these fish came from the river that runs along the border of the ranch? Her sons caught them just yesterday."

"No, she didn't tell me. Besides, we had ham. How come you're special?"

His hand touched her fingers lying near her cup and he laughed a quiet laugh. "I'm a working man and Selena looks after me."

She heard his chair move. "I could use a drink." His hand touched hers as he pulled her chair back and she took his arm as they went into the den. Seated on the leather couch, she listened to the sounds as he mixed drinks for them and smiled in his direction as she felt the cushions move with his weight.

He sighed as he placed a cool glass in her hand. "We could certainly use some of the rain but I'd like to see it spread out a little more. The news said partly cloudy and cooler tomorrow but no rain." He picked up her left hand, caressing the fingers from nails back to her hand. "I'll have to work tomorrow, maybe till afternoon, to catch up, and I hate to leave you alone. I should have asked Mother to come get you, but she doesn't trust the flash flood areas out here."

"I don't blame her, I wouldn't either," Kelly told him. "I can entertain myself if you happen to have a typewriter and some paper."

"Why, yes, I do. What do you have in mind?"

"Hap—Mr. Alston—let me off on the promise I'd write an article for him while I'm here and I can do a lot of work on that."

"All right. I'll set the typewriter up for you tonight and I promise no more leaving you after tomorrow— barring nature's wrath, of course."

Kelly finished her drink and said, "I think I'm ready for bed and I know you're tired."

He didn't deny it and pulled her to her feet, then walked with her to the door of the bedroom. "Sleep well, Kelly. I'll see you as early as I can tomorrow." He tipped her chin upward and kissed her firmly on the mouth, holding just for an instant, then released her, pushed her through the doorway, and was gone.

Kelly went to the window and stood gazing through it as though she could see the rugged outline of mountains in the distance. Her thoughts were on Jonathan and his actions around her. He seemed afraid to hold her, his light kisses only token caresses that made her want more. Until last night. His arms holding her to him were deadly serious, his kisses hungry and demanding, his hands tender as they moved at liberty over her body, a willing captive. Desire shook them both until the storm was closed out and the tumult in their own bodies the only awareness so that she didn't remember the last kiss nor how long it was before she slept in his arms. Warmth filled her body as she recalled his loving her, not quite totally, but very near to it, and she concluded that it was his choice, not hers, that called a halt.

As he had told her, he was already gone when she joined Selena in the kitchen the next morning. Putting her breakfast plate on the counter, Kelly said, "Is it really cloudy and cool?"

"Yes, quite chilly outside, but no more rain in the forecast," Selena said. "Jonathan set the typewriter up for you, so come on and I'll tell you where the supplies are."

As Kelly sat at the typewriter, Selena asked, "What happens if you make a mistake and don't realize it?"

Kelly laughed. "That's what proofreaders and editors are for. If I write the story, the least they can do is check it for me."

Left alone, she spent several minutes sorting material in her head and an hour later had her outline ready. From memory she filled in details, and hours passed as she became absorbed in the work. When Jonathan's footsteps came down the hall, she touched her watch. Four twenty.

"I thought you said an article, not a book." His hands rested on her shoulders.

"I get carried away sometimes," she told him.

"I'm dirty and starved. How about an early dinner in thirty minutes?"

"Okay." Leaving her papers on the desk, she walked arm in arm with him down the hall, Ebony joining as she came to greet them.

"I'll come by for you soon as I'm dressed."

Kelly checked her clothes, chose the navy linen

pantsuit with white lace blouse, and matching sandals. She flipped the brush through her short hair, deciding not to change the small pearl earrings, and was ready when Jonathan knocked at the door.

"Too bad you can't see your reflection, Kelly," he said very softly.

She lifted her face toward him. "Why?"

He was quiet so long, she said, "Jonathan?"

"I was trying to think how to answer you," he said, his hands resting on her hips. "You're a very attractive young lady and I like to look at you, but perhaps you wouldn't appreciate the view as much as I." He pulled her closer, bringing her fully into his arms, then bent to kiss her, his lips hard on hers, forcing hers apart.

He groaned, letting her go. "Selena's waiting for us."

"That's not fair."

"What?"

"You can see what you're doing to me, but you aren't even affected by me at all, at least not that I can tell."

"Take my word for it, Kelly, I'm affected." He tucked her hand under his arm and they went to eat.

"Did you get all the repairs done today?" she asked into the silence at the table.

"Most. The rest can be done as we go. We got the biggest rain down here, so we didn't have to worry about flash floods coming off the mountains. They usually do more damage than the rain, long after the rain is gone."

Later, as they went into the den, Jonathan asked, "Ever been fishing, Kelly?"

"At the pond on Gary's ranch, but he only stocks small bream. Robbie and I used to fish all day and think we were great fishermen if we caught one each, not big enough for the cat."

He laughed. "We can go above the dam. Should be good for catching perch and bass after all the rain."

"How far is that?"

"About ten miles from here, going through the ranch and taking the county road across the mountain. We'll have to take the Cherokee and have Selena pack us a lunch. Suit you?"

"If you don't mind baiting my hook for me."

"Don't care to handle worms and minnows?"

"I have done it, but I don't know about now. With the things wiggling, I might never get them attached."

"All right. Just for you, I'll do it." They sat without talking till he sat up and grunted.

"What is it?" she asked.

"I'm stiff from two days of pulling and lifting. Getting soft, from the good life, I suppose." He stood and she could tell he was stretching.

"I'm ready to call it a day and you need to rest so we can enjoy the fishing trip. What time do we leave?"

"Six?"

"I'll be ready." She took the arm he offered as he walked down the hall with her.

"Good night, Kelly. See you early in the morning." His lips brushed her hair momentarily before he strode away from her down the hall.

She was in bed a few minutes later, leaving the door partly open for Ebony and Tish, and when they wandered in, she was too near sleep to get up and close it.

"Up and at 'em, sleepyhead. It's five thirty."

It took a while for Jonathan's voice to break through the sleepy haze and wake her. "Be right there," she finally managed.

Minutes later the fragrance of fresh coffee welcomed her to the kitchen and she joined Jonathan and Selena for breakfast.

Selena grumbled, "Can't see going fishing before daylight."

Kelly grinned toward her. "Doesn't bother me at all." And at Selena's quick intake of breath, she went on, "Don't feel bad; it's all right."

Jonathan's hand touched hers. "Everything's ready. Let's leave Ebony and Tish here."

"You'll have to put up with watching me if Ebony's not there," she warned.

"I'll manage." They said good-bye to Selena and two unhappy dogs and were on their way.

"The longer range of the Jemez Mountains is south of us," Jonathan told her. "The one we cross is only four thousand feet elevation, and the dam's just the other side. We'll go upstream about three miles before we stop. Did you bring a sweater? It turned cooler, as promised."

"Selena gave me a Windbreaker that should be warm enough with this long-sleeved shirt."

He concentrated on driving, describing in detail any sight he thought might interest her. It was almost an hour before he stopped and said, "Looks like a good place here. Come on." She slipped from the seat into his arms and he set her on her feet out of his way as he removed their gear.

"Hold my arm, Kelly, and just follow. It's downhill, so step easy." A minute later he said, "This is fine. It's only a few steps to good fishing spots." He spread the blanket he carried. "Sit here till I get the hooks baited, and we'll go down the bank. I see some rocks we can sit on where that breeze won't hit us."

"Doesn't feel like July," she commented.

He laughed. "Give it a couple of days and we'll have eighty-five again."

Settled on the rock he found for her, Kelly took the rod Jonathan handed her, hook ready for the water.

"Cast to your left, Kelly, let it out a good bit. I'll be just behind you to your right."

Her first swing wasn't far enough and Jonathan's arms came around her to pull it back and cast again. "Let go," he instructed, and she released her hold on the rod. "Now," he said, giving it back to her.

The sun coming over the rim of the mountain felt good as it warmed the damp air and Kelly leaned against a rock behind her.

"You can't sleep and fish too," Jonathan said, quiet amusement in his voice.

"The fish don't take me seriously, anyway," she told him.

The sound of the water over stones and a ripple touching the bank were background for birds singing in trees behind them.

"Are there any puffy white clouds?"

"Some. Just to our right over the jagged peaks. They're moving fast in that wind. Why do you ask that?"

"It seems the kind of day that the sky should be so blue it hurts your eyes and a few clouds playing around, more like spring than midsummer."

He didn't say any more but she knew he was watching her. Suddenly she jumped. "My line. It's moving."

"Hang on to it, Kelly. Easy. Hey, that's a nice one. Here, I'll help."

His arms came around her, hands guiding hers as they reeled slowly until she could hear the fish flapping.

"Turn him loose," she said, dropping her hands from the rod.

"What? It's a good-sized one, Kelly, and a few more—"

"Robbie and I always threw ours back." The light brown eyes met his and didn't look away.

Without another word, he released the fish back into

the water and watched it swim away. "You're a nut," he said sounding still amazed.

"I'm sorry."

"No, you aren't, Kelly. That fish knew to get your hook instead of mine because he recognized a real softie. Admit it. Did you ever squash a bug?"

She stared into his face and laughed aloud. "No, not on purpose."

He gazed a second longer and his voice sobered when he asked, "You were very close to Robbie?"

Her smile faded and she turned away from him. "Yes." She swallowed. "Ann is five years older than I and took care of me after our parents died when I was fifteen. Robbie was almost part mine."

"Did you live with Ann and Gary?"

"No, not after I finished school. I went on to college and started teaching, but we saw each other often and I was chief baby-sitter."

"What did you teach?"

"English and journalism."

"In Albuquerque?"

"Yes."

Jonathan shook his head. "God, Kelly, there's so much I don't know about you."

"Really, Jonathan"—she could feel her whole body tense at the mention—"I don't want to talk about it. Besides, I'm getting hungry."

His lips brushed her temple as he said, "Wait here and I'll set up our lunch."

She listened to his footsteps as he walked away and a few minutes later the door of the Cherokee slammed and he came back toward her.

"Come on, I'll walk you to the blanket," he offered.

"Can I help?" she asked.

"No, today you get waited on as though you were helpless whether you think you are or not." His fingers

touched her cheek and she smiled. "Want coffee first
or wine?"

"Coffee, please." A moment later, he placed a foam
cup in her hands. She sipped the hot liquid, feeling the
steam on her cheeks as it warmed her throat.

"I'm putting your plate in front of you. Clockwise,
you have chicken—the wishbone, no less—deviled
eggs, two biscuits filled with sausage and cheese, dill
pickles, an apple, a hunk of cheddar cheese. The cake is
coconut and it's on a separate plate."

She laughed. "And the wine?"

"You get that later."

"I'm already full listening to you name all that's on
the plate. How will I ever have room for it all?"

"We'll manage. Just remember how hard we've
worked this morning and we have a couple of hours to
go before we start home." A moment went by as he
moved things. "Here's a fork but you can manage better with your hands." His fingers took her coffee cup
and replaced it with another one. "The wine. I'll put
your coffee cup to the right of your plate."

They ate, the only sound the wind sighing through
the tall pines and shorter fir trees. Birds whistled and
called to each other. The ripple of the water was loud
over the rocks.

"Why aren't you fat?" she asked.

"How do you know I'm not?"

"I can feel you." As she made the statement, her
wide-open eyes went up to meet his and a telltale blush
warmed her cheeks. She knew he was watching her and
she bit her lip.

His laugh was quiet as he said, "You haven't a
chance at hiding your blush with that skin, Kelly."

Lowering her glance, she picked up her coffee cup.

"Let me heat that up for you," he said, taking the
cup and returning it a second later.

She breathed slowly and changed the conversation. "Is Selena Spanish?"

"Yes. Her husband is Al Cardon, my lead foreman. They've been here since long before Dad died six years ago." He stood, pulling her with him. "We have to walk off some of that food."

Arm in arm, they walked along the water's edge with Jonathan telling her bits and pieces about the landscape. A few times he stopped abruptly, hooked a finger under her chin to gently lift her face up to him and place a light kiss on her soft lips, which parted willingly under his.

By late afternoon the breeze turned cool again, sending a chill through Kelly as they lay on the blanket in each other's arms. Jonathan felt the tremor and pulled her even closer to his warmth.

"I guess we should get back now. I didn't realize it was getting so late."

They gathered up the picnic things and Jonathan drove slowly back across the trail to the main county road, describing as he went along. A royal greeting awaited them from the dogs, Ebony barking to herald her master's return and Tish making herself comfortable in Kelly's arms for a free ride to the house.

Later that night, after a light supper, Jonathan said, "Let's go down by the corral, Kelly. Randall, our veterinarian, is here. He isn't around often, so I like to catch up on his ideas when I can. Ebony can visit Beowulf while I talk to him.

Ebony stayed close by Kelly's side guiding her over the unfamiliar ground, not wanting to leave her even with Jonathan there. Kelly realized when Beowulf joined them by Ebony's alert movement and she unhooked her leash.

"Go on, girl, enjoy his company while you can," she whispered as they scampered away.

"This isn't your last visit here, is it, Kelly?" Jonathan's voice startled her; she hadn't realized he was behind her.

She turned, smiling nervously, "I hope not. Why do you ask?"

"The way you encouraged Ebony to visit Beowulf sounded as though it were a last chance."

She shook her head. "I just meant while she had someone to look out for me." She accepted his arm to link with hers as they entered the stables.

"Randall?"

"Here, Jonathan," a voice answered, and they followed the sound till Kelly heard movement.

"Kelly, this is Carl Randall, vet for our outfit. Kelly O'Neil, Dr. Randall."

"Irish, I'd hazard a guess, with that name and hair." A big, work worn hand enveloped hers.

"Guilty," she admitted.

"Just a minute and I'll show you around, Kelly."

"Kelly's blind, Randall, but I wanted to ask you about the shipment due in Monday."

Even though the conversation went on, Kelly was conscious of Dr. Randall's observance of her standing near Jonathan, but he said nothing more and his goodbye was in a normal tone as they left.

They were nearing the house when she told him, "Jonathan, my eyes feel a bit irritated. I need the drops. Do you want to check the bottle before I use it?"

He didn't answer, instead turning her to face him, holding her still in front of him. She waited. "I worry about very few people, Kelly, but you, I worry about. Yes, I know you're capable of taking care of yourself, but there are a lot of things that can go wrong when you can't see your surroundings. I'm thankful you have Ebony, but expert that she is, she cannot read bottle labels."

"I'm not so sure."

He shook her and she heard his exasperated sigh. "Yes, let me see that bottle before you use it."

In her room she found the handbag, handed the bottle of drops to Jonathan and sat on the bed while he read the label.

"Do you know what these elements are?" he asked.

"I looked them up when I got the prescription, but I've forgotten the medical terms. It's only a cooling solution, no harmful chemicals. I don't use them often and I suspect the pool chlorine may have caused a little irritation. It's the first time I've been swimming in the past year."

"We'd better stay out of the pool, then. Lie back and I'll put the drops in for you."

She did as instructed, keeping her eyes wide until the cooling liquid spread over the sensitive area.

"Better?"

"Uh-huh." She heard him cap the bottle and replace it in her bag, returning to sit by her on the bed.

"I want you to go to the specialist at Johns Hopkins," he told her abruptly, and before she could protest, he went on, "All expenses paid."

"How?"

"I'll pay them."

"No." She started to sit up but he put an arm on either side of her, leaning so that his face was only inches from hers, his breath warm on her face.

"Don't be stubborn, Kelly. Let me help."

"I could never repay you, Jonathan, and if I wait for the test results, chances are they'll have an answer."

"Too much of a chance and I don't need to be repaid."

She shook her head, opening her mouth to object, but he covered the opening with his lips, and she shivered as an intense thrill pulsed through her, shaking them both. His arms tightened as her fingers dug into his shoulders and she held him to her, accepting the plundering of his kisses.

He pushed her back on the pillow, whispering against her throat, "Think about it, Kelly, and we'll talk tomorrow."

"But, Jonathan—" She stopped, still warm and wrapped up in his kisses.

He brushed her lips and said, "Good night, Kelly. I'll be out a little while tomorrow and we'll have breakfast about ten if that suits you."

"Yes." She listened to his footsteps receding, confused by her feelings and his second mention of a visit to Johns Hopkins Medical Center, paid for by him. *What do I do now?* she wondered.

She found a gown and lay down on her bed. A long time later Ebony found her there, still wondering what to do about Jonathan Heath.

Chapter Six

July weather eased its way back into existence on Friday and Kelly stayed outside in the pleasant breeze. Jonathan hailed her from the corral and she walked to meet him, turning as his arm circled her waist.

"I'm starved," he said. "What's for breakfast?"

"I smell cinnamon rolls, but stayed outside so I wouldn't be tempted to snitch one and ruin all the other goodies." She smiled up at him. "Let's go eat."

He pulled the screen door open, letting her walk in ahead of him and find the way to the breakfast nook without any trouble. As he pushed her chair in at the table, Jonathan's hand moved across her shoulder, his fingers caressing her neck under her hair.

"What would you like to do today, Kelly?" he asked. Seeing her shrug her shoulders, he suggested, "How about going up to Taos? We could go to the museum and art galleries, then stop to see Jean and Rena at the shop."

"Jean?"

"Mother. Sometimes she seems too young for me to call her Mother and I switch to Jean." He smiled at her. "We can even take the dogs with us if you like."

"Sounds great."

When they finished eating, he said, "Give me a few minutes, Kelly, and I'll be ready. I just want to call Jean and let her know we're coming."

Kelly went to her bedroom, collected a handbag, pulled the long yellow dress from the closet, took matching sandals from her case, and placed them on the bed.

"Ready?" Jonathan asked.

"Yes," she said, adding, "I don't know where Ebony and Tish are."

He laughed. "They'll find us. I have your things."

As he predicted, the dogs were waiting by the car and, as soon as the door opened, entered without an invitation, assuming they were included in this trip. They scrambled over into the backseat to make room for Jonathan and Kelly.

"We go through Santa Fe and take Highway Two-eighty-five north, then Route Sixty-eight into Taos. Jean's shop is on the northern outskirts and we'll stop by and say hello to them before we go sightseeing. All right?"

"Yes." She turned toward him. "How did they happen to open a dress shop together?"

"They've been friends for years. Rena's husband died several years before Dad, and they're both the type who need to be busy. Traveling and volunteer work wasn't enough for them after a while, so they decided Taos needed an exclusive apparel shop. They were right, I guess, because they're very happy with it, stay busy, and make some money too. They close during April and May. That's when they make most of their buying trips and have the time of their lives." He chuckled. "They enjoy life to the fullest and never seem to be bored."

And how do you keep from being bored, Jonathan? she wanted to ask. Instead, she bent her head toward Tish as the small dog jumped from the backseat into her lap.

"Here we are. Their shop is on a corner, facing east, with only one style dress, bathing suit, sandals and bag

displayed in a stark beach setting. Quite impressive."
He helped her from the car. "Step up. Take Ebony's
leash." He opened the door, letting her follow the dog
into the shop.

"Hello, Rena, you remember Kelly?"

"Yes, of course. Hello, Kelly. Jean is with a customer, but I'll call her."

Kelly felt Ebony pause by a chair, but she remained
standing, her head tilted, breathing in the smell of new
clothing and the fragrance of expensive perfumes.

Leaning toward Jonathan, she whispered, "It's beautiful."

"Why are you whispering?" he asked.

"It's so elegant, I was afraid to speak out loud."

His laugh was just for her ears alone. "Kelly, you are
a wonder."

"Jonathan. And Kelly." Jean came toward them. "I
wasn't expecting you this early."

Kelly felt the closeness as the two hugged, then
Jean's arm came around her and guided her across the
room. "You look lovely, Kelly. Come in here and we
can talk."

"I'm going to take Kelly to the museums and show
her some of the pottery the local Indians have made,"
Jonathan said. "Will you keep the dogs?"

"Yes, I'll be glad to."

"What time's dinner?"

"We should leave home about seven. I made reservations at Taos Lodge."

"Sounds good. Come on, Kelly, let's get started on
our tour."

They spent the afternoon rambling through museums, old shops, and the home of Kit Carson, with
Jonathan furnishing a running commentary. She held
the black pottery made by the Indians, hands exploring
the contours as Jonathan explained how it was done.

"This is a Kachina doll, favorite symbol of the Indians," he said, placing a small object in her hands. Her fingers followed the delicate features, the rough home-spun material of the dress.

"I remember reading a long time ago that some dolls have a meaning for the medicine man in his cures. Are these the ones?"

"Yes. This one is about twelve inches high, but there are larger ones. Do you like it?" She nodded.

They browsed for a while and when they left the store and got in the car, he gave her the doll. "You'll need a souvenir of Taos to show to Alston and your friends on the paper."

She smiled her thanks at him and leaned against the seat and sighed.

"Tired?"

"Sort of," she said.

"You can rest before we go eat. Jean and Rena will be dressed when they get home because it will be time to leave by then."

"What will you do?"

"I have some calls to make," he told her.

It was only a few steps from the car to the door of Jean's house and up three steps to the entrance. She waited as Jonathan unlocked the door and reached back for her hand, leading her through two rooms across a hallway.

"This is the room I sleep in when I stay over, which isn't often," he said, turning her to face him. "I'll get your things from the car and be right back."

She stood where he left her until she heard him return with her clothing.

"The bath is straight in front of the bed and I hung your dress in the closet to the right of the bath. Okay?"

"Yes."

He lifted her face and kissed her mouth hard, long-ingly, before he left her.

Once she was alone, her mind refused to rest as she

reviewed the week past. The visit with Ann and Gary had been an unexpected bonus, but undercurrents between Jonathan and her troubled her like so much fever gnawing inside. His restraint was obvious and he treated her more like a child than a woman in whom he had awakened grown-up emotions only hinted at by former male companions.

Fred had never been a hot-blooded lover and she smiled at that thought. There was Jesse, a fellow teacher in Albuquerque, who was fire and rain, but she hadn't been able to agree to his requests that she become his live-in girl friend. In her younger days when blood ran warm for pigskin heroes, there was Ken, her first teen-aged football idol. But no one had ever appeared to play with her heart and soul as Jonathan was doing, and she was fast acquiring feelings that cautioned her she was heading for trouble. But she pushed her apprehensions from her mind and slept.

Awake before Jonathan came to call her, she found the dress in the closet where he had hung it and was fully dressed except for shoes when Jonathan knocked. She smiled as he took her hand. "Did Tish steal my slippers?"

He laughed. "No, I had left them in the car but here they are. You look lovely. Feel better?"

"Yes, and am I awful to say I'm hungry?"

"Oh, no. Since Jean's paying, we want to eat every bit of her money's worth." He waited as she stepped into her sandals and put his arm around her as they walked into the sitting room.

Jean and Rena arrived and a few minutes later they were on their way to the Lodge. From greetings she could hear, Kelly gathered they were regular customers and she listened to conversations around her, allowing Jonathan to order for her.

They were midway through the meal when Jean asked, "Kelly, have you ever modeled?"

"Heavens, no," she said, totally surprised. "I understand you need to be tall and skinny for modeling."

"Rena and I were talking about how striking you would look in our new black line for fall. Your coloring is outrageously bold for dark colors."

She laughed. "I'd stumble and fall and ruin your entire show, Mrs. Heath."

"Call me Jean, please, Kelly, and if you lived nearby, I'd certainly enlist your help in the new season. Right now we're already into the fall and winter showings and from there, we go into spring colors. They're going to be soft and feminine this season, thank goodness." She laughed. "I really don't know how they sell some of the horrible colors and styles, but it seems women will buy anything if it's called 'style.'"

The talk went on around her and Kelly smiled to herself at the thought of modeling the exclusive line of clothing handled by the two older women.

Sounds like fun, though, but there's a job I have to finish ahead of everything else. She caught a glimpse of the darkness she still faced.

"They have a wonderful dessert, Kelly," Rena said, interrupting the younger woman's thoughts. "Would you like to try it? I have no idea what's in it besides seventy-five thousand calories."

"And five pounds per bite," Jean added.

Kelly joined in the laughter. "No, thanks. The lobster was delicious and I'm stuffed."

"When are you due to leave, Kelly?" Jean asked.

"Sunday around noon." She sighed. "I'm already sorry."

"Stay till tomorrow, Jonathan," Jean invited.

"No, thanks, Mother. Since tomorrow is Kelly's last day here, she needs to get some rest. I've been so busy repairing storm damage that I've missed some of our visiting time and want to make up for that."

A strange thrill startled Kelly at the tone of his voice

and set off an alarm of wonder. She pushed it to the back of her mind as they said good-bye, promised another visit, collected Tish and Ebony, and started back toward Santa Fe.

Fingers on her watch told her it was ten thirty. Only one more day with Jonathan, then back to regular routines from a heavenly week. A strange feeling of unreality floated around her as she realized it had been hours since she thought of Robbie or the reason for her blindness. So conscious was she of Jonathan and her yearning to be with him that her thoughts had become strictly one-way.

He interrupted her thoughts. "How about a short nightcap? You look tired and this is your vacation. If I send you back to Hap Alston too tired to work, he'll have a word to say to me."

"Not to worry, Jonathan. I finished my article and if it's what he wants, it will take up slack on the human interest sheet and soothe his feelings."

"What's your subject matter?"

"Trials and tribulations of a blind person trying to get along in a seeing world. You think of prejudices in relation to sex or race, but when you're blind, people either try to ignore the fact or they overreact and feel guilty. We don't need that. I usually try to get across in my articles the fact that we can manage with more understanding and less pity."

"May I read it?"

She turned to face him. "It needs editing, and it isn't your usual *Wall Street Journal* material."

"I read the comics too, Kelly," he said, laughing softly, adding, "May I?"

"Sure."

When they reached home, Jonathan went to the bar across the den to mix drinks, strangely silent. Kelly walked around touching tables, lamps, the mantel, reveling in the different textures of the masculine accessories Jonathan had chosen for his home. Then she felt his callused, yet soft, touch on her cheeks and she turned into Jonathan's arms. Gently, he pulled her against him, holding her without speaking. When he released her, he led her to the couch and sat beside her, leaning across her to place a drink in her hand.

"Pretty and cool," he whispered against her ear.

"Why are you whispering?"

"Because you're so elegant." They laughed together, and sat in companionable silence to finish their drinks. When she leaned on his shoulder, he shifted to allow her face to rest against his throat, removing the glass from her hand as her head went back to meet his kiss. Gentle kisses went from the curve of her cheek to throat and back again, taking her lips as she moved to meet him, her hand finding its way under his shirt, fingers tangling in thick chest hair. His left hand, in a quest of its own, found the zipper at the neck of her dress and slid it down till he reached the catch on her bra, releasing it to slide his hands around to cup the small firm breast. Her breath caught beneath his kiss as he traced the smooth skin to the tight brown center jutting outward under his manipulation.

"Jonathan?"

"Hmmm?"

"This is—could be—"

"Dangerous?" His voice barely audible, he continued to move his mouth across hers, the tip of his tongue caressing soft lips that parted, giving, accepting, expecting more.

"Y-yes."

"It's been a long time since I've been this close to danger. Let me stay," he said, his free hand in the bright tangle of hair, pulling her head back so that he looked down into her face, heavy brown lashes lying against her cheek, hiding the unseeing depths. His exploration over her breast shifted to the other one, catching the hardening tip between his fingers, rubbing with a slow rhythm then releasing it to move over her flat stomach, fingers skimming her firm flesh. His breathing was deep and steady as he watched long lashes lift and he stared into the light brown circles, seeing a luminous edge around the pupils.

"Can you see me?" he whispered.

"Yes." A slight smile curved her well-kissed mouth. A finger came up to his lips, found the groove on the left side of his face, and followed it upward to his eye. "Is that a long dimple?"

"No, it's a scar."

"A horse kicked you?" she teased.

"Nothing quite so glamorous," he assured her. "A very unglamorous car accident."

"Oh, I'm sorry," she said, attempting to sit up, but he held her close to him.

"Don't change the subject," he told her.

"What was the subject?" she wanted to know.

"Danger. Yours." He stood, and with swift steps, led her to the bedroom. The door closed behind him as he pulled the dress from her shoulders with one liquid movement. Her hands came up to stop him, but she wasn't fast enough, and she stood there in loose bra and pantyhose, unaware of the innocent look of her slender, almost too slender, body.

"Kelly." The gruffness of his voice was muffled as he suddenly laid her down on the bed, wrapped her in his arms, and buried his lips in her hair. But just as suddenly he pulled away from her, his breath uneven, his hands trembling as he disentangled them from around her.

He breathed deeply, trying to steady himself, and said, "I'll see you in the morning." Then he was gone.

Kelly stared in the direction of the door, too stunned to react. She lay a long time remembering every word they had said. None of it meant a thing, she decided hours later, when finally she slept.

Jonathan was out when she got to the kitchen the next morning.

"He said he'd be back early, Kelly," Selena told her. "He had a few things he wanted to check."

After her coffee Kelly took out her article and wrote two headings for it to give Hap a choice for the spotter. She hoped he liked it a lot, since he was good enough to let her off. She left the article on Jonathan's desk so he could read it when he found time. She was restless, wanting to run, to be able to swing her body, to reach out. For what? For Jonathan. Jonathan, who made love to her to within an inch of her life, then left her. *I hope I survive one more day,* she thought, feeling wistful and sad at the thought of leaving the ranch—and Jonathan.

"Why the pensive look?" Jonathan had approached without her hearing, so engrossed was she in her thoughts.

She smiled, not answering, accepting his arm as they went in to breakfast. The hard muscle of his arm moved against her breast as they walked, sending a thrill traveling at breakneck speed through her body as she recalled his hands on her the night before.

"Feel up to riding?" he asked.

"Yes."

The phone rang as they left the dining room and he said, "Sit by the pool and I'll be there shortly."

Ebony and Tish joined her and she sat in the first lounge chair Ebony stopped near, pushing her hands through her short hair. Jonathan promised they would ride some, and she wanted to let her horse run like the wind, let her stretch strong forelegs to pound out the restlessness that surged inside her. She hadn't run and played since she and Robbie had run hand in hand over the pastel desert flowers that spring when he would have been five, their laughter floating on the breeze that came through the mountain passes and canyons, teasing at them the way they teased at life, forgetting at those times that Robbie would never see any of it.

Her tongue licked at dry lips, and she ran her hands over her face, to the back of her neck to rub at the tension there.

"Kelly?" Jonathan's voice questioned. "Are you all right?"

"Oh. Yes, of course."

He was quiet, and she waited, not sure of whether he wanted conversation since, even to her, he seemed preoccupied. She wished she could see his expression, but she smiled toward him, remaining silent.

Big hands gathered both of hers and she moved over as he sat on the edge of the lounge. "We need to have a serious talk, Kelly," he said.

"Whatever for?" she asked. "This is my last day here and we don't need to be serious." She hesitated. "What kind of serious talk? I'm not going to Johns Hopkins. I can't pay—"

"Will you marry me, Kelly?" His voice was as even as if he'd asked the time of day.

She went still, her breath cut off by the unexpected question, and as she held that breath, she could hear him breathing, quietly, evenly. *What in the world is this?* she wondered.

"Jonathan." She stopped, then asked, "Why?"

"Why do people get married, Kelly?"

She waited for the obvious answer to his own question, and when he said nothing, she asked, "Do you love me?"

The fingers on hers tightened, hurting. "Love is a vastly overrated commodity, Kelly. We have everything we need for a good marriage."

"What do we have?" she asked, anger beginning deep inside her.

He released her hands, leaning to kiss her, his mouth gentle as the tip of his tongue caressed her lips, lingering in the sensitive corner he had found excited her. His words a mere whisper, he hesitated at the tender spot in front of her ear. "We're friends, and that matters more than love. Besides that, I want you very much and you want me, don't you, sweetheart?"

She pushed him away, almost looking straight into his eyes, knowing his were dark, perhaps moody, and her hands framed his face. "I don't believe you." She shook her head. "You want to live with me and never say 'I love you' and don't want me to say it to you? No, Jonathan, no. Love is—"

"Love is a trap that, when sprung and has maimed the victim, is then useless and discarded. Or else it's patched up and is never the same."

She shivered at the bitterness in him that was a steel sword thrusting its way through her body, tearing at the feelings he had fostered all week. She felt again the tenderness as he made love to her, pushing her away before it went too far, even when he knew she wanted him.

"Why, Jonathan?" She asked the question she knew he wouldn't answer, but she asked anyway. "Why would you marry me when you could marry any rich, raving beauty you wanted? A blind woman you'll have to lead around and watch to see that she doesn't put the wrong drops in her eyes? Someone you'll have to take everywhere she goes, always depending on you for everything. It gets old, believe me, and if there's no love...." She let her voice trail off, swallowing hard, feeling hot tears course down her cheeks.

"Are you finished?" he asked.

"I—I guess so." She sniffed a little.

"Are you in love with Fred?"

"No."

"Anyone?" he persisted.

"No." If he couldn't feel her love for him, he wouldn't believe her, anyway, so she remained silent, letting him assume she told the truth.

"Then marry me." There was the slightest tone of command in his voice, slight, but there.

Silence enclosed them, and still he waited for her
answer. Her voice, when she spoke, was steady even
though her heart had started a drumbeat all its own. "I
have a contract with Hap that terminates the end of
August. If you still want to marry me at that time, all
right."

"I don't care for such an evasive answer to my proposal." He could have been smiling.

"It's the only one I can give under the circumstances."

The silence stretched and the nerves that had nagged
at her all morning threatened to split in a screaming
torrent. Finally he said, "All right, Kelly. I can wait."
He pulled her up and steadied her. "We were going
riding. Still game?"

"Yes." What a weird situation, she thought, walking
between Ebony and Tish, till the small dog stopped in
front of her, begging to be carried.

"You have her spoiled," Jonathan told her in a normal voice.

She felt light-headed. *I could be having a bad dream,*
she thought.

"Carl rode Goldie out this morning, Kelly. I'll give
you Sable. She's a very gentle Arabian, the color of her
name."

Kelly let Sable have her head to follow Jonathan's
lead. Tish sat on the saddle in front of her and Ebony
ran ahead a short way, then bounded back to let Kelly
know she wasn't abandoned. Her thoughts ran helter
skelter, her moves automatic, glad Jonathan wasn't a
big talker. *What will we do all the time after we're married
if we're not in love and don't talk much? That leaves a lot
of time for making love together, which isn't a bad deal,*
she grinned to herself, hugging Tish.

"Why are you smiling?" She hadn't heard Jonathan
walk his horse back to meet her.

"It's a lovely day, Jonathan. I was just thinking how

hot it is in Salt Lake City compared to what—Eighty here, at the most.''

"About that," he agreed. "It's seldom higher than eighty-five degrees even in July and August."

They rode in silence till she heard his horse pause, and she pulled the reins on Sable. "Let's walk." He reached for her and she leaned into his arms, but he didn't hold her, instead turned to walk hand in hand with her, leading the horses.

"I read your article, Kelly. Your way with words certainly is graphic enough that the public should have no trouble seeing what you can't see." His fingers tightened. "Ebony puts you in a whole new world, doesn't she?"

"Yes." She didn't have to add any more if he understood her meanings in the article. Perhaps more people would be touched and she'd be doing all blind people a great service if it brought in funds for research. She could only hope.

"Does Alston know you plan to leave when your contract's up?" Jonathan interrupted her thoughts.

"Yes, he understands." For a moment she was tempted to spill everything to him, but she needed a little more time before her secret came out. She'd have to depend on his forgiveness later on. Maybe he wouldn't care to marry someone so deceitful, and maybe that would be for the best. How could you marry without love, at least to start? Love might die after too little nourishment, but to begin marriage without any at all? What a waste. *I could love him enough for both of us,* she thought and shook her head, knowing it didn't work that way.

"What are you saying no to now? I haven't asked yet."

"Anticipation," she told him, turning to smile in his direction.

He laughed. "Ready to go back? It's time for a rest before dinner."

"I knew I could say no in advance. I'm not tired."

"Sure, you are." His arm went around her waist, hugging her close, then let his hand rest casually on her hip, turning her toward Sable to help her into the saddle.

An automobile wreck, he had told her when she asked about the scar. She rode, deep in thought, wanting to know everything about Jonathan—when, why, where, how, who, and what—just like any newsperson. But her wish was for knowledge not to be published, only for her own personal use.

When Jonathan left her in her room promising to call her at six, she walked to the open window, breathing deeply of the warm mountain air. If she could talk to Ann, she thought, but even Ann couldn't decide for her what to do about Jonathan's proposal. *I want to marry him, but I can't,* she decided, knowing she'd change her mind a dozen times before the end of August. She lay across the bed, worrying her lower lip with her teeth, rolling over on her stomach, restless and lonely. Not since Robbie's death had she been so lonely, knowing deep down that Jonathan's attitude was at the heart of her problem. She slept an uneasy sleep, unrefreshed when she awoke.

A shower and dressing in the pale green dress gave her spirits a much needed boost upward, and she was ready when Jonathan knocked on the door.

His voice showed surprise. "Already dressed? Didn't you sleep?"

"Yes, but I didn't need a lot."

There was little conversation at dinner and Kelly made a pretense of eating. This should be their gaiest meal, a suitable ending to a lovely week, but she was jittery over the proposal, his insistence she go to the Wilmer Eye Clinic at Johns Hopkins, his attitude toward marriage. One wrong one had soured him. Did he still have deep feelings for his wife? *I'll bet she was gorgeous,* she thought, pushing food with her fork.

"You're playing with your food, Kelly. Don't you care for crab meat?"

"Yes." And for some stubborn reason she couldn't identify, closed her lips on that short answer.

"You don't sound certain at all."

She put her fork down, and turned her head to him. "Jonathan." No other words would come, so she swallowed and tried again. "It's been wonderful here with you, the best vacation I've had in years." He didn't help her. "I can't marry you, Jonathan."

"You promised you would after your contract expires and I plan to hold you to that. It gives you six weeks to consider everything."

"But—"

His voice was quiet. "If you aren't in love with anyone, Kelly, our marriage will benefit us both. I certainly intend it to be a marriage in every sense of the word."

"Except for love," she protested, her face hot.

He laughed. "I think you're mature enough to disregard the romantic nonsense generally associated with love and marriage."

But I don't want to, she thought, tightening her lips to prevent the words escaping. If this was logic, it was a kind she didn't know how to argue with.

They finished the meal in silence and walked outside into the warm twilight.

"It's a beautiful night, Kelly. Point-to-point stars for a million miles and a new quarter moon."

"When does your weather turn cool here?" If he wanted to make conversation, she could try.

"Not much earlier than Albuquerque although we are a couple of thousand feet higher. After Labor Day, there's usually some cool days, then in early November our snow starts. Higher up, it's plenty deep for all the ski buffs by Thanksgiving."

"Do you ski?"

It was a brief moment's hesitation, and she felt the stiffness in his answer. "I haven't been on skis in years. Probably break my legs before I got to the first jump."

They walked on down the slope she knew led to the corral, and she could hear animal noises as they got closer. From out of the darkness, Ebony came to walk beside her.

"Where's Tish?"

"Maria came after her since she's home and needed a playmate for the weekend."

"Is that Beowulf?" she asked.

"Where?"

"Nearby," she replied.

"Come on, Kelly, how would you know he's here? He hasn't made a sound and is twenty-five feet away from us."

She laughed. "Ebony told me. She reacts to him just like any female when there's a handsome male around."

Ebony stopped and Kelly did too, sensing the fence was close. Jonathan's hand guided her, and she swung up to sit on the top rail, feeling him within reach.

They sat in silence and Kelly gave up trying to make conversation. Never a talkative man, he was even more quiet tonight. If she were discussing him in a newspaper article, she would apply the word *taciturn* to his description. His kisses? Disturbing, to say the least, she decided. Provocative, exciting—mere words for a feeling she'd never experienced till Jonathan. It will be a week to remember, she admitted to herself, and take a while to forget. She sighed out loud.

"What's that for?" Jonathan asked.

"I've already said it's been wonderful, and it has. Going back to an everyday world will be a letdown, to say the least."

"Don't go back."

She turned on him. "You're tempting me, Jonathan, and you're being unfair about it."

"How so?"

"You know I have a job, a contract, to finish. Hap's been good to me—that's a pale word to use for how he's helped—and I can't just quit so near the end of my time there."

Jonathan jumped from the fence and his hands circled her waist, lifting her down, keeping her body close to him. "I'll bet if I talked to Hap, he'd release you tomorrow."

"No." She put her hands flat on his chest, her face lifted so he could see her expression.

"You're stubborn, Kelly," he informed her as though revealing news to her.

She grinned suddenly, white teeth showing in the faint light from the stars and slice of moon. "You noticed?"

"A few times," he told her, his head bending till his mouth covered hers.

She breathed deeply of the tangy after-shave she would forever associate with him and stood on tiptoes to bring him closer to her, hands going to his shoulders. His hands rested on her hips, pulling her against the hardness of his body. Gentle at first, his kisses grew insistent, the tip of his tongue forcing her lips apart, searching, finding her breathless response. His hand moved up her back, fitting her neck, cutting off her breath as he forced her even closer, tangling long fingers in her hair. She moaned as he used her hair to pull her lips away from his, his breath warmed her cheek, the harsh sound only an echo of hers.

"Kelly?" It was a question and answer all its own.

Answer him she did, finding his mouth again, nibbling the full curve of his lip, trailing kisses down to the squared chin, letting her face rest against his throat, parted lips and tip of her tongue brushing every inch of flesh above his shirt collar. Her hand came downward, searching for the buttons she could open.

"Don't do that, Kelly," he warned, his voice quiet.

Even as her busy fingers ignored him, she said, "All right."

Hands beneath the smooth material found the roughness of his chest, moving with quick familiarity over the broad expanse, under his arms as far as she could reach, lifting her face to him again. As he took her offered kiss, her fingers dug into the hard muscled back. He lifted her without effort, it seemed, and she was aware of movement till she felt straw beneath her, smelled the musky scent of hay. Her dress slid from her shoulders and his lips followed its movement, touching every part of her flesh, lingering over her breasts lifting for his pleasure. His teeth coaxed a nipple until it extended into his mouth and his tongue caressed and teased until she moaned, pressing her flat stomach against the hardness of him. He pushed her away from him, one hand coming from her hips to stroke her belly, hesitate at her navel, then finally trail down to separate her thighs. Her breath came quickly and unevenly as his fingers pressed into the firmness of her legs, lifting her hips to meet the force of his body. Sunlight and darkness mingled behind her closed lids as he whispered, "Darling," and time stood still as they gave equally to each other.

He wrapped his shirt around her, holding her tight, lips against the brightness of her hair. "You'll marry me, Kelly?"

A deep breath shuddered through her body as she yielded. "Yes, Jonathan."

Chapter Seven

Salt Lake City lay cloaked in the humid heat of mid-July, and no one seemed inclined to do much more than go to work, and head home to pools and air-conditioned homes. Kelly was no exception. After a brief flurry of interest in her return, everyone went back to their routines. Several reporters, including Fred, were on vacation. Hap read her article and, with only minor changes, printed it.

He called her into his office on Wednesday morning, closed the door, and said, "Tell me all about it."

She did—even to the strange marriage proposal—but left out the events of her last night with Jonathan.

"Are you going to marry him?"

"Yes."

"Can you settle for that, Kelly?" he asked, concern in his voice.

"I guess I have no choice. I love him, Hap, and if he'll marry me after he finds out I'm not really blind—" She stopped. "He doesn't strike me as a man who'll take kindly to being fooled."

"You had plenty of good reasons, Kelly, and so far they've worked, although I wouldn't have given a plugged nickel for the chances when you came here."

She smiled, remembering her first interview with Hap a year ago, scared to death of the stern editor but

In the Eyes of Love

determined to get a job with him, somehow. "Thanks for going against your better judgment, Hap."

In the coolness of her apartment after work she lay on the floor, Ebony beside her. Each day away from Jonathan made her situation seem more fantasy than reality. Her pulse beat faster as she thought of the hours in Jonathan's arms when she had given him her love, and he had taken her heart as a bonus. Awakening in his bed, his arms still around her, she stirred, sleepily wondering where she was.

His lips moved aagainst her cheek as he whispered, "You have straw in your hair."

Full realization of what happened came instantly and she stiffened, trying to pull away, but his hold tightened, and he said, "No, darling, you belong to me, and you aren't going anywhere yet."

They lay close together, his hard body partly covering her. His hand went slowly over her body, sliding over her hip bone, and he drew a circle around her navel with his forefinger. When she trembled, he pushed her head back and his mouth came down hard against hers. Rolling slightly, he fitted his body into hers and his thundering heartbeat, coupled with hers, drowned the soft moan in her throat. There was no doubt that Jonathan was claiming her for his own and as she had little power over her own traitorous feelings, she gave him body, heart, and soul.

It was quiet as she recalled the happy hours with Jonathan until the phone rang in the stillness, causing even the calm Ebony to jump. She was smiling at the dog's reaction as she said, "Hello?"

"Kelly." It was Jonathan and her heart fluttered as her fingers tightened on the receiver.

"Yes, Jonathan. How are you?"

"Lonesome. Are you sure you can't come home the end of July rather than August?" She could feel the smile in his voice and, suddenly she wanted to see him, really see him, and touch him all over. Her face burned at her memories. He said "come home." A thoughtless statement that made her homesick.

"You'll be surprised at how soon the end of August will come, and you'll have to put up with me from then on. So you'd better enjoy being lonesome while you can."

There was a slight hesitation before he went on. "I went shopping for your ring, and found two I like but you should have final say, Kelly. I'll bring them down with me next month."

"You're coming to Salt Lake?"

He laughed. "Don't sound so surprised. My fiancée lives there."

Her breath quickened at the words. "That has a nice sound. How did you know what size ring to buy?"

"I guessed at size five and a half."

"Good guess. Why don't you choose the ring since you can look them over better than I."

After a small silence, he said, "All right, Kelly. You can change it later if you'd rather."

"I'll keep the one you choose."

"I thought women would rather pick such a personal item," he said.

"Some would," she told him. "I trust you."

He laughed, and gave in. "Okay. I'll call later this week." He said good-bye but the thrill of hearing his voice lingered with her for a long time.

She went quietly about her work, finishing up all the articles she had scheduled for publication. Her appointment with Dr. Crane, the eye specialist, was set for August 15, and entrance into his clinic for results from her checkup would be August 17. If Jonathan knew about the appointments, he'd have plenty of questions and insist on being around. She hugged herself, trying to picture his face from her many explorations with her fingers, anxious at the same time about his reaction to her being able to see. She wrote Ann a long letter, but didn't mention her engagement, only that Hap was sure the award would be given and almost guaranteed a good-sized grant for study on blindness in newborn children.

Time flew, Ebony became as much a part of her life as her shadow, the pet of all her newspaper friends. Except Fred. He still kept his distance from them both, and Kelly made no attempt to resume their previous relationship. Her thoughts were filled with Robbie, Ann, Gary, and last, but far from least, Jonathan.

It was Saturday, a week before her first appointment with Dr. Crane at his eye clinic. The city lay under a blanket of heat, and muddy-looking clouds crowded over the mountaintops. Kelly, on her way home from the library, walked slowly, hearing Ebony panting beside her.

"Miserable out here, Ebony. Let's get home and stay there. Maybe spend the afternoon in the bathtub." She wore a pale green sleeveless cotton shirt and brief white shorts that showed off the lightly tanned legs. Her sandals were mere bottoms and one strap to hold them on.

They turned the corner a few doors from the apartment, and Ebony slowed, then stopped, and Kelly could feel her body move as she wagged her tail in a friendly greeting. Almost at the same moment she caught the familiar tangy smell of after-shave.

"Jonathan?"

"Hello, Kelly. I won't ask how you knew I was here."

She stood absolutely still, then was suddenly in his arms, held to his chest.

"Library again?" he asked.

"Yes." She was out of breath. "Where did you come from?"

"I told you it was lonesome at home." He took her

hand opposite Ebony's leash, and started walking with her. "Do you have plans for the weekend?"

She shook her head, smiling up at him. "Except to read. I have a column to finish before Sunday night's deadline."

"It may be late," he told her, squeezing the hand he held, causing her to miss a step as she took in his meaning.

Inside the cool apartment she said, "Would you like some iced tea?"

"Yes." He followed her into the small kitchen and stood nearby as she filled two glasses and handed one to him. They went back into the living room.

"Your new place is nice. More room, isn't it?"

"Oh, yes, I'd forgotten you didn't see this apartment. Ebony and I have plenty of space to wander around. Whoever made it possible, I hope he or she knows how much I'm in debt for Ebony and all this room."

"I'm sure he does." He picked up her left hand, and she felt the ring being slipped on her finger. "Will you marry me, Kelly?"

She stretched her hand in front of her, going over the ring with the fingers of her right hand. "It's an odd setting," she said.

"Yes. It's a small pearl with a diamond on each side set in platinum." His lips touched the ring. "You didn't answer my question."

"Yes, I'll marry you, Jonathan."

He held her face between his hands, kissing her with soft, brief kisses across her mouth, the tip of her nose, her closed eyes. "Do you want a big wedding?"

"No. Do you?"

"No. When?"

She hesitated. "October first?"

"Why not September first?" he countered.

"That might be rushing it some if I don't get finished here before the very end of August," she said, doing some fast calculating.

"Finished what?"

"With the paper, moving. Oh, all the things that have to be done. I need a dress."

"Jean plans to take care of that if you don't mind."

"You mean she already knows?"

He laughed. "She's my mother, whom I adore. Of course, I told her I asked you to marry me, but not how unenthusiastic you are."

"Did you tell her you weren't marrying for love? Maybe just because you feel sorry for me?"

"Kelly, stop it." His hands tightened on her shoulders. "We've been over this before."

She sat silently, looking straight into his eyes, willing him to change his mind, but she knew he wouldn't. *Now's the time to back out of this deal,* she cautioned herself. Instead, she said, "I wear a size nine dress."

"She already knows that," he informed her.

"How?"

"Remember Jean's in the dress business, and very good at judging sizes. Then, too, I looked at the labels in your dresses while you were at the ranch."

She laughed. "That's sneaky."

His lips touched hers, lingered on her temple. "Do you want to wear white?"

She went still within the circle of his arms, then moved her forehead against his lips and whispered, "I'm not entitled."

He shook her a little. "You are if you want it, Kelly."

"No. I like lavender, blue, or green." She let her fingers slide from his cheek across his mouth, spreading them to cover the firm lips, his warm breath sending tremors through her body. He kissed the fingers she held there, letting his hands go to her waist, pulling her up with him as he stood, lifting her, his long legs moving with sure stride to her bedroom. He remained standing by the bed, gazing at her face inches from his, then kissed her mouth, a brief, bruising kiss.

His voice was rough as he said, "I want you, Kelly. Don't make me wait."

She made no protest and unlike his voice, his hands were gentle as he undressed her, his lips touching every inch of her body as it was uncovered. Her breath came quickly as his kisses spread fire through her and she moved to meet him.

"Jonathan?" Her arms held on to him, nails striping his back.

"Kelly honey." His mouth, hard and possessive, held hers until he moaned with the intense emotion coursing through their bodies.

Kelly didn't recognize the feelings that Jonathan brought to the surface and guided to bring her pleasure she never knew existed, had never dreamed of. She accepted them, knowing she was heading for trouble, but fell more deeply in love with him as the night passed, refusing to look beyond the moment.

On Sunday morning, Jonathan insisted on cooking breakfast for them. "My plane leaves at two thirty so after I'm gone, you can do your column." He rumpled her hair as he passed her. "Wouldn't want you to get fired at this late date."

"Where'd you learn to cook?"

"Jean taught me years ago. Said I might one day have to cook for my wife." He laughed. "I'll have to tell her she was right."

Her thumb moved to the inside of her hand to feel the ring he had placed there. "Jonathan?"

"Yes, Kelly?"

"Are you sure?"

"Yes, I am. Now, tell me how you really feel about marrying me." He waited a split second before adding, "Not that I plan to let you out of it, regardless of your answer."

"I'm getting the best of the bargain," she told him.

"How do you figure that?"

"Well—" She hesitated, then said bluntly, "You're very wealthy, and I've never had anything extra. It's hard to comprehend having anything you want at any time."

"Is that important to you, Kelly?"

She spread her fingers. "I don't know, Jonathan, but living hand to mouth isn't fun forever."

"No, I don't suppose it would be," he said softly. "Now, eat your breakfast."

She took another bite. "What do you get out of the marriage, Jonathan?"

"You."

"Will I be enough?"

"Yes, you'll see that you are."

"How?"

"Want me to show you?" His voice was teasing.

A flush started at the low neck of her blouse and spread upward, staining her face the color of rose petals, all the way to the russet-gold hairline. She swallowed, but only shook her head.

"You've a lovely blush, Kelly," he said, his hand covering hers as it lay on the table.

The apartment was empty almost beyond belief after Jonathan left, and Kelly wandered from room to room, restless and uneasy. It seemed wrong, somehow, to plan a marriage based only on his wanting her and pity that she knew was there, despite his denial. Love didn't guarantee the survival of a marriage, he had said, and she knew he was right. Especially a one-sided love as in their situation.

I'm going to be sorry, whatever I do, she concluded, and went to bed, reliving again the hours in Jonathan's arms. His gentleness with her, even as she sensed the unleashed passion building in him as he made love to her, bringing a fiery response from her, body and soul.

Oh, Lord, I've never felt anything the way he makes me feel, and I'll never be able to say no to whatever he demands. Burying her face in the pillow, she finally slept.

"Relax, Kelly," the strong male voice told her. "It won't take too much longer."

But sitting in Dr. Crane's office, Kelly could not relax. She was tense—tense at the thought of what he would find after a year of wearing the discs that had made her blindness real to her and to the world. She voiced her concern.

"Well, it's certain to be an improvement over the past year," Dr. Crane assured her.

As he worked, removing the discs from her eyes, filling them with the cooling liquid, she thought about what Hap had told her.

"You got your grant, Kelly, and it's been given to research for blindness in the newborn with Dr. Oscar Clements at the Darbyshire Clinic. All the findings will be presented at seminars nationwide and monitored by your Dr. Crane." He was quiet for a moment. "Eight thousand dollars was paid to cover Robbie's last hospital bill and here's a check for seven thousand dollars for your use. You certainly earned it." She accepted the rectangle of paper, running her fingers across it as Hap went on. "Are you sure you want no publicity on this?"

"Yes, I'm sure, Hap, only for the research portion to the clinic and the doctors there. I have everything I need, thanks to you. If I could repay you, I would, but all I can do is give you my heartfelt appreciation."

He cleared his throat. "It's been a revelation to work with you, Kelly, and we're going to miss you at the paper."

She came back to the present as Dr. Crane said, "What do you see, Kelly?"

"Blurred gray," she said, tenseness in her voice and stiff body.

"Good enough. Come on in here and lie down for two hours then we'll put more drops in before we put the patches on."

It was after eight o'clock when she and Ebony got back to the apartment and, aside from several cups of coffee, she hadn't eaten since breakfast. More than being hungry, she wanted the seclusion of her apartment so she could cry. Dr. Crane cautioned her about rubbing her eyes and she was going to have a problem mopping up the tears she could no longer hold back. She removed the patches, keeping her eyes closed as she wet a handful of tissues, threw them away, and took more to keep against her cheek to mop up the remaining moisture, careful not to apply any pressure on her eyes. Drying the area completely, she replaced the patches held by bands around her head, glad the tears had subsided for the time being.

The phone rang and she blew her nose and cleared her throat before she picked up the receiver. "Hello?" Her husky voice sounded as though she were getting over a cold, when she was getting over a case of utter lack of self-control.

"Kelly?" Jonathan's clear voice came through her fog of emotions. "Are you all right? Where have you been?"

Her heart tripped over its own beat at the sound of his voice, but she managed to tell him the story she had rehearsed. "Oh, Ebony and I went to the county fair to cover some of the pet shows. I should have told you I'd be gone all day."

"I was a little worried since I called several times," he said. "How are you?" His voice was gentle as he questioned her.

"Okay. The weather's a bit cooler after the rains a couple days ago. And you?"

She half listened, letting his voice infiltrate her very

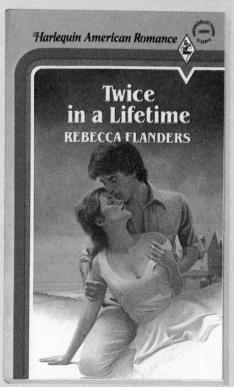

Enter a uniquely American world of romance with *Harlequin American Romance.*™

Harlequin American Romances are the first romances to explore today's new love relationships. These compelling romance novels reach into the hearts and minds of women across America…probing into the most intimate moments of romance, love and desire.

You'll follow romantic heroines and irresistible men as they boldy face confusing choices. Career first, love later? Love without marriage? Long-distance relationships? All the experiences that make love real are captured in the tender, loving pages of *Harlequin American Romance*.

What makes American women so different when it comes to love? Find out with *Harlequin American Romance!*

Send for your introductory FREE book now.

GET THIS BOOK FREE!

MAIL TO:
Harlequin Reader Service
2504 W. Southern Avenue,
Tempe, AZ 85282

YES! I want to discover *Harlequin American Romance*.

Send me FREE and without obligation, "Twice in a Lifetime."
If you do not hear from me after I have examined my FREE
book, please send me the 4 new *Harlequin American Romance*
novels each month as soon as they come off the presses. I
understand that I will be billed only $2.25 per book (total
$9.00). There are no shipping or handling charges. There
is no minimum number of books that I have to purchase.
In fact, I may cancel this arrangement at any time. "Twice
in a Lifetime" is mine to keep as a FREE gift, even if I do
not buy any additional books.   154-CIA-NAD7

Name   (please print)

Address   Apt. No.

City   State/Prov.   Zip/Postal Code

Signature (If under 18, parent or guardian must sign.)

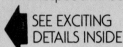

being, her body coming alive as though he had touched her. Before she said good-bye she told him, "I'll be covering some stories and gathering material around the state next week, Jonathan, and I won't be here very much. I'll call you from wherever I am. All right?"

"Call me collect, Kelly, as often as you can."

Leaving Ebony with Hap, she checked into the clinic early Monday morning and from then on never a minute was she alone, as Dr. Crane began a series of tests checking for possible cornea damage. She called Jonathan Wednesday evening, assuring him that she was having a great time.

"I'll be home late Saturday, so I'll call you then," she promised.

"Not till then?"

She laughed. "Gives you a chance to miss me."

On Thursday Kelly was allowed outside the clinic for two hours, wearing dark glasses, then more tests were taken, and after sunset she walked outside without glasses. Each time she recognized a tree or house or car, her heart hammered and her breath came quickly. She gulped, fighting back the desire to scream at the slow progress of regaining her sight. After a year of not seeing any of her familiar world, she was in a hurry to see it all.

Dr. Crane was waiting for her in the small examination room as she came back inside, and she quivered as he probed with the shaded light into her sensitive eyes. He backed away from her, rubbing his hands, hardly able to contain his excitement. "It worked, Kelly, by golly, it worked." He adjusted an illuminated screen in front of her and said, "Tell me what the third object is and the color."

"It's a red, white, and blue beach ball," she said.

"Right." He flipped the screen. "What's that?"

For a moment the screen blurred and panic fluttered

in her throat. She blinked several times and the image cleared. "A basket of red roses and a border of yellow jonquils."

Dr. Crane was quiet and she held her breath. When he touched her face, she jumped and gave a low whimper. He said quietly, "Everything checks out, Kelly, and we'll proceed with the drops at regular intervals as planned." He helped her to her feet and gave her the special dark glasses to put on again. "Keep these on at all times for protection until we finish here."

She had trouble sleeping that night. Her thoughts zipped from Jonathan to Robbie to the proposed wedding, to Jonathan to Robbie in a mad merry-go-round. Doubt chased away her joy and joy chased away the blues that threatened.

Why didn't I tell Jonathan what was happening? she wondered time and again, walking from door to window and back again, seeing enough to allow her to make the short trip several times without stumbling. *Why did I agree to marry him?* She rubbed damp palms on her pajamas and climbed into bed to twist and turn, and finally sleep just before daylight.

She was awake before Dr. Crane came in at six thirty Friday morning, but stayed in bed, the dark glasses on, her eyes squinting behind them.

"Well, Kelly, are you ready for this?" he asked.

"Yes," she told him, not at all sure of that one positive word.

A machine that resembled a word processor was wheeled to the side of her bed. "This will put the laser beams into the eyes, Kelly, to heal the tender tissues we've irritated. Only the light will touch your eye. Just lie still and you won't feel anything."

She heard the button click, then a soft whirring sound, and Dr. Crane said, "That's it." He pushed the machine out of the way and said, "One more last round of drops and we're through. All that remains is reading this last test and making the report." A cool cloth mopped at the corners and lids of her eyes. "Look at me, Kelly," he said.

Instinct had kept her eyes closed and now she let the lashes lift away from her cheeks, gazing into Dr. Crane's hazel eyes beneath bushy white brows. His ruddy cheeks were shadowed by a probing light attached around his head.

"Keep your eyes open as long as you can, Kelly, while I take a look." She held her breath until he turned the light off and smiled. "How do I look?"

"You're the handsomest man I've ever seen," she whispered.

He laughed. "I may keep you here forever." He patted her hand. "Take a shower if you like but no water in the eyes, so don't wash your hair. I want you to stay in the room all day and keep the draperies closed. I'll see you tonight."

She watched the white-coated figure walk away from her, eyes riveted on the pink bald spot on the top of his head gleaming in the dim light of the room. When the door closed behind him, she let out her breath and slid down on the pillow. Exhausted, she was asleep in seconds.

She opened her eyes slowly, the lashes sticking, then finally separating. The room was still dim with draperies pulled and she widened her eyes, sitting up to turn her head left and right to take in the room that came into focus just the way it should. The twin bed exactly like hers across the room was made up, the covers taut and sterile white. The metal cabinet by the bed was bare, and her gaze went past it to the polished floor that gave back a blurred reflection of the room. There was no bright color at all but the neutral objects were beautiful just the same.

"Star gazing?" Dr. Crane's familiar voice asked and she turned to see him grinning at her.

"It's hard to believe," she said. "It worked. The whole wild plan worked." She was trembling as she realized this was what the experiment was all about, what they had hoped to find, the ability to heal scarred eye tissue with lasers and the drops that had never been used before. She breathed deeply. "Now what do we do?"

"We go ahead with the experiments using the money you got for being a guinea pig, Kelly. It's a start and people will take notice after the reports come out in detail. I mean the people who can help further our research and get us the funds to do it." He picked up her hand. "One more day of observations and you can go home."

Using the light around his head, Dr. Crane searched her eyes for any sign that would indicate trouble but he found none. "Take it very easy the rest of the day and I'll see you early in the morning."

As the door closed behind him, Kelly lay still, her eyes seeking and finding small nail holes in the wall, the cord hanging from the light going into the receptacle a few inches from the floor. A straight chair was placed between the beds and she looked at the braces on the legs, never recalling she had ever noticed that chairs needed that much support for all the different shaped and sized bodies they held.

Her fists were clenched tightly into the white-ridged spread, and she looked at them. Her third finger, left hand, was bare. She had followed instructions and left all her jewelry at home and her heart caught as she wondered what her engagement ring was like. And Ebony. She closed her eyes, picturing the dog who was a part of her life now even though she had owned her only a few months. Robbie would have loved her. So would everyone, child or adult, who could use her as eyes and a companion so complete that loneliness was a distant thing. Her body quivered as she thought of what she had missed for the past year, but some people would miss forever.

I'll see Jonathan, she thought, and immediately felt his arms around her. A thrill shimmered through her and she turned on her stomach, her face on the edge of her pillow, and went to sleep.

She slept better than she could remember, dreaming of Jonathan, and awakened to lie smiling, eyes wide open to stare at the splotched white ceiling of the clinic. Even that was beautiful, she decided, as she padded to the bathroom to put drops in her eyes, shower, and brush her teeth.

Dr. Crane stayed with her all day Saturday, his tape recorder going as he asked her detailed questions. There was no damage to her sight from extensive wearing of the colored discs that kept her from seeing for a full year.

"You know, Kelly," he said, "if we'd had volunteers like you a decade ago, we'd be a hundred years ahead in treatment of eye diseases that cause blindness. A lot of people might see today if we could have gone this far in experimenting and had the money for sophisticated equipment." The light probed her eyes as he gently stretched the lids. "You earned every penny you received—and more." He stood up. "What do you plan to do with Ebony?"

She gazed at him in surprise. "I'll keep her. I love her too much to give her up."

"Just asking." He patted her shoulder. "Come on and let's get you on your way home."

She called Hap and he was there within fifteen minutes. He opened the door to the driver's side but Ebony was over him and bounding toward Kelly. She knelt to put her arms around the sleek neck, whispering, "You're so beautiful. Oh, I knew you would be, but you're even more so than I thought. No, I can't give you up." Ebony sat quietly, her tongue occasionally brushing Kelly's cheek trying to dry the tears that wouldn't be controlled.

"How about me?" Hap asked, and Kelly stood, arms going around the man she had never seen.

She backed away from him and said, "I pictured you as handsome and I was right." She wasn't surprised to see Hap's hair a brown-gray mixture, a crewcut much as he must have worn it during his army days, and clear hazel eyes that missed nothing. He was about five feet ten, straight and slim as a reed.

He let Ebony in the backseat and opened the front door of the car for Kelly. Ebony's head appeared immediately through the opening between the two front seats. She was keeping an eye out for Kelly as she had always done.

Hap didn't start the car but turned to Kelly. "Tell me the results."

She took a deep breath. "Dr. Crane says they have enough material from what he's gathered in the past year to show the areas of the eyes most likely to be damaged at birth. From the way the tissues form and the arteries crisscross, they can follow a healing process with laser beams and know exactly when there has been enough treatment, and if it's getting to the right places. The Darbyshire Clinic had already started tests along this line and the additional money from the fund we got through the articles will give them enough to complete their studies. Also, the nationwide attention they'll get about the success of the treatments will allow them to lobby for more funds next year and have a lot of concrete evidence to submit to back it up."

Hap shook his head. "When you first came to me, Kelly, and I agreed to give you a job, I couldn't figure out if it was you or I who was nuts. Before it was over, I decided both of us were." He looked at her. "Just goes to show you it pays to be a little crazy." He pulled the car into the street, threading through traffic, and asked abruptly, "Are you sure you're doing the right thing in marrying Jonathan?"

"Yes," she said simply in a voice that told Hap not to pursue the issue.

After Hap left her in her apartment Kelly walked around the living room, hesitating, her eyes going over the simple furniture she knew by the touch of her hand. Brown hopsacking covered the cushions on the love seat and big chair. Lamps on each of the two end tables had beige and brown shades to match, coordinated with the earth tones of the carpet. Her eyes rested on the print framed on the far wall, snowcovered mountains rising over the lush valley below, enough of blue sky to give a living glow to the scene. She walked slowly to the kitchen, leaning against the doorframe, blinking as her eyes traveled over the neat array of cabinets over the sink, the stove with the tea kettle on the front burner. The small table with imitation butcher-block top held glass salt and pepper shakers and a pale gold sugar bowl with a rim of darker flowers.

Smiling, she turned toward the bedroom to face Ebony, who sat in the center of the living room watching her. She went down on her knees and without urging Ebony moved to stand in front of her. Kelly's hands framed the wide face with the warm, intelligent eyes, remembering the animal's gentleness and sharp perception of her needs the past weeks.

"Why can't I push a button and have ten just like you for children who can't see?" she whispered. "You came out of nowhere; surely whoever performed the magic could do it again." Her thoughts swung to Jonathan, wondering why she insisted on believing he was responsible when he denied it.

Kelly went on into the bedroom, Ebony beside her. The bed was neatly made, a chair covered in gold and green chintz was placed near the window. On the chest against the far wall was a small jewel box. Her hands shook as she opened the box and gazed at the ring inside for several seconds before removing it. As she slipped it on her finger, the diamonds on each side of the tiny exquisite pearl winked at her through the tears.

Ebony's dark eyes watched her with concern and Kelly knelt down to her again. "Jonathan would kill me if he knew I couldn't make up my mind which is the most beautiful—you or my ring." She laughed and sniffled at the same time, burying her face in Ebony's strong neck. They sat a long time, Kelly trying to absorb all that had happened to her.

Finally, back in the living room, she stared at the phone, somehow afraid to call Jonathan, yet wanting to tell him her experience, wanting his understanding, and his sympathy for Ann and Gary and yes, sympathy for her too. It had not been the easiest year of her life, pretending blindness to carry out her promise to the small nephew she had loved so dearly.

Before she could rally the courage to pick up the phone, it rang, shattering the quietness, and she reached, her eyes closed as she was so accustomed to doing. It was Jonathan.

"I was just getting ready to call you," she told him. "I have plane reservations to Albuquerque on September first."

"Albuquerque?" he asked.

"Yes. I wanted to go see Ann and Gary before going to Santa Fe." She almost blurted "to pick up my car." Instead she said, "I haven't told them we're getting married."

"Why not?" There was surprise in his voice.

"Well, I thought—" She stopped then went on. "I thought it might all be a dream."

He laughed. "And now?"

She sighed. "I still wonder about it. Maybe when I see you again, it will seem real."

"I'll meet you in Albuquerque."

"No," she said, feeling panicky. "I'd rather you didn't." She hesitated, unsure how to explain her wishes.

"I don't think I can wait. For certain, I don't like it." She heard his indrawn breath. "Can we be married on Sunday? I've made all the arrangements."

"The sixth?"

"Yes. Jean has your dress finished, all but hemming and a few other finishing touches. She wants you to try it on as soon as you get here."

"Is it pretty?" she asked.

"Yes. It looks like you as a matter of fact. Don't ask the color; wait and be surprised."

"All right. I'll call you from Albuquerque."

Hap took her to the airport on Tuesday, saying little as he checked her baggage, made sure Ebony was taken care of since she couldn't travel with Kelly this time but had to be put in a special compartment for pets.

"If you ever need a job, Kelly, give me a call," Hap said.

Restraint was evident in her former boss's voice and Kelly too found it difficult to withhold emotion for the man. Promising to keep in touch she hugged him as her boarding call came over the loud speaker.

Flying this time was different from the last time she was on the plane to see Jonathan. True, she listened to the smooth drum of the engines, and felt the acceleration as the plane lifted off the ground, but then her eyes fixed on the clouds below them and the electric blue of the late summer sky. She smiled at the beautiful sight and refused to shift her gaze till the plane touched down in New Mexico.

Ann was standing just inside the roped-off area for passengers and Kelly drank in the features of her sister's face. Clear, pale complexion, blue eyes, long black lashes that matched the shiny black of her shoulder-length hair. They were striking opposites, Kelly's bright head a perfect foil for Ann's darkness.

To Kelly, it was almost like a dream to be walking up the carpeted aisle, seeing Ann waiting for her.

The sisters didn't speak, but gazed at each other a long time before Ann gathered her quietly to her and held on for dear life. They collected her bags and Ebony, and Kelly drove her eight-year-old white Mustang for the first time in a year.

Ann's eyes stayed on Kelly's face as she talked. "We got the receipt for the hospital bill, Kelly. Everything's paid off except the small amount on the ranch and that will be done in less than six months."

"I'm glad."

"Oh, Kelly we're so grateful to you. I don't know how we'll ever repay you."

Kelly reached out and squeezed her sister's hand. "You don't have to."

Stopped for a stoplight, Kelly's eyes fixed on the bright red circle, and she grinned. "You know, even stoplights are beautiful," she said.

But her joy was short-lived when, as she, Ann, and Gary had talked nonstop through dinner, her sister inquired about Jonathan.

Without preamble Kelly said, "I'm going to marry him this Sunday."

"Kelly!" Ann was stunned. "He still thinks you're blind."

"Yes."

"How are you going to explain all this to him?" Gary asked.

"Tell him the truth, and hope he understands."

"He'll have every right to be angry, Kelly."

She ran her fingers through the short russet curls, shaking her head as she did so. "I know, but I couldn't bring myself to tell him before. I know I should have."

Despite misgivings about what Jonathan's reactions

would be, she loved being with Ann and Gary. The worry over all the debts from Robbie's long illness and operations no longer haunted them and Kelly felt a surge of thankfulness that her farfetched scheme had worked.

They were getting ready for bed when Jonathan called. "I just got in from Denver, Kelly, or I'd drive down. When can I expect you?"

"Friday," she told him.

"You're cutting it close, sweetheart," he warned. "We're still getting married Sunday, so make it early Friday." It sounded like an order.

She laughed. "Yes, Jonathan. Early." Her heart was having itself a wonderful workout at the sound of his voice. "Jonathan?"

"Yes, Kelly?"

With all her being she wanted to say "I love you" but knew his response would not be what she wanted.

"Nothing. I'll see you soon." He couldn't know she meant literally.

On Thursday repacking her clothes to take to Santa Fe, Kelly told Ann, "I'll call you about the wedding, the time and all. It's going to be very small, just Jean, Rena, you and Gary at the ranch. No frills."

Ann couldn't hide her worry. "Where are you going on your honeymoon?"

"Nowhere right now. It's a busy time at the ranch, and Jonathan said we'll go somewhere later. It doesn't matter. Heath Cliffs is big enough and away from everyone else so it will be as good a place as any for a honeymoon." Her body trembled at the delicious memory of Jonathan's hands spreading fire through her. The only thing missing would be love, she thought, but Ann would never understand. Nor did she.

It was early afternoon when she left Albuquerque as she had planned, wanting to arrive at the ranch when Jonathan wasn't watching for her, gauging her time to when he usually came in. The interstate she had traveled so often stretched ahead of her, mountains on all sides, the old black lava hills that she loved.

Turning left onto the state road toward the ranch, she swallowed to relax the nervous tightness in her stomach. Ahead of her she saw the enormous posts made from whole trees that supported the six-foot wrought-iron lettering HEATH CLIFFS. Jonathan had given her directions for Ann and Gary to drive her, so she knew she was still five miles away from the house itself. She pulled the Mustang to the roadside and stopped, her eyes taking in the fertile high valley, the Jemez Mountains Jonathan described on their fishing trip straight ahead of her as the road turned southwest from Santa Fe. After a few moments she went on, past the gate and onto the land belonging to Jonathan. Minutes later, as she rounded a curve going up a hill, the house came into view.

"Good heavens," she said aloud, and Ebony, sensing the uncertainty in Kelly, stuck her nose over the seat to reassure her.

Jonathan had told her the house was all one floor, but he hadn't said how much ground it covered. The front was old southwestern adobe, ends of logs that had once been mammoth trees, extending in fortress-like fashion three feet from the wall. Five arches spanned the area, blending into the stone wall on the west side of the house where the late evening sun shone, turning it to slate-gray and cream. She drove slowly around the drive and stopped near the double garage at the side.

Excitement coursed through her, overcoming her uneasiness, and she moved quickly toward the door she knew led from a wide hallway into the kitchen.

"Selena?" she called, when a step to her left caused her to turn—right toward Jonathan.

She stared, transfixed by the sight of the man she

loved. He stood well over six feet, slim and straight, thick molasses-brown hair in rumpled waves back from a high forehead. The wide mouth that had covered hers many times was pulled upward at the left corner by the deep furrow of scar she had traced with inquisitive fingers, and as her glance followed the scar, her breath caught. The skin below the left eye twisted downward, showing a large area of white around the dark brown center. It gave him a lopsided, leering look until her glance moved to the right side to meet the direct dark gaze.

"Jonathan!" She stepped into the warm circle of his arms, on tiptoe, straining her body to his, his embrace folding her against the hardness of his body.

Suddenly he pulled away and held her at arm's length. "How did you get here? Kelly?" The questioning in his voice told her he realized she was different. He said, disbelieving, "Your eyes are green."

"Yes." She couldn't say anything more as she filled her eyes with his features. Her hands went to his face, fingers touching the scar, following it along his cheek. "Oh, Jonathan, I can see you."

His hands on her shoulders tightened to cut into her flesh. "How? When?" His mouth straightened into a tight line, pulling the scar with it, further stretching his left eye.

"It's a long story. Can we—can we sit down?"

He turned without another word, leading her as he had done countless times before, seating her on a long leather couch in what must be the den. She didn't take time to look around, but sat beside him on the edge of the couch, her voice urgent as she tried to explain her year as a blind person. His unwavering stare the entire story caused her to stumble at times, but she went on until the day she stepped into the path of his car. She stopped, uncertainty pulling at her, watching him.

"Why didn't you tell me?" he asked finally. "You

didn't have enough faith in me to trust me with the truth?''

"I wanted to, but to fulfill my contract I had to remain the year, and I was afraid that, somehow, if you knew, then I'd be more likely to forget sometimes around someone else." She spread her hands. "I tried not to get too close to anyone, or emotionally involved, so the experiment would work."

"Fred?"

She smiled. "It wasn't hard to stay uninvolved with Fred. You were my only real problem."

His eyes went over her bright hair, the green of her eyes that had been light brown as long as he had known her, the clear complexion with freckles across the straight nose.

"So, now you know the man you're engaged to marry is far from handsome. Do you still want to marry me?" A smile twisted the corner of his mouth upward.

Her voice was barely a whisper. "You aren't angry with me?"

The heavy brow lifted over his good eye. "Shouldn't I be happy you can see, Kelly?"

"You've no further reason to feel sorry for me," she said.

"I never said I felt sorry for you. That was your idea. Don't you recall the reason I asked you to marry me?"

Overjoyed at his reaction to her confession, she slid back on the couch, turning into his arms. "Yes, Jonathan. Please kiss me."

Chapter Eight

Jonathan's arms around her couldn't control the trembling in her body as she fully realized they were together. He had listened to her story without speaking, his mouth a straight line except where the scar pulled it upward. She hadn't been able to hide her shock at the sight of one side of his handsome face set apart by a deep, twisted groove, his left eye forced to remain partially opened all the time. Knowing there was a scar and seeing how bad it was were two different things and she knew a deep sympathy for Jonathan and how he must feel. She had done him an injustice by pretending blindness and not explaining that she would be able to see him.

She lifted her head from his shoulder, pushing away from the couch, and green eyes met dark brown ones, narrowed almost closed. Her smile was tremulous, eyes misty, as her hand went to his face. He flinched as she touched the scar and her eyes widened in surprise. She had caressed the groove many times but he had never pulled away from her.

"It doesn't matter, Jonathan," she told him and took a deep breath to go on, but he cut her off, his voice like cold steel.

"Doesn't matter, Kelly? You can sit there looking at me and tell me this hideous apparition doesn't scare you? You mean you won't mind being seen in public with me and watch reactions when people get a glimpse of both sides of my face?'' His laugh was soft but watching him, she shivered. "You're very kind, Kelly." His hand on her waist tightened, pulling her back to him and he bent his head, his mouth hovering near hers. "Now that you know how my mouth is shaped, do you prefer to be kissed from the right or left?"

She held him away, eyes going over the wide firmness she knew so well, the touch she would be able to identify to her dying day even had she never been able to see. She shook her head as she deliberately went over the ropy skin with two fingers.

"I knew the scar was there, Jonathan, and even though Ann described it to me and it's worse than I imagined, it doesn't change my feelings for you." She met the glittering black eyes again. "I was blind and you weren't ashamed to marry me; your scar isn't as big a handicap as blindness if you just think about it. You weren't ashamed to marry me, were you?"

"If you'll use some common sense, Kelly, you'll see there's quite a bit of difference in the two situations."

She shook her head. "I'm so happy about having my sight back, being able to see you and be with you again, that neither my blindness nor the scar seem important enough to fight over."

Long fingers tilted her chin. "All right, Kelly, we'll be married as we planned." His voice was matter-of-fact, jolting her with its coolness, and her lips parted to question him, but his mouth covered hers, stilling her protest. His fingers spread from her waist, curving over her breast to move across the firmness swelling against the T-shirt she wore. Biting her full lower lip with soft nips, he moved to the corner she loved for him to touch, the tip of his tongue fondling her. His arms tightened as he pushed her back on the couch, his hard body pinning her beneath him. She moved to fit her slimness beneath him, hands working under the thin material of his shirt, probing into the hard muscles of his back.

With a sudden movement he stood, leaving her staring up at him, puzzled at his reaction. He reached, taking her hand to pull her up. "I think everyone will be delighted to hear you've regained your sight, Kelly."

The explanation from Jonathan that treatments had given Kelly back her sight as inexplicably as it had gone was accepted by everyone. He even gave them the information that colored lenses had been worn to protect her sensitive eyes from light thereby explaining the green eyes. The news made the activities more festive as they made ready for the weekend wedding.

Jean was rapturous. "I didn't think to pray for such a miracle, Kelly, but someone must have." She slipped the dress she had made over Kelly's head, straightening the skirt as it slipped over her hips. "This color is perfect for you."

Kelly was standing on a dais, turning so Jean could pin the hem straight. The dress was pale lavender with a tulle lining, a tight waistband attached to a billowing full skirt. The bodice fitted closely over her small bust, buttoned down the back with tiny covered buttons.

"I'll have to hem it and take it in some in the waist, but that's all," Jean assessed.

Kelly could contain her curiosity no longer. She blurted, "Jean, what happened to Jonathan's face?"

The older woman faced her. "He didn't tell you?" As Kelly shook her head, Jean went on. "No, he never would talk about it but I thought with you maybe he would. It was a car accident three years ago when he was married to Lola. They were going home from a party in Santa Fe. Lola was driving and was angry with Jonathan because he objected to her flirting with other men whose wives were there watching. They were in her car, a Mercedes, going nearly one hundred miles an hour when she lost control. Jonathan was badly hurt and in the hospital for weeks, leaving him disfigured as you see him now. One leg was broken and he has never been able to ski since then, something he always loved. Lola was only scratched. She couldn't stand the sight of him after that, and a year later they were divorced."

Kelly stood silently as she listened to the story, and felt a deep hatred for the woman she'd never met. *I hope I never do,* she thought. *I think I'd be tempted to strangle her.*

The silence went on until Jean said, "How do you feel about the scar, Kelly?"

She said slowly, "I don't blame Lola for leaving him." At Jean's sharp glance, she continued. "If I looked at Jonathan every day and knew I was responsible for that scar, I couldn't stand it either." She looked straight into Jean's eyes. "I love Jonathan. If it hurts him, it hurts me."

Jean Heath kissed her cheek and, without a word, went on with her work.

At ten on Sunday morning the small group gathered in the huge living room, and Judge Wallace Creighton, an old friend of the family, performed the ceremony, making her legally Jonathan's. His kiss held the promise of a more thorough one later and Kelly smiled at him, green eyes loving him, forgetting for the moment he only needed her for his physical well-being.

The reception was a big family-type affair that afternoon with all the employees of Heath Cliffs gathered to join in the celebration.

Dr. Randall, the veterinarian, stood talking with Ann and Gary. Kelly was surprised that he was young, probably no older than Jonathan and handsome in a dark gray suit, pale blue shirt, and darker blue tie. His dark hair was thick, gray at the temples, gray-streaked eyebrows over blue eyes that twinkled at Kelly.

"Sure will be nice having a pretty face around here," he said as she joined them. "It gets dull during the winter."

She laughed with them and turned when she felt Jonathan's hand slide around her waist. She was on his right side and couldn't see the disfigured eye. He must have been very handsome, she thought, and caught her breath as he looked down at her, his fingers caressing under her arm just touching the swell of her breast.

Then everyone was gone, leaving their best wishes for happiness with them, and Kelly walked with Jonathan to check doors before going to their room.

"Drink?" he asked.

At the tone of his voice, she looked hard at him. "No, thanks, I've had enough. Are you tired?"

"No." He bit out the harsh word.

"Jonathan?" Her hand went out to him and he caught it, yanking her roughly into his arms.

"Are you happy now, Kelly?" he asked softly, his eyes dangerously bright, the injured one narrowed a little. "You're married to a very rich man, no more pinching pennies. You can see all the things that belong to you, including the ugly face of your husband."

Sucking air into her lungs, she struggled as his arms tightened, one hand tangling in her hair to hold her head back, the other spread against her hips as he pressed his hard body into her. Gasping, she said, "I don't understand. Please."

His mouth barely touching hers he ground out, "You don't understand? Oh, but I do, Kelly. You're a liar and a thief and you'll repay everything on my terms. Ebony. The apartment house I bought so you'd have a place for her. I even have an appointment for you at Johns Hopkins Medical Center next month to see if they could help you. Ah, yes, you have a large debt to pay, starting now."

"I never lied to you deliberately, Jonathan. The experiment was almost over when I met you and I couldn't do anything to ruin that. I thought you—"

He didn't let her finish. With cruel deliberation he kissed her, his mouth no longer recognizable as the gentle one she remembered. His tongue forced her lips apart, and she felt his teeth against hers as her hands uselessly tried to hold him away. She went limp in his arms and they dropped to the floor almost in slow motion. He took her with savage delight and she watched with wide eyes the hate in the disfigured face as she framed it with her hands.

Hours later after he had carried her to his room, asleep after possessing her as he would any article of his choice, she lay awake, her body aching with protest. Her suspicions had been confirmed—he had given her Ebony and provided for her, had arranged for the apartment and for Chuck Benson to give them instructions. She thought longingly of the weeks she had known him, her idyllic vacation at Heath Cliffs when he had protected her, seen to her every need, worried about her.

She turned her head to look at him, his face only inches away. Even as he slept, his left arm lay across her, holding her within his reach for his satisfaction. The scar kept his mouth from relaxing, holding it forever in a twisted grin. His left eye didn't close completely, but long thick lashes covered the gap between lid and cheek, hiding the white area. Her right hand went out to touch his cheek, and her fingers brushed the scar down over the squared chin to his throat to his chest, curving in the thick curled hair. His indrawn breath brought her eyes back to meet the dark, hostile gaze.

"Please," she whispered as his arms closed around her, turning her body to him, a hard leg across hers to hold her immovable.

"I can please both of us." His low voice was harsh

on her temple and even as a slow flame kindled in her body, she struggled. He laughed. "I like a little fight, Kelly. Come to think of it, I'd probably get very tired of a sweet little wife who always did the right thing. This is better for both of us."

Closing her eyes to the dislike in his, she held on to him, willing him to be gentle, to love her as he took her, but she knew he never would.

When she awoke, she was alone. Down the hall in the bedroom where she had slept before she found that Selena had unpacked for her and put out a blue-checked sundress. Simply made, it had probably cost a pretty penny at Jean's shop but it was one of many that Jonathan had provided for her. As he said, she had a lot of things to pay for, an insurmountable debt she would never live long enough to repay. *I don't believe any of what's happened,* she thought, glad of the numbness that kept her from reliving her wedding night. A chill shook her body, freezing her. She needed something warmer than that sundress.

In the closet she found a pair of jeans and a thin print shirt with long sleeves, slid her feet into sandals, and rehung the dress. She stood gazing around the room where she had known some very happy times. It was bigger than any apartment she had ever had and almost as big as Ann's entire house. The creamy white wallpaper had ivy leaves spaced just enough to give it living color, and drapes at the wide bay window were the same print; the spread and thick carpet the palest of greens. She walked down the hall, carpeted with the same rich green as her bedroom, then turned into the slate tiled entrance to the kitchen.

"In here, Kelly," Jonathan said and she turned to the dining room where he was seated, coffee in front of him, the silver pot on the table close by.

"Good morning," she said as he stood to pull out a chair for her, bending to kiss the top of her head. She didn't look at him, nor did she react to the embrace, realizing he would make some effort for appearances' sake.

He sat down, poured coffee for her, and said, "It's a little warm for long sleeves."

"The blouse is thin," she told him, her mouth still tender from the night's bruising kisses, burning as she sipped coffee. He would never understand how cold she was, she thought, as she raised her eyes to meet his. He had seated her on his right side so the scar wasn't within her view but she knew it was there and that he would never let her forget it. The bitterness he felt for her had to be an extension of his feelings about the scar for surely her masquerade wasn't as bad as he made it out to be. It had been, to her, done for a purpose that would help so many children, her deception could be justified. Not so for Jonathan; he was taking it as a personal insult to him.

"Jonathan?"

"Yes, Kelly."

"We don't have to live like this, do we?" Her green eyes pleaded with him.

"Like what, Kelly? We're husband and wife and that's the way we'll live." His hand covered her left one as it lay on the snowy-white tablecloth. "You'll have everything you need and so will I." He lifted her hand to let his lips trail across her fingers, and a tremor of warm desire for him slid across the bottom of her stomach.

"Let me explain," she started.

But Jonathan didn't want to listen, instead he pushed back his chair and stood looking down at her, the scarred eye hooded at that angle. His voice was quiet steel and just as cold. "There is no need for further explanations, Kelly. The past is past and we'll go on from here. I have work to do but I'll be back for dinner."

She remained at the table, her eyes staring unseeing into the dark depths of her cold coffee. Some honeymoon, she thought later as she wandered down to the corral, Ebony and the irrepressible Tish romping beside her. She found Carl Randall working on the injured leg of a prize Brahma bull.

He greeted her, smiling. "You mean Jonathan is working today?" And at her nod he shook his head. "What a nut."

She walked around with him, listening with interest as he talked about the ranch, the workers, the animals, and Jonathan.

"Jonathan probably works harder than the rest of us combined even though he has capable people handling all the jobs. But no honeymoon?" He shook his head again.

She smiled, hoping he couldn't see beyond it. "He said we'd take a trip after the fall roundup was finished. Sounds like something out of a B movie, doesn't it?" They laughed.

"What's that?" she asked, pointing to dropped pipes with spouts at regular intervals, running the length and width of the building that housed the animals kept in the corral.

"That's the automatic sprinkler system. We're so far from any fire hydrants that if we were ever unlucky enough to have a fire, trucks could never reach us." He stared up at the complicated network of pipes. "There's nothing worse than a fire with animals." He was quiet a moment, then went on. "The system is activated if heat reaches a certain temperature and we have the manual switch on the outside of this building should the automatic set not work for some reason."

Her curiosity about the ranch and seeing everything hidden from her during her first trip kept her busy so that she was surprised when she saw it was four o'clock. She checked with Selena and found that Jonathan usually ate around seven when he was working, so she went to her room to look for a dress suitable for a new bride to appear in before her husband. Not that he would notice she was a new bride wanting to be treated as such.

A simple black sheath with long full sleeves of a diaphanous material caught her eyes. She showered, dressed, and sat by the window, waiting for her hair to dry. Thoughts of the previous night invaded her mind. She didn't want to be an object Jonathan possessed only for his pleasure. She wanted him to see her as Kelly. She shivered, swallowing around the lump in her throat.

The door opened and she looked up to see Jonathan. "Waiting for me?" he asked softly. He had already showered and changed and was wearing dark gray pants and a white shirt. One step brought him to her and he reached to pull her up to him. His mouth covered hers hungrily. She tasted the mint of the toothpaste he had used and opened her mouth to accept the onslaught of his kisses, drowning in the desire that swept through her, yet denying to herself the hatred she felt in him.

Freeing her lips, she whispered, "Don't hurt me."

"Hurt you? But you don't care how *you* hurt, do you, Kelly?"

"Never intentionally, Jonathan." Her hands reached out and cradled his head.

He was still for only a moment then his breath caught as his eyes traveled over her body, taking in her small firm breasts, flat stomach, and firm thighs outlined so clearly in the black dress. He continued to stare at her, his lips curved in a sardonic smile.

The dark gleam in his eyes was not love, Kelly knew, but desire. She broke from his hold and backed away from him.

"I need a drink," he said abruptly and walked determinedly out the door.

He was standing at the bar, looking into the half-empty glass he held, when Kelly entered the den. Without a word he handed her a frosted glass, waiting till she sat in the club chair before he went to the couch.

She put the cool drink to her mouth, feeling the sting of alcohol on her lips where his kisses had bruised them. He watched her, making no attempt at conversation, and she asked, "If you're going to work all the time, what can I do to help and keep busy?"

He leaned forward, eyes narrowed on her. "You don't *have* to do anything, Kelly. I know money is important to you and now you have plenty to do as you please from the accounts I've opened in your name. Do whatever you want to do as long as you're here when I want you."

"And when you no longer want me?" she asked.

He smiled, the full lower lip twisting as the scar pulled it upward. "I'll let you know."

She tried again. "I love you, Jonathan," she said, trying to make her voice even.

"Don't bother, Kelly. We both know where we stand." He looked over his drink at her. "You do your part and I'll do mine. Nothing more is required of either of us."

The very softness of his voice sent shivers through her. She had lived with Robbie's death, temporary blindness, gone without meals many times, and God knows what else without thinking twice, sometimes making hasty decisions, depending on logic and gut feeling in the absence of surety. Staring at his uncompromising expression, she thought, *I was one hundred and eighty degrees wrong about Jonathan when I thought my love was enough but one-sided love makes everything unbalanced, not equal.*

He stood up, ignoring her plea. "Shall we eat?"

That set the pattern of their days as the summer drew to a close, and Indian summer brought lazy shimmering days to northern New Mexico. Left alone much of the daytime hours, Kelly drove into Taos at least once each week to visit with Jean and Rena. Jonathan never asked where she went nor what she did and she never offered him any information. Jean was a lovely person, easy for Kelly to like, seeming to return the affection Kelly felt for her. Her silver-gray hair was short, always in place, framing the handsome face that showed few wrinkles.

They were getting ready for their show for the summer line of dresses and sportswear for the coming year and Kelly stood fingering the lightweight cotton material Rena was draping around a mannequin.

"How would you look in that pale yellow, Kelly?" Jean asked, coming up behind her.

Kelly laughed. "I'd blend right in with the landscape," she said.

"I don't know. The shades of green build up a background of color. Here, let's see."

She took a fold of material and wrapped it loosely around Kelly's shoulders then pulled a corner over her hair like a scarf.

"Not bad," Rena said, nodding with approval. "Let's use a live model." So Kelly stood for hours as they twisted her, pinned, wrapped, and rewrapped. When they finished, the dress was basted and fitted to Kelly's small waist.

"Go look," Jean told her.

Kelly turned to the mirror and smiled at her reflection. The thin material draped around her slimness, a boat neck that came just below the hollow of her throat, cap sleeves that hit midway between shoulder and elbow. A full skirt floated from a tucked waistline. Her red-gold hair, growing long enough to be turned under into a pageboy, complemented the colors in the dress as Jean had predicted.

"Well, Kelly, that dress would be wasted on anyone

but you." She laughed delightedly. "I'll send Jonathan the bill after we deliver the dress, okay?"

It was still early as she left Jean's shop, heading south on Highway 68, driving slowly on the uncrowded two-lane road. It was in between seasons with the summer crowd gone and the ski crowd not yet in sight. School had started and few children were in evidence as she entered the four-lane highway into Espanola, the small lovely city twenty miles or so north of Santa Fe. It was an area she never tired of and she loved the mountains that could be seen all around as she drove into the city limits. Maples were blazing scarlet, aspen trees shimmered in waves of gold, and rust-colored chamiso rolled over the valleys. Adobe chimneys gave forth the sweet scent of piñon as fires were lighted for the first time in the cool afternoons and evenings.

On impulse she turned left at a stoplight onto a street that zigzagged through a section of short lanes in an old part of the town settled by families with neither wealth nor worldy possessions. She slowed to a stop as she saw several small children running along the sidewalk, shouting as they rode stick horses across the broken asphalt.

As the group ran between two houses and disappeared, Kelly started on down the narrow street, following the curve around a fenced yard, and made a forty-five-degree turn into a less settled area where the road ended abruptly. She pulled over to the curb to stop.

Sprawled across the end of the street was a large building painted the dull yellow that so many of the older adobe and block homes used, possibly because the paint was cheap. It rambled across the fenced lot, strips of dirty white showing where the yellow paint had peeled from beneath the overhang at each corner. It was old, she could tell by the full red-tiled roof, the type no longer used on regular homes due to the expense. The size puzzled Kelly since it was three times as big as any of the neighboring houses.

Straightening over the wheel, she let her gaze go to the high wrought-iron gate, reading a sign that said: BE CAREFUL—BLIND CHILDREN. She stared at the blunt statement painted in big black letters and looked back at the desolate structure. There wasn't a sign of life anywhere.

Glancing at her watch, she saw it was nearly three thirty. Opening the car door, she slid out, uncertain what she intended to do but knowing she was going to knock on one of those doors. The hinge on the gate screeched as she pushed the latch upward, letting the weight pull it open for her. She pushed it shut behind her and leaned against the iron, warm in the afternoon sun. The walkway to the front door was made of coarse sandrock, as was the yard, and her sneakers made no sound as she moved from there onto the cement porch. A small sign on the heavy wooden door stated: NO SOLICITING. She pushed the bell at her eye level but heard nothing to indicate it worked. She frowned and raised her hand to knock when the door opened.

"May I help you?" The woman who faced her was tall and wide shouldered with Indian features and heavy braids of brown-gray hair wound around her head. Dark brown eyes surveyed Kelly without smiling.

Kelly wet her lips, realizing she hadn't given a thought as to why she had entered the yard and knocked on the door. "I'm Kelly Heath," she said and smiled at the stern-faced woman. "I saw the sign." She half turned, indicating the sign on the gate she had opened.

"Yes?" The dark eyes questioned a lot with that single word.

"Do you have blind children here?" she asked, knowing the question was impolite.

The woman continued to stare at Kelly. "Yes, I have six children. Why do you want to know?"

Kelly took a deep breath. "May I please come in?"

After a moment the woman moved and opened the door for Kelly to enter. As she pushed the door closed, she indicated chairs in the room in which they stood.

"I'm Angela Nunez," she said, "Please sit down."

Kelly sat in a club chair that had seen better days as had all the few furnishings in the room. An old brown mohair couch was pushed beneath the two windows that faced the street. The chair in which Kelly sat was the only other furniture except for a small table near the couch. The floor was partially covered by a faded rug, tattered at the edges, but everything in the room was clean; no dust, no clutter. She looked back at Mrs. Nunez.

"Are the children all yours?"

"Are you from the Department of Human Services?" she asked.

Kelly smiled. "No, I'm just interested in blind children. I turned down the street not knowing it was a dead end and saw the sign on the gate."

Mrs. Nunez relaxed a little. "What is your interest, Mrs. Heath?"

"Please call me Kelly." She sat forward on her chair. "My nephew was blind and we were always trying to find ways to make it easier for him and wondered about all the children who went through life not seeing."

"*Was* blind?"

Kelly nodded. "He died about two years ago."

The dark eyes softened. "Would you like some tea, Kelly?"

"Yes, thank you."

She followed Mrs. Nunez across the room and down a short dark hallway into another room so unlike the bleak living room that Kelly stopped and blinked. It was big with windows down the entire wall she faced. Bright red gingham curtains covered the bottom half of the window and were parted to let in the late fall sunlight. Three long trestle tables sat three feet apart in the middle of the room. Two old gas ranges were in the corner with cabinets above and below the counter. Kelly took it all in as she waited for the tea.

The woman moved quickly to take the whistling kettle from the burner and reach in the cabinets above the stove for cups and saucers. She was aware of Kelly's curiosity and smiled.

"This building was once a mission but the congregation outgrew it and my husband and I took it to convert into a house big enough for all our children." She placed the tea in front of Kelly. "Do you live in this area?"

"No, I'm from south of Santa Fe. I've been to Taos to see my mother-in-law and took a detour at the stoplight." She leaned forward. "Where are your children?"

"They're all in school. I have five boys and one girl ranging in age from ten to fourteen. They ride a bus into Santa Fe and won't be home until five."

"Do they go to public school?" Kelly asked, surprised.

"No, that's why they must go into Santa Fe. There are no special schools near us."

"Are they all blind?"

Mrs. Nunez smiled. "Yes. The children are mine only because they're throwaways no one else wanted. We about keep body and soul together, but we do have each other."

Kelly continued to look at her and Angela went on. "While my husband was alive, we did all right and we manage now, but it's harder."

"Can you get state help?" she asked, remembering all the efforts they had made in trying to get funds.

"Only if I consent to put the children in full-time schools or homes, because that's where the available government money goes."

"Why don't you?"

Mrs. Nunez got up to refill their cups. "Would you have put your nephew somewhere out of the way?"

Kelly didn't answer, knowing the woman expected none. She felt familiar anger at her own helplessness and she wanted to cry out in protest at the unfairness of it all. She looked around at the pleasant room they sat in, guessing that a big part of the family's at-home time was spent here. "How do you manage?" She smiled before Angela could answer. "You could tell me it's none of my business."

Angela smiled back at her. "If you weren't interested in the situation, you wouldn't have stopped at all, Kelly." She went on to tell her what she wanted to know. "Each child draws a small check from Social Security because of blindness and I have a small pension from Tomas. The church helps a lot and I work part-time at the school cafeteria nearby and they give us a lot of leftovers."

Kelly finished her tea and stood up. "I wish I could meet the children but my husband will be worried." She took her cup and saucer to the sink, rinsed them, and placed them on the wooden counter, which was scrubbed spotless. "May I come back?"

"Yes, of course." Angela related her work schedule to Kelly as she walked the younger woman to her car.

Kelly slid behind the wheel of her little Mustang, waved to Angela Nunez, and pulled into the street, trying unsuccessfully to miss the potholes. In the rearview mirror she saw the woman standing on the porch until she rounded the curve and she was lost from sight.

The clock on the Bank of Commerce building showed four thirty as she entered the four-lane highway into Santa Fe. She would be later than usual getting home but Jonathan wouldn't miss her—not until bedtime.

She drew her mind away from him and went back to the children. Thoughts of them kept her company until she pulled into the yard. Ebony and Tish bounded over and Kelly opened the car door for them to clamber in, pushing the automatic garage door opener and letting the dogs ride in with her.

"You're nothing but pests," she said affectionately, hugging Ebony and cuddling Tish under her chin.

Emotionally, she was exhausted. Her visit with Angela Nunez had brought the tragedy of Robbie back into sharp focus, pushing her own private misery aside. Surely there was more that could be done than she had accomplished. There was money for research into small segments of eye diseases but the here and now needed to be dealt with. She ran her hand back to front through her hair, a habit she had of tumbling it when she was uneasy over something she couldn't name.

As she went down the hall, the door to Jonathan's bedroom opened and he stood there, anger showing in the tightness of his mouth. "Where have you been?" he asked.

She had stopped short when the door opened, surprised to find him already home. "I was in Taos to see Jean and on the way home, I stopped in Espanola and stayed longer than I meant to. I'll be ready for dinner in a few minutes."

He gave her a dark look. "I'll be in the den," he said and strode past her down the hall.

When she joined him twenty minutes later, he was standing at the wide windows, whose drapes were still open even though it was dark outside. "Come here," he told her.

As she stood beside him he reached and the lights went out. Her eyes, becoming accustomed to the dimness, could make out the snowflakes just beginning to cover the ground.

"I thought it was too warm for snow. Isn't this sort of early?"

"It's almost Thanksgiving and we usually have snow by then. The ski lodge managers are doing snow dances tonight," he laughed, looking down at her.

It had been a long time since she had seen him laugh. She wanted to reach up and touch him but she knew his reaction would be instant and harsh. Better still, she wanted to kiss him, which would bring an even more violent response. She looked back at the outside spectacle, feeling an excitement at the thought of a big snowfall.

"If we get lots of snow, will you work tomorrow?"

His arm came around her, holding her against his hip. "Probably not, but you can entertain me."

The old familiar ache started deep inside her and she turned away, but he pulled her back, tilting her face up to his and she stood on tiptoe to meet his kiss. His mouth was gentle on hers and she responded to it, the tip of her tongue tracing the outline of his lips. His hands went upward, thumbs moving across her breasts, hands circling her to spread over her hips, holding her flat stomach against the hardness of his. He lifted his head, watching her through half-opened eyes, his breath coming quickly. Kelly's breath was uneven and her lips parted, inviting his kiss again.

A soft knock came and Selena said, "Dinner's getting cold, Jonathan."

"We'll be right there, Selena," he said, continuing to look down into Kelly's upturned face. Then abruptly his voice roughened. "Come on."

As he pushed her dining room chair forward, Jonathan's fingers went under her hair, tracing the hairline around to her ear. She held herself erect, hoping he wouldn't feel the tremor pass through the length of her body all the way to her toes.

"You're letting your hair grow?"

"Yes, I've always worn it shoulder length till I—"

She stopped, reluctant to mention things she had done in the past. Taking a deep breath, she went on. "It was easier to take care of short when I couldn't see."

He was quiet but she felt his eyes on her as she concentrated on the food on her plate. "It's becoming that way," he said and after a moment added, "We have Thanksgiving dinner here for everyone. All the hands and their families, Jean, Rena, and Judge Creighton. Would you like to invite Ann and Gary?"

"Yes, I would, thank you, Jonathan."

"Why thank me, Kelly? You're mistress of the house, which allows you to invite anyone here you want to."

She lifted her head. "I don't feel like mistress of the house. Just yours."

Jonathan was silent.

"Jonathan." She said his name but her eyes were on her plate. "I want to ask a big favor."

"You can ask," he told her.

"Will you let me mate Ebony with Beowulf?" She held her breath.

He laughed. "That should make a beautiful litter and I don't see any reason why we can't do that. Carl can help you."

Her fingers tightened on her fork as she looked up at him. "Would you give the puppies to be trained as seeing-eye dogs for children?"

His gaze went over her bright head to her mouth, back to meet her questioning green eyes. "You don't want much, do you, Kelly? Do you have any idea how much a litter from those two would be worth?"

"Yes, I do, but it would be worth much more than that to a child who can't see."

He shoved his chair back. "I'll think about it."

She sat with bowed head after he left her alone at the table, knowing full well she'd pay for her request later. *If I get what I want, it's worth it—I guess,* she conceded.

Doubt lay heavy on her chest, but in the back of her mind she saw the shabby living room and the three trestle tables in the big dining room at Angela's.

The snow amounted to only an inch or so, not enough to interrupt the ongoing work at the ranch and Jonathan worked all day with Al Cardon and his two sons down on the southern end of the ranch, repairing fences and filling hay racks. Kelly spent most of the day with Selena, planning the holiday meal and seating arrangements.

"How many people will there be, Selena?" she asked.

"About the same as the wedding reception."

"Where do you feed all those people indoors?"

Selena laughed. "We put tables on the patio, in the den, the bigger living room, Jonathan's sitting room. You name it—we have a table in it."

It was good being busy and late in the afternoon she bundled up, running with Tish and Ebony down past the corral and back. The weather turned cold and nasty, but she loved it. Fires burned in fireplaces all through the big house, and Kelly kept a book near her as she lay in front of one or the other in whichever room she stopped. She had wandered into the sitting room adjacent to Jonathan's bedroom and was lying in front of the fire, a small book of poetry open near her outstretched hand. Half asleep, she stared into the dancing flames.

"Would you like me to read to you?"

Startled, she rolled over to look up at Jonathan. He hadn't changed from his jeans and flannel shirt and was even still wearing his heavy boots. She was looking at the handsome, unscarred side of his face with a good view of the firm mouth that more often than not was ruthless and hurting on hers, but she remembered that he could be gentle.

She nodded and he sat down, leaning against a big

chair, and picked up a book. As he began reading, she
turned back toward the fire and closed her eyes, the
deep resonance of his voice soothing her.

"Kelly?" He turned her to him, pillowing her head
on his arm, fingers tracing the outline of her face to her
lips, across her nose and back to her shoulder, letting
his hand slide downward to rest on her hip.

Feeling sleepy and warm, she smiled into his black
eyes, bringing one leg up between his and pressing
close to him. She unbuttoned the heavy shirt, pushing
it aside to put her face against his chest, the thick hair
rough on her cheek.

His breathing changed but he didn't speak as he
cupped her hip with a big hand, bringing her body
closer to let her know what she was doing to him. He
kept her there until it was time to dress for dinner.

When Selena said "Dinner in twenty minutes," he
stood, pulling her with him.

"See you at dinner," he said, and went into his bedroom, closing the door behind him.

Still feeling warm and trembly from his caresses, she
went to her own room to dress.

Chapter Nine

Thanksgiving Day dawned clear and cold. Kelly was awake early, excited at the thought of seeing Ann, wondering briefly if she would know her marriage was a farce. Jonathan could act along with the likes of John Barrymore, so it was unlikely any of his real feelings would show.

Gary's pickup turned into the drive just before one o'clock and Kelly was out the door, running to meet them. Ebony was there barking her welcome, tail wagging with the excitement Kelly transmitted to her.

"Kelly," Ann said, catching her hand, holding her. "I'm pregnant." Her blue eyes flashed at her sister. Kelly stood still an instant, then grabbed Ann in a bear hug. Many times she had wondered if Ann would be brave enough to have another child after the tragedy of Robbie.

She pushed Ann away to look at her. "Are you all right? When?"

Ann laughed. "I'm fine. June."

They all talked at once, standing there, till Jonathan came out of the house. "Let them in out of the cold, Kelly," he said, shaking hands with Gary, hugging Ann.

A car drove in and Jean, Rena, and Judge Creighton joined them. The halls, dining room, and patio became a madhouse of people, until hours later, when it quieted down and they were alone again.

Jonathan brought her a glass of wine and placed it near her as she sat on the floor in front of the fire. "Did you enjoy yourself?"

"Yes, it was fun but I ate too much." She turned to him. "Ann's expecting a baby in June."

"So Gary told me. Are they worried?"

She shook her head. "No, I don't think so. What happened to Robbie was a tragic mistake and, hopefully, only once in a lifetime."

"What do you mean, a mistake?"

"Robbie was blind." She hugged her knees. "There was something wrong with his eyes when he was born but no one made any notations about it and it was never treated. It could have been corrected except for the wrong diagnosis. The research I wanted done was in the area of cornea damage that causes complete blindness. They can remove the damaged area with lasers now and replace it. They've come a long way and the money I got as a grant will extend that study."

"What grant?"

"Hap's paper was awarded a grant for research after I did the series on blindness."

"I didn't read anything about that. Anything of that nature usually gets a lot of publicity."

She shrugged. "We didn't want any publicity."

"Who didn't?"

"I—that is, Hap—neither of us cared to have any public fanfare except for the researchers and Dr. Clements at the Darbyshire Clinic. They're the ones who command the funds when attention is focused on the need for them and that's what we were betting on. If the paper had been brought into it, the fact that I wasn't really blind would have caused some people to consider it getting money through false pretenses when all we cared about was the funds for the research." *Like you,* Jonathan, she wanted to add but she didn't.

"I see."

No, you don't, she wanted to tell him. *You don't see at all, along with millions of other sighted people.* She saw the gathering anger in his face as he remembered being taken in by her seeming helplessness.

With an abrupt change of subject, he said, "Randall and I are going to Quebec Saturday to a veterinarian's conference for him and I'll be looking at equipment and, possibly, some animals. I intend to do some Christmas shopping. What would you like?"

She looked at him wishing for the nerve to say "Only your love, Jonathan," but knowing the answer to that, she asked, "Can I have anything I want?"

He smiled. "Within reason."

"I want you to go to a plastic surgeon and have that scar removed."

He stiffened and the smile faded from his face as his voice changed to the deadly cold she hated, "I said within reason, Kelly." His fingers gripped the glass he held. "Are you sick of looking at me?"

"It doesn't bother me nearly as much as it does you."

"What makes you think it bothers me?" His voice grated.

"You hate it and draw attention to it when I don't even notice it."

His laugh was ugly. "You mean each time I kiss you you don't close your eyes to avoid seeing me?"

"I close my eyes to hide the dislike in yours, Jonathan." She stood up. "What do you feed your hate on, Jonathan? What changed you from the person you were in July to what you are now? Not my deception, as you claim. I was working for something I thought might benefit someone in the future and, yes, I went to the extreme to get it, but I only hurt myself. Not you, Jonathan, not ever. Let me tell you how much I—"

He was on his feet too, the glass falling from his hands as he reached for her, amber liquid spilling over the front of her dress, making a path of ice between her breasts as the glass rolled to the floor.

"Don't tell me anything, Kelly. If there's anything a woman can do better than a man, it's lie. And cheat. And run away." His mouth was hard on hers as he finished speaking, punishing her for she knew not what.

For a moment she yielded to him, then anger coursed from his mouth through her body. In one quick motion she broke free from his grasp and ran to her room. Tears coursed down her cheeks and sobs racked her body until she could feel no longer and gave in to the peacefulness of sleep.

Jonathan was moving quietly around his bedroom, dressing in the semidarkness of early morning, when Kelly entered. As he sat down to put on his boots, she spoke, "I'm going to leave you, Jonathan."

He lifted his head, looking at her a long moment, then went on lacing the heavy work boots. "No, you aren't, Kelly. What would you do to earn all the money available to you now?"

He stood up, hands hooked in his pockets, his twisted mouth almost a straight line.

"I've always worked for a living and it won't hurt me to do it again," she said, sitting down on the bed.

"I'll make sure you never teach again nor work as a journalist." He smiled. "You know money does anything you want it to and I can blacklist you anywhere I choose."

"Hap will hire me again no matter what you say about me."

"Newspapers can be bought, Kelly. You wouldn't want Hap to lose his job for hiring practices, would you?"

What he was saying dawned slowly and, horrified,

she stared at him. "I don't believe you, Jonathan. How can you do something like that? I'm your wife, you don't want me but you'll still keep me around. For what?" Her voice was incredulous.

"The reason should be obvious by now," he told her, walking over to stand by the bed.

"I can always go back to work for McDonald's. For what they pay, they don't care what I've done, short of murder."

"That's quite a comedown for you, isn't it?"

"I paid my way through college working there and I ate Egg McMuffins every day when I could afford it." She swung her legs off the bed on the opposite side from him. "I can't stay here any longer." She had tried to tell him how much she loved him, and had he listened, he would probably have laughed. There was no way she could reach him, her love not enough incentive for him to withdraw his bitterness.

"No, Kelly." At the tone of his voice, she looked over her shoulder. "If you do, I'll foreclose on RAG Ranch."

The charged silence choked her until she finally managed, "What are you talking about?"

"Gary mentioned expanding his ranch a little, plus adding a room since the baby's coming, and I offered to lend him money with the ranch as collateral. Leave me and the ranch is mine."

The bitter taste of defeat kept her quiet. *I should be used to it by now,* she thought, hurt clamping itself around her heart, squeezing life from it. Her eyes fixed on her rings, the beautiful and unusual setting that she loved because Jonathan selected and gave them to her.

"All right, Kelly?" he asked.

She turned to look at him but his features blurred and she spoke with great effort, her voice dull and lifeless. "For whatever the reason you want me to hate you, it's working. When the transition is complete, I'll be the happiest woman on earth."

Jonathan just laughed and left the room.

It was light when Kelly stared out the window in the kitchen, helping herself to a cup of Selena's fresh coffee. Clouds hung in dirty gray tatters across the mountains, swinging in reluctant groups ahead of a northwest wind. She was watching Ebony loping toward the corral when suddenly a thought hit her. One of Angela's children would have a wonderful companion if she gave him Ebony. She rejected the thought immediately—because of her own feelings surely, but there were six children who needed dogs. She made a mental note to talk to Carl about the breeding just as soon as he had enough time. Her eyes narrowed as her thoughts ran on. *Whatever happens I'll go on from there, even if I have to fight Jonathan from here to eternity.*

Her thoughts returned to Angela and the children. Throwaways, she had called them. Kelly knew they would probably all be at home today because of the Thanksgiving holiday. She quickly collected her handbag and jacket and started on the forty-five-minute drive to Espanola.

Turning right at the stoplight, she drove slowly down the narrow street, recognizing the turn ahead of her that led into the dead-end street where Angela lived. She stopped her car by the gate and let her gaze go to the dull yellow structure with its peeling paint, as pathetic looking as when she first saw it two weeks ago. Glimpses of movement, denim-clad legs flashing in and out of sight, and the noise of boisterous children came from the back of the house. She got out of the car, uncertain what she should do, then made up her mind and walked around the side of the building.

Three boys in their early teens stood in various positions under or near a basketball net mounted on a pole thirty feet from the six-foot chain-link fence that enclosed the big backyard. One of them, a slender blonde who looked to be about thirteen, was crouched twenty feet or so in front of the pole, and as Kelly watched, he bounded up, releasing the basketball he held. It sailed into the air and came down with a solid bump on the rim of the basket, teetering for a second before it rolled off and away from the goal. An involuntary groan of disappointment came from Kelly's throat and three heads swiveled in her direction.

"Hello," she said, smiling at them, knowing they could hear the smile in her voice. "I'm Kelly Heath."

Three pairs of eyes stared and the blond youth spoke. "I'm Joshua. The tall dark one is Tony, and short stuff there is Alec." He straightened, the basketball momentarily forgotten. "Are you lost?"

"No, I was here several days ago and met Mrs. Nunez. Is she at home?"

The tall, dark one Joshua identified as Tony, cupped his hands to his mouth and yelled, "Mom!"

Angela came out of the back door. "Kelly. Come inside. I see you met my boys."

They went into the kitchen, which Kelly remembered as big and bright. Warmth from the cook stoves where something was steaming in a big black pot came to meet her but there seemed little other heat.

At one of the trestle tables sat a girl and a boy. The boy was blond and looked to be about ten years old. He was peeling white potatoes. The girl, perhaps thirteen, was washing and stringing celery.

"Kelly, this is Marta," Angela said, touching the dark pigtails on the girl's shoulder. The girl smiled and nodded as big brown eyes met Kelly's. A tingle ran along her spine, looking into the clear darkness of the sightless pupils. Marta's slim body was beginning to show the first signs of developing womanhood.

Angela stood by the small boy's chair and said, "This

is Andy, who celebrated his tenth birthday yesterday."
Andy didn't raise his head to look toward Kelly but his
hands were still on the potatoes as he murmured,
"Hello."

"Would you like some tea, Kelly, and will you stay
for lunch?"

"Yes to both questions." Kelly took the chair Angela pulled out from the table for her, feeling the
emptiness from skipping breakfast. "Can I help with
anything?"

"No, Andy and Marta are taking care of everything
right now. We're having leftovers from yesterday.
Father Dunne gave us a
the trimmings."

"You said you had six children," Kelly said as Angela placed a steaming cup in front of her and sat down
at the end of the table.

"Yes, Edward is helping Father Dunne clean at the
mission today. Edward, Alec, and Tony are fourteen
years old. Marta and Joshua are thirteen. Andy and
Joshua are brothers and I've had them for seven years
and the others I've had ten years. They have no family
except me."

"They're lucky at that," Kelly said.

"Amen," Marta said and grinned as she patted
Andy's shaggy head. He gave her a shy glance, a brief
smile, and returned to his work but still didn't look at
Kelly.

"And you, Kelly, how much family do you have?"

"Not many in numbers, Angela. One sister and
brother-in-law and one husband, Jonathan." She laughed.
"One beautiful black German shepherd and a poodle,
litle rascal named Tish, who really belongs to Jonathan's
mother but stays with us."

Andy dropped the potato he was holding and his
small hand groped to find it where it rolled on the table.
Kelly pushed it within his reach without comment.

A flurry of noise, laughter, and general roughhousing filled the room as the three boys came in from the yard, shedding jackets, filing alongside the far wall, reaching out to contact hooks for their coats.

"There's hot chocolate left if you boys would like some," Angela said as they turned with almost precision timing and walked in step to the second table, pulling the long bench out and dropping onto it.

A chorus of "Yes, please" accompanied their hand rubbing to get warmth back into them.

A moment later Angela placed mugs of chocolate in front of the boys and returned to her chair. "You've all met Kelly. Would you like to know what she looks like?"

They each assured her they wanted to know Kelly's description, all except Andy, who still sat with downcast eyes, peeling potatoes.

"Let's see, where shall I start?"

"Eyes." This request came from Joshua.

"Very bright green, almost like the fir trees in late spring when the sun shines on them."

"Hair," Alec said.

"That's going to be hard to describe. Well, perhaps it isn't quite as bright as your basketball, but almost," Angela said and laughed. "A cross between gold and orange if you can imagine that. You remember the color of pumpkins, Alec, from the time when you could still see colors."

"Yes, I remember," Al told her. "She must have freckles."

Kelly laughed with the rest of them. "Right the first time, Alec."

Marta asked, "Is she tall and skinny?"

"No, she's about Joshua's height—five feet five or six inches. Is that right, Kelly?"

"Five five," she told them. "And I weigh one hundred ten pounds."

"You're skinny," Marta said, a little envy in her voice. Her still-filling-out figure showed a more ripe fullness than Kelly's but she was far from overweight.

Angela leaned to touch Andy's hand. "What would you like to know about Kelly?"

The smaller boy raised his head and looked toward where Kelly sat across from him and Kelly was shocked to look into the deep blue eyes so like Robbie's that stared at her unblinking. "Is she pretty?"

There was a brief silence as each one looked toward Angela, who tilted her head as if to observe Kelly better. "Do you really think that's a fair question, Andy? If I say no, then I'll hurt Kelly's feelings. If I say yes, it may make her too proud. What do you think?"

"Mom!" came a chorus of protests.

Angela laughed. "Kelly's blushing a very pale peach that goes well with the freckles. Yes, she's very attractive." She stood up. "Enough of this. Get the tables set for lunch and let's feed her so she won't be too skinny."

Each child had his duties, and in record time the table was set for seven people and the big pot of turkey soup and rice were on the table. Marta stuffed the celery with peanut butter and honey.

Angela took the potatoes Andy had been peeling and put them on the stove. "These are for tonight and tomorrow," she said. "We try to get things done ahead when we can."

Kelly watched as Angela served each child and she helped Andy with his plate. She could remember how many times she had missed her plate when serving herself while the discs were in her eyes and smiled at the memory, sobering as the fact that these children would never see hit her again.

After Kelly helped clean the kitchen after lunch, she reached for her jacket on the hooks by the others. "I do appreciate your having me for lunch. I'd love to come back."

Angela followed her to her car after she said good-bye to the five children. "It was a nice break for them, Kelly. They don't have many visitors."

She smiled into the kind brown eyes. "I'll certainly be back."

On the way home her thoughts were filled with the family she had just left, and she came into sight of Heath Cliffs before she knew it. A sigh of relief was expelled when she saw the Cherokee wasn't in the yard. Jonathan wouldn't know she had been to Espanola and she could get a shower before he got home.

The following day Jonathan and Carl left for Canada as they had planned, and that night snow moved into the mountains, canceling any plans she had for returning to see Angela and the children. For the next few days she spent her time walking in the snow, sometimes leading Sable and Goldie to give them exercise. Jonathan and Carl were expected back on Wednesday but it was still early and she was surprised to see the Cherokee they had driven to the airport parked in the drive as she came up from the corral.

The door slammed and Carl Randall came down the steps. "Hi, Kelly. You look like the original snow maiden."

"Hello, Carl," Kelly responded. "How was the trip?"

"Great." He stopped. "I found a saddle that Jonathan expressed interest in and managed to get it ordered without his knowing. It will be sent to me."

"Oh, thanks, Carl."

She had talked with him about a new saddle for Jonathan for a Christmas present before they had left for Canada but had forgotten about it. She'd have to remember to write Carl a check. It would have to come from her award money since that was all she had. An errant thought struck her—the checkbooks that Jonathan gave her that lay somewhere in her dresser drawer—but she quickly pushed it from her mind.

Shaking the excess snow from her heavy coat, she hung it on the hook on the back porch and pulled off her boots. She was suddenly caught from behind and turned into Jonathan's arms.

"Hello, Kelly," he said. Before she could respond, his mouth closed over hers, then moved slowly over her cheek to the top of her head. "You're wet. You'd better dry your hair before you catch cold."

She hadn't spoken but nodded as she went on into her room. It was the most gentle kiss she could remember in a long time and touched her lips with shaky fingers, longing for her love for Jonathan to be returned. Maybe in the next world, she thought wistfully, as she turned on the hot shower.

A few minutes later she found him in the den. He stood by the mantel watching her walk into the room, her bright head held high, her slender body straight, but her lips still tingling from his gentle kiss.

"Lovely," he said. "I missed you." His dark eyes went over her, coming back to meet the green of hers but she said nothing, waiting him out. She wondered how true his declaration really was.

He handed her a drink he had placed on the mantel and touched his glass to hers. "To us, Kelly, now and for many years to come."

She sipped her drink and turned to sit on a footstool close to the fire.

"Where were you in this weather?" he asked.

"I walked Sable and Goldie and threw some bread out for the ducks on the pond on the south side of the corral."

"Alone?"

"Ebony was with me." She kept her eyes on her glass to keep him from reading anything in them.

"I'm glad you decided to stay, Kelly," he said, his voice quietly mocking.

Her head jerked up and she saw the knowing look on his face—he could get a reaction from her when nothing else would. Her lips parted as her throat closed, angry tears near the surface, and she swallowed hard, looking into the fire. "I decided I couldn't stomach any more Egg McMuffins."

"Yes, it's quite easy to get accustomed to lobster and filet mignon and an unlimited bank account." His voice cut her and she winced, wondering what the bank books he had given her showed as a balance. The same old pain surfaced as she recalled the day he had handed her the two leather-cased books.

"These are yours, Kelly," he had told her, his disfigured eye hidden by long lashes as he slanted a glance at her. "You're earning them so do as you please with the money."

She had never touched them, never so much as opened them to see what was in either of them. They lay somewhere in her dresser drawer where she had thrown them and gone immediately to wash her hands, feeling as though she had handled something dirty.

She came back to the present as Jonathan said, "I checked on what you wanted for Christmas."

Her eyes questioned him. "I went to see Dr. Hotchkiss, the plastic surgeon, and while I was there, went through X rays and an examination to see if he can repair the damage to my face."

"Why? What made you change your mind?" She held her breath waiting for his answer.

He shrugged. "He may not be able to help so don't get your hopes up too much."

"Why?" she insisted, watching him, seeing his lips tighten.

"I took a good look in the mirror and decided you were right. Even a golddigger deserves better." He walked over to her and knelt in front of her, two fingers holding her chin.

Kelly didn't deny the accusation, deciding that wasting her breath got her nowhere.

"I'm glad, Jonathan. When do you go?"

"I'm going tomorrow for a look at the X rays he took and if he's happy with them, I'll go into the clinic Friday evening and he'll operate Saturday. If he does operate, you'll have your Christmas present on time."

She caught her breath at the rapid movement of things. "How did you get an appointment so quickly? Where does he work?"

"He has a private clinic in Santa Fe and the fee he charges lets the patient have any appointment he wishes." He took the glass from her hand, placed both glasses on the hearth, and pulled her with him to lie on the thick carpet. Her hands automatically reached to frame his face and she let her fingers trace the scar that pulled his lip upward, trying to imagine the firm mouth without the disfigurement left by the accident. It had the power as it was to turn her into someone without a will of her own and she couldn't begin to visualize what it would be like straight against her own soft lips.

His arm pillowed her head as his hand slid under her sweater, his fingers going unerringly to the back fastener on her bra. He cupped her breast, massaging with slow movements until the brown tip hardened in his fingers and her breath came quickly through parted lips.

She unbuttoned his shirt and splayed her fingers along his hair-roughened chest. She could feel his heart beating beneath her hand. Their warm breaths mingled as the tip of his tongue traveled lightly across her mouth. His teeth pressed gently into the corner, nibbling back to the center, keeping their lips a tantalizing breath apart.

"Jonathan." Her voice came out a whisper and she pressed into the angles of his body, drawing her left leg up between his, wanting the tender byplay to continue.

His ragged breath stirred the tendrils of hair as he trailed light kisses over her ears. She moved her lips over his chin, feeling the stubble of beard, still with the faint tangy smell of his after-shave. He pulled her up onto his body and she looked down into his shadowed eyes, lowering her face to kiss him, openmouthed and seeking.

He moaned deep in his chest as her tongue invaded his mouth, his arms tightened as he rolled over on her, frustration at being unable to get to her causing him to swear. Raising himself on one knee, he lifted her and pushed upward to his feet, carrying her easily. As he placed her on his bed, she steeled herself for the roughness of his lovemaking but his hands were gentle as he undressed her, dark eyes examining her body as if for the first time, fingertips trailing on her skin as he lay beside her. He pulled her closer, and their bodies fit together like pieces of a well-made puzzle, the softness of hers blending into the hard-muscled frame of his.

His whisper was warm in her ear. "I'm sorry I've been rough on you, Kelly. I shouldn't blame you for wanting all you can get."

She stiffened, resenting the intrusion of his belief in her guilt that she had married him for money. "No, Jonathan—"

Her protest was lost as his mouth closed over hers and she could make no sound in her defense. It wasn't needed.

"Hold me, Kelly." It was a gentle, undemanding entreaty, his voice soft against her mouth, and she heard the sounds he made deep in his throat as her fingers explored his rib cage, drifting in slow motion over the high bone of his hip, across the tautness of his stomach, into the crease of his thigh. The sharp intake of his breath parted her moist lips and her body pressed closer as his kiss became demanding, his hands insistent in their probing, seeking, taking, and giving. Jonathan loved her the way she had known his love could be, bringing to reality her dreams of being held the way he was holding her tonight. It had taken three months to fulfill the sweetest of her dreams but it was all there as he claimed her for his own, and she slept the night through wrapped in his arms.

Chapter Ten

Kelly sat quietly in the waiting room, a magazine open in her lap, but she didn't see the pages in front of her. Nerve ends vibrated as she waited to talk to Dr. Hotchkiss. It had been six hours and the operation was only supposed to be four or less. "It might not work." Jonathan's words echoed in her head and she tensed at the thought that something had gone wrong.

She could no longer sit still, flipping through meaningless articles and advertisements. She walked over to the window to check on the snow that had been falling all through the night and morning. It seemed now that the weather forecasters were right: The snow was falling heavier, depositing new layers on the half foot already on the ground. Perhaps she should have listened to Jonathan's advice that she stay in the room he had reserved for her at the Ramada Inn near the clinic and had Dr. Hotchkiss call her when the operation was over. But she knew she had to be here, had to see Jonathan when he woke up.

As if she willed it, the door to the waiting room opened and Dr. Hotchkiss walked toward her. Kelly stood there, eyes wide, holding her breath.

"He's all right, Mrs. Heath," the doctor assured her. "It was more complicated than we suspected because of the severity of atrophied muscles in the cheek. Had he done this two, even one year ago, it would have been a lot simpler." He smiled. "He'll be fine. Right now, he's a little groggy but you can see him a few minutes."

"Oh, thank you." Kelly's breath expelled and she followed him on legs that trembled. She stood by the bed looking down at Jonathan, a long thin strip of bandage on the left side, his mouth covered completely except for a small opening on the right side where she could see crusted blood. It was unnatural to see him lying there, unaware of what was happening. She swallowed and reached for his hand, which lay outside the white spread, squeezing the long, slim fingers, caressing the hand still tanned from summer outdoor work. The feel of bristly hairs somehow comforted her ragged nerves.

He groaned and stirred, his fingers moving to close around hers, and she bent closer as he tried to speak.

"No, Jonathan, don't talk. Lie still," she murmured.

"Darling," he said, moving his head on the pillow.

Her heart thumped as she put her lips to the unbandaged cheek, loving the sound of the endearment she had never heard him use.

His left hand came up, catching her shoulder, and her hand slid beneath the covers to the waistband of his pajama bottoms. "Sweetheart," he whispered again and she could smell the medication, a strong, sharp odor, but she didn't move, wanting to savor the words he would never say to her when he was conscious.

He moaned and she bent to whisper her own endearments but his voice was harsh as he said, "Lola. Lola, no." He twisted away and Kelly let him go, staring down at the half face visible to her, feeling the blood drain away, leaving a crushing vacuum in her chest.

A moment later she stumbled away from him and made her way back to the small, sterile waiting room, crumpling into the same straight-backed chair she'd been in all day. At last she realized that Lola was the reason he had no use for love. The reason he insisted love wasn't necessary to a good marriage. He still loved her, no matter what he said, no matter how much he denied having any use for love, and since she was gone, he didn't want love from anyone else. After all this time, two years since the divorce, he still called for her. "Love is a trap that maims the victim and deserts," he had said. He was the victim and Lola had deserted him. He was right, she concluded, feeling the crippling pain left by her own love for him. Using Kelly, he vented his outrage at Lola's treatment of him but, though he hated, he still loved the woman he had first married, still dreamed of her enough to call out for her. Kelly was the weapon he used against her, not caring that the weapon had feelings too. In his tender moments she had believed that he would someday come to love her as she loved him. Her naiveté had been her open invitation to hurt, which Jonathan accepted and returned with a vengeance.

Tell me, Jonathan, she thought. *Why am I punished for my deception when you are equally guilty? Perhaps you too have a guilty conscience.*

She was still sitting stiffly in the same position when Jean came. "Kelly," she said, holding out her arms, and Kelly went into them, seeking refuge from the pain that engulfed her.

"What's wrong?" Jean asked. "You look terrible."

Kelly pulled the older woman to a chair and said, "No, nothing's wrong. The operation was a bit more complicated than Dr. Hotchkiss thought at first but he believes it's successful. It took longer to complete, that's all." She smiled. "I am tired from sitting around waiting."

"Have you seen him?"

"Yes, for a few minutes. He's still dopey." She took a deep breath to still the trembling through her body and asked, "Aren't the roads bad between here and Taos?"

"Not too bad but I came with Judge Creighton. He had to go to court. The main roads have been salted and I could have driven myself." She continued to look at Kelly's pale face. "Have you eaten?"

She shook her head. "I'm not hungry."

"I'm going to see Jonathan then we'll get something."

As Jean went in to see Jonathan, Kelly went to the restroom and splashed cold water in her face, holding a wet paper towel to her eyes for several seconds. Using her small purse brush, she fluffed the russet waves of hair around her face, hoping to hide the hurt from Jean. The staring green eyes and soft lips pressed together in a thin line were unrecognizable as hers, and she used her fingers to rub her cheeks, bringing temporary color back to them. She lifted her head and straightened her shoulders, telling herself it wasn't the end of the world—*not mine, anyway, because I never belonged to Jonathan's world*—and admitting that darkened the shadow already enclosing her. She was standing by the window gazing at the somber cloud-covered mountains when Jean returned.

"He's half asleep and Dr. Hotchkiss says he won't really appreciate visitors before tomorrow." She pulled on her coat and gloves. "There's a small café not far from here."

"I have the Cherokee and there's a nice restaurant at the motel. We can get something to eat there and stay in our room for a while before coming back here." Now Kelly was glad Jonathan had insisted they take the four-wheel-drive Cherokee when they left the ranch yesterday.

When they were seated in the dining room, Kelly glanced at her watch to see that it was four thirty. She was aware of the empty gnawing in her stomach, still nothing appealed to her, and the giant-sized knot in her throat would make swallowing difficult.

"Just soup for me, Jean," she finally decided. "My stomach has a million butterflies in it."

"All right." She looked at Kelly, concern in her eyes. "Why don't you go to dinner with us when Judge Creighton picks me up at seven?"

"No, thanks, Jean, I'll stay at the clinic a while."

"Do you want me to stay all night with you?"

Kelly laughed a little. "I must seem an awful baby to you but I'll be okay, Jean. You'd better go home while you have someone to drive you. Those clouds look mean and the forecast I heard last wasn't too promising."

They finished the light meal and went through the lobby to Kelly's room. Jean sat by the window, and Kelly lay across the bed, remembering the night Jonathan had held her and loved her as though it meant something to him.

"He'll be all right, Kelly," Jean tried to reassure her, misreading the lost look in Kelly's green eyes shadowed with light gray smudges underneath.

"Yes, I believe he will. I can hardly wait to see how he'll look. He was very handsome, wasn't he?"

Jean laughed. "At the risk of sounding like a prejudiced mother—yes, he was a very handsome man."

"And Lola?"

Jean drew in her breath, looking straight at Kelly. "Lola is more beautiful than anyone has a right to be. Black hair, clear olive complexion, big brown eyes with incredibly long lashes, and a figure designed by Venus." She stopped.

Kelly's fingers dug into the spread but she had to ask the question. "Jonathan loved her very much?"

"Yes," Jean said simply, her face showing nothing. She leaned forward. "That was years ago, Kelly, and he hasn't seen her since the divorce. He is certainly devoted to you."

Yes, Kelly wanted to tell her. *Devoted to making me*

pay my way by satisfying his need for Lola. "Where is she now?"

"She's an operatic star, living in St. Louis, appearing in her own productions. Jonathan met her when she was just starting out at the Santa Fe Opera and she stayed here as long as they were married. She's very talented."

There was no indication in Jean's voice of like or dislike as she talked about her former daughter-in-law. No bitterness surfaced because of what had happened to Jonathan. Jean was a strong woman and must have accepted it long ago and made her own adjustments to it. Perhaps she had forgiven her for what had happened to Jonathan because of her but Kelly believed she would always hate her for it.

Each word of Jean's information trampled into Kelly's already scarred self-image. That was why he would never go to the opera with anyone until she came and he supposed, rightly so, that she would never recognize the name of Lola Kendricks as his former wife. *Talent. Something I have so little of it wouldn't register in milligrams. Beauty. Nonexistent as far as I'm concerned.* Apricot hair like Tish and freckles. Jonathan had found in her someone who would never remind him of Lola. Never in a lifetime.

At six thirty they went back to the clinic and found Dr. Hotchkiss still there. "You can see him. He's wide awake and wondering where you are."

Jean patted her shoulder and said, "I'll see him in a few minutes if he isn't too tired."

Much of the bandage had been removed from his jaw and the blood cleaned from his lips. A white liquid covered the thick red streak where the incision had been made and the skin pulled together and clamped. A white patch covered the area around the left eye but she could see the black stitches in the soft flesh beneath it. She walked around to his right side, stopping far enough away so that he could focus on her without moving his head.

"Kelly?" As he spoke, he opened the one eye, blinking to get it wider. He snorted. "How in hell did you go a year without seeing at all? This is driving me crazy." His hand went toward the small bandage but she caught it.

"Don't be so impatient. The doctor says you'll be beautiful in no time." She held on to his hand. "Jean is outside and wants to see you before Judge Creighton picks her up, so I'll be back after she leaves. Stop trying to talk, you may rip stitches."

"Bossy," he said but he sounded tired and she left him to give Jean a chance to talk for a minute. Judge Creighton came by to pick up Jean promptly at seven and Kelly promised to call as soon as she found out when Jonathan would be discharged.

He dozed as she sat beside the bed, holding the hand that kept going to his face. She wondered if he was dreaming of Lola and if Lola would come back to him once he no longer carried the deep scars she hated.

Once he muttered "Kelly?" and she leaned over him, her fingers resting in the hollow at the base of his throat, feeling the pulse she loved to put her mouth against and feel the pumping of his heart as he made love to her. At least she could cause a change in his heartbeat, even if it was only the normal desire of male for female—any female.

It was ten o'clock when she let herself into the motel room and much later when her tired mind and body gave in to sleep. The telephone woke her.

"Good morning, Kelly." Jonathan's voice sounded wide awake.

"Jonathan. What time is it?"

"Seven thirty. You mean I woke you?"

"Yes. How are you?"

"My face feels like it's been chewed on by lions and the eye that shows is black."

"What does Dr. Hotchkiss say?"

"He's pleased with the results, but I reserve judgment."

"Till when?" she asked.

"Till you give me your opinion." His voice changed and grew distant.

Involuntarily she stiffened. "Can I see you now?" Her hands clenched into fists, she wondered how she would face him now that she knew the reason he forced her to stay with him—she was the insulation needed to protect him from his feelings for Lola.

"Yes, I may be able to leave later today."

"I'll be there as soon as I can," she told him.

Lying back on the pillow, she faced with horror the thought of staying on at the ranch as though she had learned nothing. *Does he dream about her? Does he pretend I'm Lola when he makes love to me? Would he take her back if she wanted him?*

Having no answers readily available, she dressed and drove the few blocks to the clinic. The snow had stopped before she went to sleep last night, and the roads were clear, but she still noticed heavy dark clouds in the sky as she parked the Cherokee.

Jonathan was sitting up in bed, pale against the pillows. The patch had been removed from his left eye and he now sported two black eyes.

She kissed the top of his shaggy head. "Is that all?" he asked.

"I'm afraid to touch you," she said, then bent to kiss the corner of his mouth.

"A little better," he grumbled, his hand reaching for hers.

She laughed, hoping it didn't sound as hollow as she

felt. "You're like a spoiled kid. Haven't you ever been indisposed before?"

"Never, and I'm not interested in a lesson in patience." His dark eyes glinted at her.

She sat on the bed, his hand on her thigh. His fingers slid in tantalizing slow motion from her knee to the fly front of her jeans, hesitating to move over to pick up her hand and hold it. He pulled her toward him and her parted lips touched his mouth, tasting medication.

There was a knock on the door and she lifted her head as Dr. Hotchkiss came into the room. "Let's have another look, Jonathan." He waved his hand as Kelly rose to leave. "Stay here, Mrs. Heath, I'll only be a minute." To Jonathan he said, "I want you to stay here tonight." When Jonathan started to protest, he said, "Yes, I know I said you could leave today but after the trouble I had with that tendon, I'd rather you stayed one more night. The weather's getting too nasty for you to drive back to the ranch, anyway." He straightened. "You know this won't make a completely new face, Jonathan, but the smaller scar will work into the folds of your cheek."

Jonathan's eyes turned to Kelly but she ignored him and asked her own question. "How much scar will he have after the healing is complete?"

"It will never go away completely, Kelly, but as I said, the cheek fold will hide most of it and the mouth will follow its natural line. There will be two sessions of dermal skin abrasion and X ray therapy to slough away the dead skin and smooth the texture of the new skin that will replace the part over the scar. Those sessions will be scheduled about a week apart, according to the way the healing progresses. Each case is different, but Jonathan has the type of skin that takes to the stretching required. The scars in the eyelid won't be noticeable at all.

"I must caution you, Jonathan, about going out in the cold and there's to be no physical work until I tell you. If you must go outside, stay only a very short time and cover your head and face."

After Dr. Hotchkiss left the room, Jonathan closed his eyes and lay back against the pillow and Kelly could feel him withdrawing from her. After a moment he said, "Doc's right, Kelly, go on back to the motel before you get stuck here too."

I wouldn't mind being stuck here with you, she wanted to tell him. But was he thinking about Lola and wishing she were there instead of her? Would she be happy with Jonathan's new face and be able to look at him again without showing revulsion?

Back at the motel that night Kelly called Jean to tell her what Dr. Hotchkiss had said, smiling as Jean's deep breath of relief came over the phone. "We'll be in Santa Fe until tomorrow and if the weather isn't too bad, we'll come up to see you before going to Heath Cliffs."

Jean's laugh was delighted. "Maybe I can use my influence with the weatherman, Kelly, so I'll be able to see you two before Christmas."

The silence of the empty room closed in on her and she wished for Jonathan's long body next to hers in the bed, wondering dully if he compared her almost straight body to Lola's, which Jean described as being designed by Venus. How could he not compare them? Jean's voice had been expressionless as she described her former daughter-in-law, but every word was burned into Kelly's mind, striking at her every thought.

Well, we won't get to the ranch today, she decided the next morning as she looked out the window. The snow had begun again during the night and showed no signs of stopping. She wanted coffee in the worst way but waited for Jonathan's call before leaving the room.

It was seven when the phone rang and Jonathan said, "Good morning, Kelly. Looks like we're in for another day in town but I'm free if I can get to the motel."

"How's your face?"

"Stiff and sore. Purple eyes instead of black but only one small bandage left." His voice showed no emotion whatsoever.

She stared at the wall in front of her, the ache inside of her a physical thing. "I'll come and get you."

He hesitated. "Aren't you afraid to drive in this?"

"If I can get out of the motel parking lot, I can make it all right," she told him with more assurance than she felt.

"I'm not sure it's a good idea, Kelly, but I'm ready to get out of here."

"Watch for me," she said.

Pulling on her boots and coat, she wrapped a scarf around her head and walked out into the winter wonderland. *Should be Christmas Eve,* she thought, *It's so beautiful and I'm getting my Christmas present early.* She refused to think of Jonathan preferring to give it to someone else.

It took several minutes to clean the overnight accumulation of snow from the Cherokee and when she finally cleaned her boots enough to get inside, the motor had warmed sufficiently to keep it from stalling.

During the night the parking lot had filled with people stranded by the storm and it was difficult to maneuver between cars and drifts. It took fifteen minutes to get into the street and fifteen more for the few blocks to the clinic.

Jonathan had been watching for her and came out of the clinic as she stopped. A woolen scarf over his head and jaw hid his face from her but when he climbed into the passenger side of the car he said, "Are you okay?" At her nod, he said, "I had some drugs this morning and I'd better not drive."

"Are you in pain?"

"No, but Dr. Hotchkiss says there's a little danger of infection from cold so he gave me some antibiotics."

The drive back to the motel was easier and she pulled back into the parking place she had left, the only one available.

"The storm's helping business anyway," he said. "Have you had breakfast?"

She shook her head.

"Come on. I could use a good cup of coffee."

Inside the dining room only a few people were eating or just sitting, talking about the storm. As Jonathan removed the scarf and his jacket, Kelly stood watching. Aside from the dark purple under his eyes, only a wide red line ran down the side of his face to a one-inch bandage that covered the left corner of his mouth almost to the edge of his nose. Along the red line the flesh was gray-white and rolled up to make the scar fit into a deep furrow. The left eye that had never closed completely was exactly like the right one, the long-lashed lid coming over it as he looked down at her. Only the stitches were visible. His mouth was a firm, evenly molded line, the lower lip fitting under the upper one that had been stretched upward by the scar. He smiled, the tender flesh showing only a little stiffness.

"Oh, Jonathan," she said softly and continued to stare.

"How would you like to get out of that coat, Kelly?"

"Oh." She turned so that he could take the snowy coat from ner and she removed the scarf, shaking her head to free the bright hair from her collar. Even seated, she couldn't take her eyes off him. "It's the best Christmas present I could get. I can't believe that's all that will show."

"You do like your expensive presents, don't you, Kelly?" he asked.

"Don't you think it's worth it?"

He shrugged. "I didn't have to look at me but if you say so."

She felt helpless anger. No matter what she said, she turned into a money-hungry female. Taking a deep breath, she said, "Thank you for the present, Jonathan," and looked at the menu the waitress placed in front of her. His face wasn't perfect but the difference was startling and Dr. Hotchkiss said the dermal abrasion treatments would smooth the rough, hilly texture of his cheek.

She didn't look up at him again until he asked, "What does the weatherman have to say about the storm?"

"Ten inches or more," she said. "If it keeps up like this all day as predicted, I'd venture to say 'or more' would fit the situation."

"Going to Taos is out of the question," he told her. "I'd like to try to get home before it gets worse. Are you game to try?"

"Do you really think we should?"

"I've driven in much worse," he said, looking through the front window of the restaurant at the leaden sky. "I'll need to get some feed down to the south pasture by tomorrow."

"Jonathan, Carl and the others will take care of that."

He grinned, wincing a little as he did so. "I know that but I thought I needed an excuse to be foolhardy. The truth is I'm homesick."

"I can believe that," she told him, not admitting she felt the same. Even knowing she didn't belong at Heath Cliffs didn't keep her from feeling that it was home.

They were waiting for their check and Jonathan was standing to put on his coat when a low sultry voice said, "Hello, Jonathan."

Kelly, looking up at him, saw him stiffen and the

color drain from his face as he turned toward the woman who had spoken. No more than five foot two at the most, she was the most beautiful woman Kelly had ever seen. Black hair braided in thick loops around a small head, creamy olive complexion, and black eyes that smiled into Jonathan's face. Small white teeth showed between perfectly shaped crimson lips. She wore a white fur wrap that touched the top of dainty red leather boots. Kelly didn't need anyone to tell her the woman was Lola Kendricks.

When Jonathan spoke, he sounded as though he'd been running. "Hello, Lola." They stood looking at each other until the waitress offered Jonathan the check. He took it, turning to Kelly. "Lola, my wife, Kelly."

Kelly was aware of her bulky turquoise sweater, heavy gray and turquoise plaid slacks, and the serviceable black cowboy boots she had worn since college days. Feeling awkward and ugly, she said quietly, "Hello, Lola."

Lola's glance went over her briefly and she nodded, looking back into Jonathan's face. "You don't look the same, Jonathan."

"No?" He had recovered from his shock and his voice had ice tags attached. He reached to pull Kelly to her feet and helped her with her coat. "I'm surprised you remember what I looked like, Lola. The accident was a long time ago." He tucked Kelly's arm in his and turned. "I hope you won't be detained too long in Santa Fe," he said, pulling Kelly with him as he strode from the dining room. She was aware of the quiet fury inside him as they walked through the lobby to their room.

They packed in silence and he carried their bags to load them in the Cherokee. She locked the door and went to help Jonathan clean the snow from the windows and windshield. It collected behind them almost as fast as they removed it. Behind her, Jonathan dusted the snow from her coat and helped her inside before he got behind the wheel.

"Do you feel like driving in this?" she asked, studying the tense lines in his face, the thin-lipped grimace, hearing again his anguished cry of Lola's name. She shivered.

"Yes." He glanced at her. "It'll be warm in here soon." She didn't bother to tell him the chill came from something besides the weather.

Once they were on the highway where plows had been, they had no trouble, but on the range road the snow had not been disturbed and it was impossible to tell where the road was except for snow markers. Jonathan drove as though he could see and she guessed he had done this same thing many times. As they went through the gate posts, the Cherokee slid sideways and he fought the wheel, finally straightening back onto the road. He was breathing hard and sweat stood out on his upper lip. She continued to watch him as he concentrated on getting them home and she saw his face begin to relax when the house came in sight. It had taken them three hours to drive less than twenty miles.

Selena had fresh coffee ready and she brought it to them in the den. "You're beautiful, Jonathan. I'm so glad." Even before the healing was complete she knew the operation had made a big difference and it was obvious she remembered how he had looked before the accident.

He smiled at her, taking the plate of cookies she extended to him. "Thanks." He bent and brushed her cheek with his straight mouth.

Kelly looked around at the bright decorations, already giving the house a definite holiday look. "Who did all this?" she asked, delighted at the scene. She had asked him about decorating just after Thanksgiving but he had said, "Let Selena do it," not knowing she loved the warm smells and hustle and bustle of the excitement around the holidays. The operation had overshadowed everything and she had forgotten all about wreaths and candles. At the Thanksgiving dinner Carl had told her that they cut their Christmas trees from near the river but it was usually done closer to Christmas Eve.

"Selena. Hastings. Probably Carl helped," he said, standing by the mantel, still holding the coffee cup.

"You look tired," she told him.

"Exhausted, as a matter of fact. How about you?"

"You drove; I just rode. Besides you're still weak from the operation, whether you admit it or not." There was still something she had to bring out into the open and she went on before she could change her mind. "Lola is very beautiful."

She flinched away from the abrupt stiffening of his body but she made herself watch him, hearing his indrawn breath, looking straight into the dark eyes that narrowed, hiding his expression from her.

"Yes, she is." His voice was cold and hard as stone. "She always was."

He turned away from her and went to the window but she knew he saw nothing beyond his mind's eye. He rubbed the back of his neck and when he came back toward her it was as if they had not mentioned Lola's name. "I think early to bed for me after dinner." He didn't look at her, his expression telling her he was miles away.

She slept alone that night, one of the few times except for his hospital stay since they were married. She spent a lot of time alone the next few days, wrapping presents, walking with Ebony and Sable, sometimes joined by Beowulf, who trailed quietly watchful behind Ebony. She didn't know how Jonathan passed the time but he no longer made love to her. She was conscious of the emptiness, knowing it shouldn't matter since she now knew how very far down she was on his list of priorities. Perhaps he might even agree to releasing her from their marriage without foreclosing on RAG Ranch. His face was healing, the stark white and red over the scars gradually fading, and she was sure the skin would soon be healthy-looking again, handsome enough to get Lola back.

They were at breakfast one morning when Jonathan said, "I'm going in for the skin abrasion this morning, Kelly. If Dr. Hotchkiss is satisfied with the way the skin has healed, it will be the last one. Don't expect me home until late." His voice was coolly detached, denying her any part in his thoughts or activities.

She put her fork down. "I'll drive you into town." He hadn't worked any outside since the operation but had stayed in his study going over papers and books, sometimes with Carl or the foreman joining him.

"No, thanks, there's no need for you to sit all day just waiting for me."

"You may not feel like driving home," she protested.

"I'll manage." He had already shut her out and she sat in silent frustration until he excused himself and strode from the room.

She walked to the window and watched him back the Chrysler from the garage, wondering why he didn't drive the Cherokee, which he usually preferred. Perhaps he was meeting Lola and the car was more elegant, she thought, her heart a leaden weight in her chest.

She shook herself away from Jonathan and Lola and looked to the southwest at the Jemez Mountains, snow-capped and imposing in the distance. Her thoughts had all been self-centered lately and she had pushed Angela and her family into the back recesses of her mind. It was only a few days till Christmas and she found herself wondering what kind of holiday the six children would have.

In the Eyes of Love

She went in search of Selena. "I'm going into Taos since Jonathan will be gone all day. I'll take Ebony and I should be home by five at the latest."

She dressed for the cold weather in brown wool pants, a tan bulky turtleneck sweater, and brown boots, and wrapped a plaid scarf around her neck. She stood by the chest of drawers looking at the neatly folded sweaters, most of them gifts from Jean. She pulled a light green one out and held it up. Marta could wear that easily as well as the brown and beige tweed blazer. Jean would never miss them and wouldn't mind anyway, she was sure.

She picked up the bank book from Albuquerque and dropped it into her handbag, then slung her jacket across her arm, went through
a soft whistle for Ebony, smiling as the animal loped toward her.

She rubbed the big head. "Gonna have some beautiful babies for me one of these days, Ebony?" she asked, receiving a friendly kiss as she bent to the dog. As Kelly opened the door, Ebony bounded into the front seat of the Mustang, assuming a regal pose on the passenger's side.

Her mind on everything but her driving, Kelly headed toward the downtown area and the Bank of Santa Fe. She went in and transferred her award money from her account in Albuquerque, then checked her balance after she wrote two checks, one for twelve hundred dollars to Carl for Jonathan's Christmas present, the other for five hundred dollars. Putting them into her handbag, she returned to the car.

"That's that, Ebony. Let's go see Angela." The traffic was heavy as she turned north on the interstate and it was nearly eleven when she stopped by the gate at Angela's. The grim yellow walls looked even more desolate under the dull sky with the fine sand blowing in the cold wind. She shivered and turned to hook the leash on Ebony's collar. She left the sweater and blazer she had picked for Marta in the car and went up the dirt walk. As she reached the steps, the door opened and Angela came out.

"Kelly, how nice to see you. How did you know I was home?"

Kelly smiled. "I took a chance you'd be home."

"The children are at school, but Andy has a very bad cold and I stayed with him. Come on in." She stood aside for her to enter and saw Ebony for the first time.

Kelly hesitated. "I hope you won't mind, Angela. Ebony has had training with blind people and I thought the children might enjoy her."

Kelly followed Angela into the kitchen, Ebony at her heels. She looked around. There was no sign of Christmas decorations and the room was chilly. She sat down as Angela returned with her ever-present hot tea.

Angela reached to pet Ebony. "She certainly is beautiful."

"Yes," Kelly agreed. She leaned forward. "What about Christmas, Angela?"

The woman looked at her cup, then the warm brown eyes met Kelly's. "It will be the same as today, Kelly. The children understand."

"I don't," Kelly said, her voice tight. She took a deep breath. "I have some money I want to spend on the children for Christmas. I know they can't see decorations but they need something extra. I want a list of clothes they need and sizes to go with the list."

"I won't refuse it, Kelly. They need everything."

"A grocery list too."

"What will your husband say about this?"

Kelly shook her head. "He wouldn't care but he won't know. The money's mine."

Angela rose to refill their cups and brought back a pad of paper. "I'll name what we need and you write till you have to quit."

Kelly did as she was told and twenty minutes later looked up at Angela as she paused. "Now, clothing for the children."

Angela hesitated then, mouth set in a firm line, went through items and sizes. "The colors won't matter but Marta loves green and Andy loves red."

Kelly smiled, understanding in a way that Angela would never know. "Tell you what. I'll be back in a couple of hours with some groceries, but I may not have time for clothes shopping this time."

She stood up and turned to see Andy just inside the kitchen door, his blue eyes bright with fever, staring uncertainly. "I heard voices." He wore a faded flannel robe two sizes too big for him and was barefoot.

"Yes, Andy, it's Kelly, remember?"

His shaggy blond head barely moved as he nodded. Kelly released Ebony from her leash and went toward Andy, taking his small cold hand. "This is Ebony. She's a black German shepherd. She weighs more than you but she's very gentle. Rub her head."

The small hand found Ebony's ears, rubbing behind them, and a half smile touched his lips. Kelly stepped away, leaving him with the dog. "She can stay near the bed with you till I get back, Andy. You'll catch more cold in those bare feet."

"All right." He turned back to the door. "Mom, may I have some hot tea? I'm cold." His voice was husky with deep congestion.

"I'll bring it to you, Andy."

Kelly followed the small figure down the dark drafty hall, Ebony by her side. He went through a doorway, hands outstretched to guide himself, crossed the narrow room, and crawled into a cot pushed near a window. Kelly wrapped him in an old worn comforter and pulled another thin blanket over his small figure.

Angela came in behind her with a mug of tea and placed it in Andy's hand. He sat up, snuggled under the skimpy covers.

Kelly's glance took in the other two small cots and the chest of drawers that made up the room's furnishings. "Stay with Andy, Ebony," she said, "and I'll be back for you."

The dog obediently sat close enough for Andy to reach her when he finished his tea. "She'll share your bed and keep your feet warm if Mom doesn't care, Andy."

The little boy's face lit up. "Can she?"

Angela laughed. "Of course, but don't spill the tea."

Smiling, Kelly said, "Well, I'd better get started. I'll probably be gone a while, Angela. I haven't shopped in ages."

She followed Angela's directions into town, her mind running through the shopping list. A glance at her watch showed twelve thirty when the Mustang pulled into the mall parking lot. Enough time to complete both shopping lists.

An hour and a half later the salesclerk in Penney's directed her to Customer Service where she waited for her purchases to be wrapped in bright holiday paper. The children couldn't see it but they could feel it. She left all the packages and drove her car to the delivery door where they were brought out and packed into the backseat, filling it. Kelly had been away from buying things for so long that she was in a state of shock over the price of clothing for the children and blankets for seven beds.

In the grocery store she studied her list, wondering if she would run out of money or trunk space in the car first. An hour later a young man packed the groceries in the trunk, placing two fifty-pound bags of flour in the front seat with Kelly, crowding her against the door. She felt slightly light-headed as she parked as close to the back gate of Angela's house as she could. There were eighteen dollars left from the original five-hundred-dollar check.

Angela came to meet her, eyes widening at the packages in the small car. Together, they carried in the groceries and as Angela put them away, happily stacking packages of meat, boxes of noodles, and cans of vegetables, Kelly lugged the other purchases in, placing the boxes and bags on the last trestle table, and the boxes with the blankets on the floor. "Let's keep everything except the blankets separate so we can surprise the kids Christmas morning."

Kelly was breathing hard and dropped onto the wooden bench. "Whew! Am I out of shape." She shrugged out of her jacket and wiped her forehead. "You'd never know it's freezing out there."

Angela turned away and Kelly saw her hand wipe at the tears on her cheeks. She started to speak when the door to the hallway opened and Andy stood there, tousled blond head tilted to one side, his cheeks flushed—whether from fever or pleasure, Kelly didn't know.

The sightless blue eyes sparkled. "Ebony's swell." It was the first time he had expressed enthusiasm at anything. Ebony stayed at his side as he came to the table. His small hand found the bench and he sat by Kelly.

"She is nice, Andy," Kelly agreed, looking down into the eyes that reminded her so much of Robbie.

"Where'd you get her?" The face that lifted to hers could have been Robbie's in a few years.

She swallowed hard. "My husband gave her to me."

Andy's hand slid along the bench and Ebony's nose found it. He grinned and his fingers ruffled her thick fur.

"Oh, Angela, in that bag with the fruit there's aspirin and a bottle of cough syrup the pharmacist recommended. It's especially for children if you want to try it on Andy." She stood up. "I wish I could stay to see the others, but I'd better go." She picked up the sweater and jacket she had placed with the other clothes. "Marta can use these, Angela." She smiled at the older woman. "I hope the clothing fits, but keep the tickets and I'll be back to exchange whatever needs it." As she turned, she was near the big wood-burning stove and her hand went toward it, feeling no heat.

"The stove was given to us but the wood ran out last week," Angela said simply.

Kelly slid her arms into her jacket, wrapped a scarf around her neck, and bent to touch Andy's cheek. "Take care, Andy. I'll bring Ebony back when you're feeling better."

"All right," he said, dipping his head back toward the table and reverting to his usual shy self.

Angela followed her to the back door. "Kelly—"

Kelly looked up at her and smiled understandingly. "I'll see you soon," she called as she ran to the car, Ebony romping beside her.

As she turned into the interstate, she drove automatically, her mind on Angela and the children.

Where can I get wood for that stove? she wondered, eyes checking the time on the bank clock as she left Santa Fe behind her. *Four forty-five, and I told Selena I'd be home at five. I won't be very late.*

Wood. Eyes narrowed, she pictured the trees on Jonathan's land, knowing the wood for his fireplaces was supplied from them. Al Cardon could help her if he weren't so loyal to Jonathan. But Kelly wasn't surprised. Jonathan was generous where his employees were concerned. *He's even generous with his wife except for what she really wants,* a tiny voice reminded her.

She pulled into the yard, pushed the garage door open, and breathed a sigh of relief when she saw the empty spaces. Sitting there a moment, she wondered again if Jonathan was seeing Lola. Surely the skin treatment couldn't have taken all day. She shrugged as she watched Ebony jump out of the car and lope toward the corral in search of Beowulf, no doubt.

Smiling, she closed the garage and walked through

into the house, stopping by the kitchen door. "I'm home, Selena."

Selena smiled at Kelly as she unwound the scarf from her neck and took off her jacket. "Jonathan called earlier and said he'd be home by six thirty. Did you have a good day?"

"Sure did, but I'm tired. I'm going to start doing some work to get in shape. Can't even fight the Christmas crowds without wilting and I remember when I could work all day, shop half the night, and still stay awake, but not anymore." She stretched. "I'd better move if I'm to be ready for dinner when Jonathan gets home."

The morning paper lay on her dresser and she flipped to the classified section. Under Services, she found what she was looking for and placed a call to the number listed.

"Mr. Quantzal, please," she said when a voice answered.

"This is Quantzal," he said.

Kelly explained what she wanted and when it was to be delivered. "I'll mail you a check tomorrow for two cords of wood to be delivered to 110 Lansdale." When Mr. Quantzal agreed, she took a deep breath. "Could you please bring a small Christmas tree, about five feet tall? I'll also need a stand for it." His voice was pleasant as he said, yes, he could do that, then he gave her a total price.

She hung up the phone, pressing her lips together. So, the children couldn't see a decorated tree, but their presents had to go somewhere.

A warm shower helped ease her tired muscles. She was slipping into a warm velour robe when her bedroom door opened. It was Jonathan.

Her eyes went to his cheek, covered by angry red streaks fanning from eye to chin, and her breath caught. He said nothing, his glance going from her damp hair down the length of her body and back to meet her eyes. He held a big gilt-wrapped box in his hands and extended it to her.

"I went to see Jean and she sent this to you."

Her hands went out to take the box but her eyes remained on his face. "What does Dr. Hotchkiss say about the results of the treatments?"

"Not much. Evidently, he's satisfied that the operation did as much as he expected." His voice was cool and detached but somehow not as icy as it usually was. "The dermal abrasion treatments take up where the operation left off and he'll know more after the scar has healed some. He'll keep a watch on it a few weeks in case part of it has to be redone."

She continued to hold the box, staring at him, until he said, "Open it, Kelly."

"Oh," she murmured, turning to place the box on the bed and slide her finger under the gold cord to release the top. She pushed the blue tissue paper aside and lifted the garment to spread it on the bed.

An unfamiliar desire to cry touched her as she fingered the lounging pajamas of navy blue chiffon, lined in soft cotton, pants with wide legs pleated to fall like a skirt and a tunic top shirred below the rounded yoke of tiny navy and white figures with a wide sash of the same print.

"Jean has good taste," he said, looking over her shoulder. "Wear them tonight." She heard him walk away and the bedroom door close behind him.

Her fingers clenched in the soft folds of the material as she stood with head bowed for several minutes. Jean had meant for the outfit to be worn for a romantic evening but all Jonathan saw was something to enhance the body he claimed as his own.

Jonathan mixed a drink for Kelly ready to place in the blender with ice when she finished dressing. He poured bourbon and water over ice for himself and leaned against the mantel, staring into the fire. He was tired and his lips tightened as he admitted to feeling that way a lot lately.

Seeing Lola at the motel just after his operation had churned his insides and brought back the hatred he had felt for her after the accident when she left him alone to make the long climb back from the very gates of hell. Made him remember the stares when he was in a crowd if he turned his face the wrong way so the light showed the scars in their glaring ugliness, and the indrawn breaths when he ran into people they had known during their years of marriage.

It had taken a long time to become hardened to the stares and whispers but he had managed. Since that time, he had never wanted another woman, not until Kelly came along, and even then he convinced himself it was sympathy for her that made him propose marriage.

Kelly's reaction to meeting Lola had been curious, as though it was something she was expecting, and she had become quiet and withdrawn, leaving him alone after the operation. Occasionally he would catch her eyes on him but she made no point of talking about the scar nor of his discontinuance of any type of harassment or lovemaking. She was waiting, but he had no idea what she was waiting for.

That chance meeting with Lola at the motel had been all but forgotten in the ensuing turmoil of his mind since the operation until today. He had left the doctor's office after the treatment, wanting a drink badly, when Lola walked out of an adjoining office.

"Jonathan," she said, smiling, tilting her head, and lifting her face for him to kiss her. He stared down at her, took a step backward, and was rewarded by seeing the color come into her face.

She laughed, biting into the ripe fullness of her lips. "Oh, I forgot, you're married." Her voice sounded breathless. "Where's your wife—Kelly, isn't it?"

"Kelly's at home," he said shortly.

"Jonathan." The soft hesitancy in her voice had intrigued him for years, but it seemed affected now, or maybe he was so accustomed to Kelly's normal voice and straightforwardness that it only appeared that way. "Your face is healing well and you'll be back to your former handsomeness very soon." She smiled and extended a small hand out to him. "I'm sorry I was such a coward. I should have been brave but I couldn't bear the thought of your suffering and you looked so terrible, all because of me...." Her voice trailed off as he continued to look down at her.

"The treatments seem to have helped and Kelly deserves to have something better to look at since she didn't run the first time she saw me." He opened the double door leading from the professional building and waited for her to walk out in front of him. In the parking area he stopped by the blue Chrysler he had bought after the accident that totaled the Mercedes and said, "Good-bye, Lola."

"We could have a drink," she suggested.

He shook his head, opened the door, and, ignoring her, started the car and drove away, not even tempted to look in the rearview mirror. By the time he reached Taos, the desire for a drink had diminished and he wished he had gone straight home. He hadn't seen Jean since Thanksgiving, though, except for the few blurred minutes at the clinic, and he admitted to himself he had missed her. Besides, she would be pleased with the way the healing of his face was progressing.

Jean accepted the improvement to his face as she did everything else, with ease and understanding, although he knew by the smile on her face that she was impressed. She kissed him. "Dr. Hotchkiss did a splendid job, Jonathan. You should have done this years ago."

"I didn't have Kelly to nag me years ago," he told her.

"Good for Kelly," she said, smiling as she remembered Kelly's expression when she said, "I love Jonathan. If it hurts him, it hurts me," way back in September when she fitted her wedding dress. "How would you like to take her something?" She left him, to return with the box and said, "One of my customers special-ordered this, then decided not to take it."

"What is it?"

"Dinner and lounging pajamas. You know, flowing and sexy." She laughed. "Kelly will do a lot more for them than Mrs. Conley."

"Do I get billed?" he asked, watching his mother, who delighted in seeing that Kelly got plenty of nice things.

"Of course. You wouldn't want your old mother to take a loss, would you?"

He hugged her. "We'll see you Christmas?"

"Yes. If we don't get snowed in," she assured him.

The drive home seemed to take forever and he noted with impatience that it was six o'clock as he passed through the small town of Espanola. He breathed a sigh as he entered the four-lane interstate heading toward Santa Fe, the signs reflecting from headlights in the early darkness of the winter day. On his right he saw the luminous sign that announced the Santa Fe Opera House, and remembered Kelly's first visit to Heath Cliffs.

He shook his head, recalling how young and innocent she seemed, helpless yet independent in her blindness. In retrospect he wondered if his chagrin at having a redheaded woman fool him so completely had made him try to hurt her. Knowing he had someone who would never see his scarred face, never make demands on him he couldn't meet, be there when he wanted her in exchange for his giving her everything money could buy, had seemed an ideal solution.

Until Kelly turned the tables on him: She could not

only see, but she loved him, wanting his love in return; and his money meant only one thing to her: Ebony could have puppies and she could donate them for her main passion in life—children who couldn't see.

He reacted the only way he thought he could even the score, taking her body whenever he wanted, and when she threatened to leave him, gave her the ultimatum: Stay or I'll foreclose on RAG Ranch. When he taunted her about his ugly face, she stood her ground, daring to tell him it didn't matter to her, finally demanding a Christmas present he was sure she would never get.

Friday morning after Thanksgiving he had left her in his bedroom after laughing at her when she told him she'd had enough and was leaving. He drove the Cherokee to the south pasture where they were planning to add to the corral, and sat a long time thinking about Kelly. It had been a long time since he thought of hating her or of resenting her ability to see. It was then he made up his mind to see a plastic surgeon and at least hear an opinion about surgery to remove the scar or to improve the looks of it.

When he returned to the house, Kelly's car was gone and he had called Dr. Hotchkiss for an appointment on the day he was due to return from Canada. He had not believed much could be done, had not been optimistic about the results, but as the days passed after the operation and Dr. Hotchkiss talked to him after the treatment today, he was slowly coming to terms with the fact that, if not perfect, his face would no longer be enough to frighten little children.

The door to the den opened and Jonathan watched Kelly walk toward him. His body came alive at the sight of her slim figure held erect, her small chin pushing the bright head back as it lifted in defiance of a husband who refused to bend in any direction for her. He was unaware that his own body stiffened nor that the gleam of pleasure at seeing her in the navy blue lounging outfit Jean sent her would give Kelly the impression she was a well-dressed article to use as he saw fit.

The navy and white yoke flowing into the fullness of the tunic she had belted loosely around her brought out all the burnished lights of her russet-colored hair, and the pleated folds of the pants flowed over her hips, emphasizing the curves, falling to the floor to show only the toes of silver sandals. His eyes went back to her face, and green eyes met his for an instant, then looked away, the dark brown lashes throwing shadows against her cheeks.

He had not touched her since the operation and his male appetite was well aware of that fact. The pain in his face had not been severe after the operation but the physical exhaustion had surprised him, and he was forced to admit that it had taken a toll on him emotionally, as well. He couldn't bear the thought of Kelly's fingers touching the new and smaller scar when he remembered her obsession with the disfigurement before she could see and afterward. She demanded—and he had never thought of any other word that suited her request—that he give her a new face as a Christmas present and his resentment had taken a path he hadn't tried to control. He wanted to hurt her for daring to ask and he was sure he had succeeded in doing just that. His threat to foreclose on RAG Ranch was his only hold on her and he knew it, knew for certain the luxuries she enjoyed on the ranch did not impress her even though he taunted her with her enjoyment of those things. If not for her concern for Ann and Gary, she would be gone in a minute.

Often he wondered where she spent her time, but he would never ask nor would he stoop to following her. She usually visited Jean and Rena at least once each week, but other than that and the times he saw her wandering the ranch with the dogs and horses, he had no idea what she did with her time alone.

He turned the blender on to mix her drink the way she liked it and handed it to her. As he released the glass to her, their fingers touched.

The sudden desire for her that catapulted through him was unexpected and he had no control over the emotion that showed in his voice as he spoke her name. "Kelly."

He stared into green eyes that shimmered with a suspicion of tears and took her glass from her hand, placing it with his on the mantel. Her face was below his chin and she came up on tiptoe, her lips parting for his kiss. She smelled the antiseptic odor from his face and hesitated.

He stiffened and pushed her away. "The smell is rather offensive," he said.

She shook her head. "No, I was afraid it would hurt you." But he moved toward the door, ignoring her plea. She watched his uncompromising figure walk away from her, shrugged helplessly, and followed him to the dining room.

Chapter Eleven

The next afternoon Kelly stood by the pond, watching the ducks swimming in the part of the water not frozen over. Smutty clouds clung halfway down the mountainside, obscuring most of the seven thousand feet, and the wind came from the southwest, cold and damp. Forecasters predicted snow but they could be dreaming of a White Christmas, two days away.

Her thoughts went to Jonathan with his almost-handsome face that he kept closed from her. Her efforts to behave the way he demanded were being pushed aside by the love she still had for him. No matter the circumstances, she still loved him. She thought that should be a good enough reason for them to try to hold their marriage together, but truly knew that if *he* wasn't interested in her, then he had to let her go, to salvage her own life.

Kelly hadn't been able to caress the small scar already fading at the corner of his mouth, nor touch the ridge left by the skin abrasions, which was becoming less and less noticeable. He never mentioned Lola but he might as well have printed her name in giant-sized letters between them, a living reminder of his indifference to Kelly. The scars didn't bother him, because he shaved regularly, using her favorite tangy after-shave. She smiled, remembering her first introduction to that scent so long ago.

A small, warm thrill touched her stomach and she pressed her hand against it. *I need you, Jonathan, and it's Christmas. Surely—* She turned, starting at a run back up the hill toward the house, her breath coming quickly as she imagined his hands on her body, his mouth hard on hers. If he wouldn't come to her, she'd go to him. If he wanted to pretend she was Lola—She stopped thinking. *He'll know I'm Kelly and no one else,* she vowed silently. *I'll tell him how I feel and he'll listen, even if he throws me out afterward.*

Ebony raced with her the last few yards to the house and they landed on the porch, where Kelly flung her jacket on the hook and kicked her muddy boots into the corner.

"You stay," she told the wet Ebony and ran down the hallway to the door of Jonathan's sitting room. She stopped, breathing hard from the run up the hill. The door stood partly opened and without knocking, she pushed it inward, stepping across the threshold onto the heavy carpet. Her mouth opened to call his name, but she remained frozen, making no sound, as the scene in front of her etched itself in flaming outlines through her mind. Jonathan and Lola, holding on to each other, dark head bent to dark head, unaware of any world but the one in which they stood.

He hasn't even kissed me with his new mouth, she thought irrelevantly. *And here's the reason he wouldn't kiss me last night.* If she had ever entertained any doubts about Lola wanting to come back to him, she had her answer now.

Leaving the door as she had found it, Kelly made her way back to the porch, where Ebony stood waiting, highly insulted at not being dried and allowed into the house with her. She put her boots on, but left off her heavy jacket and took off with long, swinging strides toward the corral. It didn't seem as cold without the wind from the icy pond and the bulky gray sweater she wore was warm enough, perhaps because she no longer felt anything.

The thin afternoon sunshine that had struggled for survival all day gave up and disappeared, leaving semi-darkness in its wake. Kelly's eyes fastened on the flickering light partly covering the inside wall of the stables, and she wondered how the sun managed to find a last spot through the cloud of darkness to cast a beam. A crackling noise seemed to keep time with the movement of the light, and Kelly grew curious. The low growl in Ebony's throat brought her attention to the dog standing by her side, the thick fur bristled. She looked back at the light, which had climbed higher on the wall, and her body jerked with realization.

"Fire! Oh, my God!" She was at the stable door, her hand on the heavy latch but the wood was warm to her touch and she hesitated. In an instant her mind pictured the fire-prevention classes they held regularly in school. Find exits and fire extinguishers. Don't panic. Don't open hot doors. What was it Carl had said? There's nothing worse than a fire among animals. If we're ever unlucky enough to have a fire—Sable! Which stall was she in? Why hadn't the sprinkling system worked? Carl had said the manual switch was on the outside of the building but which side would that be from where she was now? She had no idea.

Her brain racing, she moved from the hot door, hearing a whinny close by. She turned to the dog at her heels. "Ebony, go get Jonathan. Carl. Go get help." She didn't know who was around this close to Christmas but someone had to be. Interrupt Jonathan and his lady love, damn them anyway. Ebony was off like a streak toward the house.

Smoke rose to meet her as she turned a corner but she could see Sable, head jerking, eyes walling at the feel of heat and smoke. She opened the crossed-panel gate. "Come on, Sable, I need you." She threw her boots aside and, placing her toes on Sable's foreleg, swung up on her bare back. Holding on to the silky mane and keeping her own head down, Kelly prodded the horse. The feel of Kelly's hand steadied Sable and though she snorted, she walked as she was guided by Kelly's pull on her mane. So far, the fire was contained in one stall and Kelly could see no animals there but she heard the frightened noises of others nearby. Suddenly the flames erupted in front of her and Sable reared, scraping her side and Kelly's leg against the wall. Grimacing with the pain, Kelly held on and guided the frightened horse to what she hoped was the outside wall. Then they were out, but the darkness was total. Feeling along the wall, she found the spikes she had seen the day Carl explained the sprinkler system to her. They were warm.

"Steady, Sable, steady." The horse was breathing hard, her big body trembling, but somehow she knew Kelly was depending on her. Kelly's hand caught a spike and she swung her leg over, placing her foot on another spike.

"Go, girl, get out of here." She slapped the horse on her flank and, gratefully, saw her head away from the stables. Two spikes up her searching hands made contact with the heavy switch.

"Work, damn you," she whispered, swinging her full weight on the metal handle. It gave, and Kelly hung on to it until it moved all the way from the upward position to straight down. She stayed there, listening, hearing only the crackling of flames till, suddenly, water rushed through the opened valves, splattering and hissing.

She took a deep breath and choked as the acrid smoke filled her lungs. A dizzying pain shot through her head and she fought to hold on to the spikes

though her legs and arms were numb. Her fingers came
loose and she dropped to the ground. A second later,
gulping for air, she was up and stumbling through
dense smoke and heat, finding latches, shoving them
loose, pushing animals toward openings she hoped
weren't dead ends. Heat fanned her cheeks and she
smelled singed hair—whether hers or animals' she
couldn't tell. She could no longer see anything.

A dark form brushed against her legs and she caught
Ebony's tail and half-crawled to follow her. The sound
of her name came muffled through the blinding smoke
but her tongue was thick and she couldn't answer. A
blanket was thrown over her and she was lifted to be
put down some moments later.

"Kelly?" Jonathan's voice penetrated the gloom but
instead of seeing him she saw the two figures locked in
close embrace. A chill invaded her body and she murmured, "No."

"Are you all right? Kelly, answer me." The urgency
in his voice was lost on her.

"Yes." She wondered where Lola was and started
shivering.

"Don't move," he ordered and was gone.

She watched the flickering flames and heard people
shouting, animals protesting in fright, and felt apart
from it all. Her face stung, there was no feeling in her
lips, and the smell of scorched hair stung her nostrils.

A form came from the darkness to kneel beside her.
"Kelly, it's Carl." His hands pushed the blanket aside
and a flashlight shone nearby but away from her face.
"Are you hurt?"

"Are all the horses out? Is Ebony all right?"

"Ebony's fine. Thanks to her coming for us, we got
to you. Tell me where you hurt."

"My hair."

"Your hair?" he repeated.

"Yes, it hurts. I must have burned it." The statement didn't make sense to her but she didn't know how to correct it.

The light came to her face and she closed her eyes to shut out the brightness, hearing his muttered exclamation.

"I'm going to take you inside, Kelly," he said.

She didn't protest as she heard him barking orders to someone and she was put on a makeshift stretcher and carried. Sounds of fire and activity faded as they left the corral. Selena met them at the door and Kelly was conscious of conversation that she didn't understand.

Kelly opened her eyes to see she was in Jonathan's bed and she tried to explain that she would have to be moved, but it was too much effort. A small Christmas tree stood on the sill of the bay window, blue lights reflected in the glass to give an illusion of two trees. It would be Christmas Eve in a couple of hours but she had lost interest in the holiday. Her Christmas present arrived early and had been given to someone else before she claimed it for her own.

He was never mine, she thought. *I belong to him, but he belongs to Lola.*

Carl was holding her left hand, working her fingers, putting thick cream on her arm. "That stings," she managed.

"I know, Kelly. I don't have any pain killer but Dr. Sells will be here soon and he can give you something."

Jonathan strode into the room. His face was smudged, his hair wet, water running in smutty rivulets down his face. He knelt by the bed.

"How is she, Carl?"

"Not bad, Jonathan, but a doctor should look at her hand. How's everyone else?"

"All right. The fire's out and the animals are safe. They're being put in the back stalls where there's no damage." Jonathan touched his wife's cheek with one finger. "Your hair, Kelly. Oh, honey." She felt his lips against her cheek and wondered what was wrong with her hair aside from smelling like singed chicken feathers and hurting.

Just then Dr. Sells arrived and Kelly watched his movements through half-closed lids.

"The rings will have to be cut to treat her hand, Jonathan. They won't come off without tearing the flesh."

Jonathan's voice was cold and unfeeling. "Cut them."

She felt the cool touch of an instrument, and a sharp pain pulled at her fingers as the double platinum band snapped. A touch on her arm, the sting of a needle, and gradually everything faded.

She turned restlessly during the night and Jonathan was there but he didn't touch her. "Do you want some water?" he asked.

"Please." He held the glass and straw for her. The water hurt her throat and her eyelids felt as though they were lined with sand. Her hand throbbed.

"Sable?" she asked.

"Fine, thanks to you."

She wanted to inquire about Ebony and the other animals, but her lips could not form the words, so exhausted was she from the shock and medication. She gave in to sleep.

Hours later her eyes opened to see Jonathan's head on the pillow next to her. It was the first time she had seen him asleep since the operation and she examined the rugged features, the firm mouth relaxed, no scars, no twisted lip, and wondered as she often had if his kisses would be different with such a beautiful mouth. Her own soft lips twisted, remembering what his kisses had always done to her.

He woke without warning and instantly withdrew, sitting up. He was fully dressed except for slippers.

"How do you feel?"

"Sore. My hand hurts." She used her right hand to push her hair back and felt a brittle crunch as she did so. She turned her hand to look. It was full of tiny pieces of burnt hair, scorched brown and black instead of its usual russet. She looked at Jonathan. "I want to go to the bathroom."

"I'm sorry, Kelly. Your hair was beautiful and I know you wanted it to grow longer." Jonathan helped her to her feet and she swayed, but then had no trouble walking, even though her hip was stiff and sore where Sable had sidled into the wall. He flipped the light switch and stood watching as she turned to the mirror.

After one brief glance she said, "I'll be out in a moment." Later, as she opened the bathroom door, he was there to help her back to the bed. She sat on the side of it and said, "I'm ready to get up."

"Kelly—" he began.

She didn't look at him as he got her robe and slipped it on her right arm, helping maneuver it around the small, loose bandage on her left hand. Even with her eyes closed, she could see what she looked like. The red-gold of her hair, grown almost shoulder length, had been singed away to her ear on the left side, not quite so bad on the right. Her face had an angry red streak from her nose back to her hairline on the left side. She remembered the spikes and heavy switch feeling hot, couldn't remember her face burning, but her left side had been turned more to the building where the heat was intense. She knew her hair would grow back and her face would heal in time. All things heal with time, she told herself.

"Do you want breakfast?" Jonathan asked.

"Yes." She looked up at him. "Is Ebony all right?"

She didn't know if she had asked that question before or not but it was important enough to repeat.

"Yes, Kelly. If hero awards were given out last night, I'm not sure who'd get the biggest—you or Ebony."

She shrugged and bitter laughter crowded into her throat. Their being heroes was the result of an accident. Unlike the fire, the accident was fatal to her, killing all hopes she might have harbored.

At the table he asked, "Do you want to talk about it? How did you discover the fire?"

Which fire? she wondered but shook her head and concentrated on eating. A lot of concentration would be required if she was to survive the coming days.

Selena came to stand across from her. "Kelly, I can trim your hair and shape it if you like."

She nodded. "Thank you. I wish you would."

"I need to go check on things, Kelly. Will you be all right?" Jonathan rose and pulled back her chair. "You really should stay in bed."

She shook her head. "I don't want to."

He stood with his hand on her shoulder and said, "Take it easy then and I'll be back as soon as I can."

When Selena finished cutting her hair, Kelly gazed at her reflection again, smiling a little. Short hair was much easier to care for, anyway.

Until then, she had refused to think of the fire and her part in it, or the tragedy that was somehow averted. But now she went to the back porch and looked toward the corral. Snow had started falling and she couldn't see any damage to the buildings from her vantage point, but figures moved around going in and out, already working to clean and repair. Ebony trotted toward her and she smiled as she opened the door to let her in. She knelt, hugging the big dog, not caring the thick fur was layered with snow.

"You're just beautiful, Ebony. Remind me to be nice to you." She let her go into the house with her, wet feet and all. Jonathan could afford to have his carpet cleaned for what Ebony had done for him.

The phone was ringing and Kelly hesitated, thinking Lola might call for Jonathan. She stiffened and picked up the receiver.

"Kelly? I just heard. Are you all right?" It was Jean.

"Yes. A little the worse for wear, lucky and thankful. How did you know?"

"Jonathan called earlier but I wasn't here. Rena told me but she was so excited, she didn't remember any of the details. Tell me."

Kelly sat down and related the events, beginning when her unseeing steps led her to the stables. By the time she finished the story, she was trembling and had broken out in a cold sweat as she relived the horrible experience of the fire.

"I'm coming down and stay tonight, Kelly. Tell Jonathan. Take care and I'll see you."

She was still sitting there, face buried in her right arm, when Jonathan came in. Without a word he picked her up and took her into his sitting room, holding her close, rocking her as he would a child. When she stopped trembling, he brushed the hair away from her face.

"What happened?" he asked.

She shook her head and buried her face against his cold throat. After a few minutes while his hand smoothed the fabric of her robe over her hip, she said, "Jean called. They'll be down tonight instead of tomorrow."

"Good." His lips brushed her short hair. "If you've looked outside, you know we're going to have a White Christmas."

"Yes," she whispered, tightening her arms around him, ignoring for a little while what she knew she would soon have to face. Gradually her body relaxed and she drifted into sleep. Some time later she woke alone on the couch, covered by a blanket. Through half-closed lids, she watched the orange flames of the fire in the hearth, wondering how they could be so beautiful and so ugly too.

The stable fire had put a damper on the holiday spirit around the ranch, but Jonathan had not canceled the Christmas Eve open-house that had been planned for weeks, and by two o'clock the house was coming alive. Selena helped Kelly with the dress of royal blue velveteen that Jean had made for her. Even with her scorched face, the blue was becoming, showing off the bright green of her eyes, and bringing out the highlights in her hair. The dress had a soft round collar, long full sleeves, a fitted bodice that hugged her close, and a long skirt that swirled to the floor. Dr. Sells came and removed the loosely rolled gauze bandage, replacing it with a smaller one that protected only the portion of her fingers that was blistered, and that was less awkward for her.

"Burns aren't covered by anything that will rub them too much, Kelly," Dr. Sells told her. "This is so you'll remember to be careful with your hand more than anything else. The salve will keep it protected, but pamper your arm for a few days, okay?"

She nodded, laughing as Selena came with a blue ribbon to tie on her wrist. "It matches your dress," Selena said, and for an instant as their eyes met, Kelly saw worry in the dark eyes and knew she was thinking of what could have been the end of the story.

Rena, Jean, and Judge Creighton arrived at six o'clock and Jean demanded a full accounting from Jonathan of what happened. *No one knows the full extent of damage but me,* Kelly thought as she listened to Jonathan tell them that the fire had been confined to one side of the stables, fortunately where no animals were housed. Although the insurance investigators would be coming after Christmas Day, Jonathan guessed at a wiring shortage as the cause of the fire. She ignored the praise given her, remembering only the reason she had been there at the right time.

The crowds were gone, leaving only Rena, Jean, Judge Creighton, Jonathan, Carl, and Kelly in the large living room near the front of the house. "Will Ann and Gary be up, Kelly?" Jean asked.

Before she answered, her glance went to Jonathan, meeting his dark eyes that told her nothing, then back to Jean as she said, "Yes. Tomorrow, if it isn't too bad. Ann worked today." *If you leave me, RAG Ranch is mine,* she heard Jonathan's voice clearly. With Lola back in the picture—and his arms—he would probably change his mind about her having to stay on the ranch. *Maybe he'll even pay me to leave since I put so much store in his money.* At the same time she remembered she still hadn't looked at the bank books to see what Jonathan had deposited for her.

At midnight, they drank toasts to each other and to many more Christmases, and gathered around Jonathan and the huge tree to open the presents. Carl handed Jonathan a small box and in it was a note directing him to the patio at the side of the house. He came back carrying the leather saddle Carl had ordered for her while they were in Canada, and placed it in the middle of the room. Polished black leather, plain except for a silver braid and brads across the horn. It smelled clean and expensive.

He looked at Kelly after reading the card that said simply, "Merry Christmas, Jonathan. From Kelly." "How did you get this? The only place that makes this type of saddle is in Canada."

She smiled at him, teeth biting into her lower lip, wishing she had the nerve to kiss him, but said only, "It was easy." Everyone laughed as he bent to kiss the top of her head. For her, he had selected leather boots with a purse to match and she couldn't keep from comparing them to Lola's dainty bright red size fives.

When all the gifts were gone from under the tree, Jonathan said, "One more." He went to the hallway, then returned with a full-length gray leather coat with matching fur collar. He held it out to Kelly till she slipped her right arm through, then draped it over her left arm.

"It's beautiful, Jonathan." It was. The elegant material caressed her body, molding itself to just the right places.

"Goes well with apricot hair," Jonathan said, smiling down at her.

Jean found rooms for everyone to sleep and shooed them to bed. Kelly stood up to go to her room but Jonathan touched her uninjured arm.

"Drink?" he asked.

"Yes." She sat back down on the couch.

When he handed her the glass, he sat on her right side when before he made sure he was on her left side, his scarred face away from her. He didn't have to hide from her anymore although she could have told him it had never made any difference to her. To her, he had always been Jonathan, with the same appearance he'd had when she could only touch to see his features.

"Merry Christmas, Kelly," he said, kissing her cheek.

"Merry Christmas, Jonathan." She turned her head so that her lips brushed his. "I like your mouth," she whispered.

"Will it hurt if I kiss you?"

"No."

He started on the opposite cheek from the burn at the sensitive corner of her mouth that always excited her, lingering, his breath warm in her mouth as her lips parted in anticipation. The tip of his tongue entered quickly, forcing her lips further apart, and as her hand moved on his leg, he pushed her head back, long fingers on her neck sliding down to spread beneath her breast. With the gentleness she remembered from long ago, he explored her throat, the hairline from there to her ear, his teeth grazing her skin. His hand went beneath the full skirt, bunching it as he moved to her thigh, on to her flat stomach, fingers hesitating at the top of her pantyhose.

"Yes," she whispered. "Yes." His mouth came back to hers, tender in the fierceness of their kiss and flames erupted inside her from long-banked fires.

His mouth left hers and he murmured, "You could have been badly hurt, Kelly. What were you doing at the stables?"

Her eyes opened wide as she heard the question. Lola. The stables. The fire. Lola. A strangled sound came from her throat as she pushed him away, struggled to her feet, and ran from the room.

The snow had stopped but sleet was falling when the household came awake. Ann called to wish them a Merry Christmas and say they wouldn't be there. It was the only time Kelly could ever remember being glad she wouldn't see her sister.

"The weather's so bad and the road conditions are even worse," Ann said. "I hate to miss seeing you, but we'd better not."

"I know it would be foolish, Ann," Kelly told her. She hesitated, then related the news about the fire, afraid she might hear it from someone else. She didn't mention her part in it, just the damage to the stables. Ann sympathized, glad there were no serious injuries.

"How's the baby?" Kelly asked.

Ann laughed. "Both of us are fine. I'm going to have to be careful how much I eat. I've gained three pounds already." She bubbled on. "We've already had the foundation laid for the new room, Kelly, and Gary's starting to get the material together so he can start work as soon as the weather improves."

Kelly's heart twisted at her enthusiasm, aware of the

price she was paying for Ann's happiness. If Ann knew, it would tear her apart, and there was no reason to cause her any more hurt. Kelly sat by the phone thinking thoughts that could never be construed as "good will toward men."

Selena fixed a very late breakfast for all of them, and as they sat with coffee, Jean looked at Kelly. "How did you get Ebony to leave you and what did you tell her to do?" Her mother-in-law was well aware that Kelly didn't want to talk about the fire, but she thought it was because she was still upset over the fire itself and talking it out would be good for her.

Kelly understood what Jean was trying to do and made herself think only of Ebony's part in obeying her as she related what she remembered. She turned to Jonathan. "Ebony should have something special because she's really the one who saved the stables."

For a moment his dark eyes questioned her, recalling that she ran from him without explanation the night before. His expression changed and he grinned, looking boyish with his unblemished jaw. "Tell you what. We'll mate her with Beowulf as a reward."

The general laughter covered Kelly's silence as she drank her coffee. A quiet thrill went through her as she realized he was granting the favor she had asked of him weeks ago.

The group of visitors left early, giving themselves plenty of time to reach Taos before dark, and the big house seemed empty and echoing. Jonathan stood with his arm around her as they watched the car pull from the yard.

He looked down at her. "I'm going to give Carl a hand, Kelly. Go rest a while. Okay?"

"Yes."

Back in the house alone, Kelly wandered from room to room, admiring the holiday decorations. Some of the candles and homemade items were from Jonathan's childhood, Selena had told her, some his father and

grandfather had designed and made when stores weren't
filled with gaudy plastic and tin ornaments at any price.
She picked up a tiny cradle, barely two inches long,
carved from a cedar sapling many years ago. It held a
miniature replica of a baby covered with a blanket of
faded blue wool. Would Jonathan ever have children to
enjoy the treasures? She shivered and walked on into
Jonathan's sitting room, going to rest on the wide sill of
the window. The sleet had stopped and the setting sunlight sparkled on icicles hanging from the eaves. She
heard Jonathan's boots on the porch, and a few minutes
later he came through the doorway.

They stared at each other till he said, "You must be
tired, Kelly, with all the excitement and company. How
does your hand feel?"

"It doesn't hurt and didn't look too bad after Dr.
Sells popped the water blisters."

He had fixed them a drink without asking and he
brought it to her where she sat by the window. It was
growing dark now, and their shadows reflected in the
glass.

"We haven't had much chance to talk," he said,
smiling at her. He settled himself on the floor. "Tell
me how you discovered the fire. You don't mind talking about it now, do you?"

She shook her head and sipped her drink, looking at
the dark head near her knees. "Ebony and I were walking down to the corral. Ebony growled and bristled all
over and when I looked to see why, I saw the fire."

Jonathan turned his head to watch her when she began talking, but she was gazing into her drink. "Your
coat was on the porch. You took it off and walked to the
corral that way?"

She hesitated. "We had been to the pond and it
didn't seem as cold as it had been, so I took off the
heavy coat. I had on a thick sweater."

"You didn't come inside the house?"

"Yes, I was inside, Jonathan," she told him, her

teeth clenching. "I came back to tell you something I thought was important, but you were busy so I went on to the stables."

"You could have interrupted me. What was I doing?"

"Making love to Lola." It was a bald statement that hung between them.

His head jerked upward, dark eyes narrowed. "Is that what you thought?"

"That's what I saw," she corrected him.

He watched her, not bothering to deny it, and she stood up, moving away from him. He hadn't asked what important something she had to tell him nor would he have been interested to hear it.

From the center of the room she looked back at him, her voice soft so that he couldn't tell how it hurt her throat to speak. "Our marriage has been a circus from day one, Jonathan. I know every circus must have an orange-haired clown, but I don't care to be your freak show." She took a deep breath. "If not for you and Lola, Ebony and I would never have been near the stables to see the fire, so give the credit to the ones who deserve it—you and Lola." She placed her drink on the lamp table. "It was as natural as breathing for me to love you, Jonathan, and it will be difficult to stop, but I have one thing going for me—I no longer *want* to love you." She walked from the room, leaving him staring after her.

She went about the process of undressing and putting on a long flannel robe with a sense of finality. As soon as she could get away from Heath Cliffs, she would leave Jonathan. It was a simple solution. They would all survive, no matter what.

Breakfast was the same as it had been for weeks, silent. Kelly was conscious of Jonathan's watchful eyes but she ate a little, then picked up her mail Carl had left on the table and went back to her room.

There was a late Christmas card from Angela with a note enclosed.

Santa Claus came to our house in grand style this year, Kelly. He's very knowledgeable, having guessed all correct sizes of our clothing. We had a fire in the stove and put up the tree by the big window. We made popcorn balls for decoration and, if it was a little lopsided, no one noticed. I must say that I'll probably be deaf by next Christmas with six radios on six different stations turned to full volume. Oh, Kelly, it was wonderful. The only thing missing was you.

Kelly smiled, thinking of the celebration they had, and went to dress. Outside, she whistled for Ebony and ran with her down the hill toward the pond. It was cold, but clear, and they rambled the lower pasture as Kelly tried to make a final decision to leave Heath Cliffs. It was late afternoon when she raced Ebony back up the hill again.

Head bent against the wind coming out of the west, she went around the east side of the house just to look at the mountains before going on to take her shower and dress for dinner. As she paused and looked up, a sleek Cadillac pulled into the drive, and Lola stepped daintily onto the walkway, starting toward the center archway that led across the foyer to Jonathan's sitting room.

How dare he invite her here again, she thought, a searing anger starting in her midsection as she stepped forward, cutting off Lola's path.

"Looking for someone?" Kelly asked, not trying to hide her dislike.

Startled, Lola looked up at her, the beautiful face a mask of aloofness. "I'm here to see Jonathan."

"Why?"

A perfectly shaped eyebrow arched upward. "I'm sure if Jonathan wants you to know what we discuss, he'll tell you."

Kelly braced her feet apart and her words came out with a hiss. "Get back in your car and leave."

Lola smiled. "I was invited here by Jonathan, who owns the place, in case you've forgotten."

"No, I haven't forgotten," Kelly told her. "Perhaps you've forgotten that I'm mistress of the ranch now and there's room for only one at a time. When Jonathan wants to make an exchange, he'll inform me, and until he does, get off this property."

Lola drew her dainty figure to a haughty stance, moving toward the door as she did so. "Don't be absurd. I belonged here long before you did."

Kelly stepped in front of her, blocking the entrance. Her voice was cold fury as she said, "Leave, before I throw you off the place myself."

Lola laughed and Kelly took a step backward, saying softly, "Ebony."

The black figure moved to her side and her fur bristled, making her look twice her normal size. A low growl came from her, and huge white teeth bared behind a snarled lip, making Ebony look nothing like the gentle animal Kelly knew her to be.

The woman hesitated. "You wouldn't dare."

"Try me," Kelly told her, smiling, her eyes narrowed.

They stared at each other, hate a viable thing between them, until Lola made her decision and turned back to her chauffeured car. "Jonathan will hear about this," she protested.

Kelly shrugged. *So maybe he'll throw me off the ranch,* she thought. Her mouth twisted. He had called Lola to come home, wanting her back now that she could stand to look at him again. *The least he could have done was get rid of me first,* she thought, bitterness at Jonathan making her shiver. A pain that was almost physical in its intensity struck her slender body.

She watched the big car move down the driveway and started around to the back of the house to go in through the porch where she could remove her boots.

Jonathan stood near the edge of the side yard watching her, his dark eyes going from her to the car disappearing down the drive. She met his glance, wondering how much he had heard and not caring, feeling so cold her body was stiff.

She paused by the kitchen door. "I don't feel well, Selena. I don't want any dinner." Without any excuses, she went on to her room, using the lock for the first time. She wasn't sure why she bothered, Jonathan didn't even come around anymore, not needing her now that he had Lola back.

Standing in the middle of her bedroom, she said aloud, "You've made a believer out of me, Jonathan, and I'm finally getting around to hating you, although I'm not the happiest woman alive, as promised."

Unable to avoid thinking of Ann and Gary, knowing if she left Jonathan—as she surely must—they would lose everything once again. From the sadness of having Robbie born blind to losing him to meningitis, they were about to be saddled with a loss big enough to bury the strongest, just when they had happiness within their grasp—the new baby, an addition to the house, and out of debt after such a long struggle. It was a choice Kelly must make. They would lose RAG Ranch or she would lose her mind loving a man who used her body to satisfy his longing for another woman. How long he would allow her to deny what he termed his rights she wouldn't pretend to guess. Even now she wondered at his lack of demands, wondered why he no longer took her when he wanted as he had before his operation. Because of Lola, of course. It was as though he had wanted to punish Kelly for being able to see his twisted face, and now that he was as handsome as he could ever have been, didn't care that she had deceived him into believing she was blind and never mind the reason she had for doing so.

Her disjointed thoughts rambled on and she made no effort to stop them. Didn't it all seem a long time ago? The newspaper, kind and generous Hap, and his gruffness to cover his feelings. Fred, who had been good to her, even if he was somewhat stuffy. Cora, who separated her clothes and laughed about Jonathan propositioning her while she visited him on her vacation. Chuck Benson with his delightful southern drawl. Ebony.

She lay across the bed until daylight, not closing her eyes. After she heard Jonathan leave through the back, she got up to watch him walk with long strides toward the corral. A little later he and Carl came back, got into the Cherokee, and drove south toward the Jemez Mountains. Kelly watched until the vehicle disappeared, straightened her shoulders, and moved quickly. Whatever he did about the loan for Gary would have to be dealt with, but not even Ann's welfare could keep her at Heath Cliffs without shattering her completely. It was the end of a deep, dark tunnel that ended in a fathomless pit.

It didn't take long to fill two suitcases with her old clothes and a few of the new blouses Jean had given her. She looked at the leather coat Jonathan had given her for Christmas, never worn, and thought, *That's mine, it goes,* and placed it on top of the luggage. From her nightstand she took the folder with the articles and journal she had been writing about working with the blind, planning to put it together and send it to Hap one of these days.

She opened the top drawer of the dresser, looking for earrings and there lay the two bank books she had never opened. The top one was a green leather wallet with the initials KOH printed in gold on the corner. She flipped the top, reading the account number and below it the balance of ten thousand dollars. The second book was brown with her full name spelled out and inside on the first line was the figure fifty thousand dollars.

Stunned, Kelly held the books away from her, then dropped them back into the drawer and pushed it closed. Enough money to last her for years. Surely enough to pay off the lien he held on RAG Ranch. No doubt he would have her arrested for grand theft if she used any of the money, capable of doing anything to her with his financial connections and he surely wouldn't hesitate to show her how powerful he was. She backed away from the dresser, forgetting her earrings.

The Mustang hadn't been driven for several days so she started the motor to let it warm, then went back to sit on the edge of her bed. She had tried all night to decide how to say good-bye to Jean and Selena, deciding against calling Jean. The less she knew, the less she'd feel guilty if Jonathan asked her about Kelly. From the beginning, Kelly had loved her; as a mother-in-law, there was none to equal Jean, she was sure. The two of them had become very good friends, Jean returning Kelly's affection in full.

There are a lot of people and things I'm going to miss, she thought, *not the least of all a man called Jonathan.*

She carried the bags to her car, switched off the engine, and went back to the kitchen. "Selena."

Selena turned around, smiling. "Breakfast in a moment, Kelly." Here was a woman she would surely miss. Selena, who had accepted her without question, when she could see and when she could not. And the man she loved had never accepted her; at least, not for what she was. For what he wanted, no doubt.

"No, Selena." She went on before she could change her mind. "I'm leaving."

"What time will you be home?"

"I'm not coming back, Selena. I'm leaving for good."

Selena stared, dark round eyes in the smooth tanned skin questioning her. "Why?"

"There's no place for me here," Kelly said.

"I don't understand. Does Jonathan know?"

"I don't understand either, Selena. As for Jonathan knowing, I'm sure he wonders why I'm still here." She put her arms around the woman, hugging tightly. "You've been wonderful to me, Selena. I'll keep in touch." She ran from the kitchen, back to her room, where, after one last look around, she closed the door.

Ebony raced to meet her in the hopes that she could go wherever she went in the Mustang. She hugged the dog, refusing to think how she would miss her, then got into the car and backed out, having automatically opened the garage door via the control button over the visor.

She didn't need that anymore either, she thought, but left it there and drove away without looking back. Her vision blurred as she went through the big gate but she bit her lip and drove on, breathing a deep sigh as she reached the interstate.

There was one more task she needed to do before she headed south, and her lips stung as she bit into them again. According to her checkbook, about five thousand dollars remained in her account after her shopping sprees over the holidays.

I'll split it with Angela, she decided, and remembered the bank books in her dresser drawer, flinching at the reminder that Jonathan felt he had paid well for the use of her body.

Few people were in the bank and she withdrew twenty-five hundred dollars for herself and made out a cashier's check for the balance in Angela's name. She walked across the street to the post office and bought a

stamped envelope. On a piece of paper from her handbag she wrote a brief note.

Angela;
    I'll be out of town for a while and will see you in
a few weeks, or I'll write. I hope the money will be
enough to see you through the winter. Give my
love to the children.

Kelly

Dropping the note into the "Out of Town" slot, she
went back to the car and drove back the way she had
come, chewing on her lips, fighting tears. With an uncertain future stretching with dull emptiness in front of
her, it didn't seem quite the time for tears. There
would be plenty of time for them later. As she passed
the turnoff to Heath Cliffs, she averted her head, staring straight ahead at the highway in front of her.

It was eleven o'clock when Kelly reached the city
limits of Albuquerque and checked into a motel just off
the interstate. She carried her two bags into the single
room, put them in the closet area by the bath, and, with
a brief look around, left again, locking the door behind
her. She went across the lobby into the dining room,
picking up a morning paper from the rack on her way.
A young girl placed a cup of coffee in front of her as
she sat down, and she gave her order for French toast
and bacon, and opened the paper to the "Apartments
for Rent" section. After circling a few of the items, she
turned to the employment advertisements. McDonald's was still recruiting for help. Later she folded the
paper, concentrating on her breakfast.

Back in the room, she stretched out on the single
bed, staring at the ceiling, fighting with her mind to
keep it from returning to Heath Cliffs. It was over and
the future stretched into infinity, she acknowledged to

herself, but the past had to be left behind. She slept, only to wake hour after hour to stare at the same ceiling, tired and disoriented.

A place to live was first priority and Kelly picked up the paper in the morning to look over the rental section again. The ads she had marked were in a section of the city she knew well, and gathering up her handbag and keys, she left the motel to go look at the locations.

It hadn't changed much in the months since she had left Albuquerque. The apartments listed were neither excellent nor very bad and the third place she visited, she rented. A small one-bedroom apartment, living room/kitchen combination, and a bathroom she could turn around in if she didn't stretch her arms out too far, but it was clean and reasonable. She paid her first month's rent, and the landlady, a small woman with wispy, gray hair and a bitter mouth, told her she could move in on Monday.

Back in the motel room she called Ann. She had been postponing the inevitable but it had to be done.

Ann's happy voice when she heard Kelly changed to uncertainty as Kelly explained that she was in Albuquerque without Jonathan. "Why, Kelly? I thought you were so happy. I don't understand." The same old refrain she heard everywhere.

When she finished explaining as best she could, Kelly was exhausted. Ann didn't understand. Selena didn't understand. Kelly didn't either. Perhaps Jonathan understood, whether or not anyone else did.

She read the newspaper want-ads each day, finding the same ones over and over. A smile tugged at her lips when she read the ads for a topless bar. With her loss of weight, that was about what she was—topless. No experience necessary, the advertisement said. *Oh, I have experience,* she thought. *What kind would you like? Loving someone who doesn't give a damn about you but can use you for any purpose he chooses? Like forgetting his real love.* She choked and threw the paper on the floor.

She moved into the small apartment on Monday and made the rounds with her résumé of experience. She stopped by the Lions Club and left some of the articles she had written about seeing-eye dogs and Braille printing services for the blind. The secretary there told her they could use the articles in their monthly newsletter, but there was no pay. Kelly left them. The information she had in them would get to a lot of people through the Lions Club and that was what she wanted.

She wrote Hap, telling him briefly what had happened and asking if he could use any of her collection in his syndicated columns. The one she hoped he would use was the one about Angela and her family. Hap was a pushover for emotional human interest stories.

She couldn't stand the small apartment any longer and on Saturday drove to RAG Ranch, dreading the thought of what was to come.

It had been almost two months since she had seen Ann and Gary. "You've put on weight, Ann, but it's becoming," she told her sister. It was. Her cheeks were blooming, eyes sparkling. What would happen to her when Jonathan took the ranch? Kelly shuddered at the thought but she would never tell them. Jonathan could do his own dirty work.

Ann had made coffee and they were sitting like old times. Not exactly like old times, either. Gary glanced at his wife, then at Kelly. "Jonathan came by yesterday."

"Jonathan was here?" she asked. Already? She thought he would call but hadn't even considered the fact that he would drive down to the ranch. Of course, he planned to find her and drag her back to Heath Cliffs, to humiliate her and prove he could do as he pleased. Her lips tightened and anger shook her slim body. *That's what you'll have to do, Mr. Heath,* she vowed silently. *If you think I'm going back up there and play second fiddle to Lola*—Her thoughts broke off as she came back to what Gary was saying.

"He didn't believe us when we said we had no address for you." He stood up and went into another room, then returned with a small leather box in his hand, holding it out to Kelly.

At her questioning look he said, "Jonathan brought it and asked us to see that you got it. He thought you might need some of the things." Gary's voice and face were studies in concern. "He looks so much better with the smaller scar. I don't know why he didn't have that done years ago."

Kelly swallowed over the dryness in her throat and nodded. "He is handsome, isn't he? The operation was my Christmas present." Her fingers moved over the box in front of her.

"Then why—" Ann stopped when she saw the look on Kelly's face.

Kelly shrugged. "Some people make mistakes, and then there's me."

The catch on the box opened as she pressed a button and she lifted the lid to stare at the two bank books she had left in her dresser. She didn't touch them. A small velvet case was in one corner and inside were her wedding rings. The bands, cut when she had burned her hand, had been repaired. She looked a long time at the sparkling beauty of the set, closed the lid, and pushed it back into the corner near the bank books. A piece of heavy bond paper was folded on the bottom and her breath caught as she recognized the legal letterhead paper normally associated with lawyers. He wasn't wasting any time filing for divorce. Maybe that was why he was looking for her—to tell her she was free, and good riddance.

With unsteady fingers she unfolded the paper and read the fine print through, then reread it. She handed it to Gary when she finished, but her eyes went to Ann. Kelly's clenched fist lay near her coffee cup and Ann placed her hand over it, smiling with sympathy at her younger sister.

Gary cleared his throat. "Do you know what it means, Kelly?"

"Offhand, I'd say the loan you got from Jonathan for the ranch has been paid in full."

"What?" Ann's eyes were huge blue orbs. "Let me see."

The three of them sat there, then Ann asked, "Why?"

Kelly shrugged, unable to shed any light on it for them.

Gary read the paper again. "We can't accept this, Kelly."

"I had nothing to do with it, Gary, and let me tell you this: Jonathan Heath is so stubborn, once he makes his mind up, it takes a better person than I am to change it. I've tried." The last two words were tight with bitterness. *How I've tried,* she thought.

Though they discussed all the information they had between them, they couldn't reach any conclusion, and Kelly told them, "Accept it. He can afford it. Maybe he figures it's worth it to get rid of me." She shoved the leather case toward Gary. "Would you put it in your safety deposit box?"

"Don't you want your rings?" Ann asked.

"No," Kelly told her.

"The bank books?"

She thought of the money that had been in her name for four months and that she had never even touched. When you had everything, you didn't need money, she thought. It was only when there was a dime left and it was two days till pay day that it mattered. She had been in that vicinity many times.

"I don't need them," she said.

"What are you going to do, Kelly?" Gary asked that evening after dinner. "What are your plans?"

"I don't have any. It's too late to try for a spring teaching assignment." A fall assignment was still a long way off; maybe by then she could be managing a McDonald's and get all her Egg McMuffins free. They should help put some weight back on her bones.

Against Ann's protests, she returned to Albuquerque early Sunday afternoon, promising to call during the week. Heavy clouds hung over the Sierra Blanca range straight ahead of her and she imagined the ski lodge managers doing a snow dance.

Jobs were hard to find and she was beginning to think she would really have to apply to McDonald's when she got a call from John Rabon, president of the local Lions Club.

"We'd like to use two of your articles in the Albuquerque paper to head up a program we're just starting. Can you come by sometime today?"

She was in his office in thirty minutes, landing an assignment to write an article each day in the coming month as the Lions Club prepared for their yearly drive for funds for the blind. With a lot of material already written that she could draw from, she was elated.

Keeping busy kept her mind off Jonathan until nighttime. It was now four weeks since she had left Heath Cliffs and he was still there, lurking in the edge of her thoughts, tormenting her, taking over her dreams. Bitterly, she gave up fighting her losing battle, stopped wondering if Lola had moved back to the ranch.

She dropped her articles off at the paper and returned home. There was a letter from Hap in her mailbox and she lay across the bed to read it.

It was brief, typically Hap. "I'm sorry about your marriage, Kelly." She smiled at the cryptic statement. Hap would never lower himself to say "I told you so."

"I used the articles you sent, Kelly, and will use any others in the same vein. A check is enclosed, and anytime you want a job, come on out." She ran her fingers over the generous amount of the check.

"You wouldn't want Hap to lose his job for hiring practices, would you?" The voice was clear and she swallowed, rolling over to bury her face in her pillow.

The knock on her door penetrated through her misery and she sat up, rubbing her hand across her eyes. "Who is it?"

"Jonathan."

She didn't move nor answer him until the knock was repeated and the familiar voice called, "Kelly?"

She stood up, smoothing her hands over the front of her jeans and brushing her hair back from her face. She wet her lips and went to open the door to face Jonathan, her nemesis.

They stared at each other until he said, "May I come in, Kelly?"

She pushed the storm door open and stepped aside as he walked past her into the small room. His glance went over the simple furnishings, the neatly stacked papers on the tiny dinette table at the edge of the living room area. The dark eyes came back to Kelly, still standing by the door she had closed.

"How did you know where I lived?" she asked finally.

"Ann and Gary weren't very helpful but I have friends in the State Highway Patrol who kept a lookout for your car."

"What do you want?" She went to the club chair, motioning him to the couch.

He remained standing, watching her. "May I inquire what your plans are?"

She shrugged. "Did you buy up all the McDonald chains?"

"Be reasonable, Kelly. Come back home."

"'Be reasonable,'" she repeated. "'Do it my way.'"
She didn't try to keep the bitterness out of her voice
and her eyes went a darker shade of green as she went
on. "I've always considered myself a generous person,
Jonathan, but I draw the line at sharing my husband.
I'm old-fashioned enough to want mine on a one-to-
one basis. You know, the old hackneyed phrases that
say 'Let no one put asunder...till death do us part.'
You can't have us both at once, I don't care how powerful you are."

"It wasn't the way it looked to you, Kelly." Jonathan
stood facing her, big hands clenched into fists at his
sides.

"No? It was quite an exhibition if it wasn't the real
thing."

"I had congratulated her on her big success in St.
Louis and she's the one who kissed me. I didn't kiss her.
If I appeared to be holding her, it was to keep both of us
from falling." He ran long fingers through his hair in an
agitated gesture. "I was not making love to her as you
accused me of doing." Unaccustomed as he was to explaining his actions to anyone, Jonathan was finding it
difficult with Kelly's accusing eyes watching him.

"What was she doing there in the first place?"

"I didn't ask her what she wanted because I wasn't
interested." He moved toward her. "Kelly—"

She threw up her hands as if to keep him away from
her. "She said you invited her back the day after Christmas."

He nodded. "She had some things stored there and I
told her to come get them or I'd burn them. Some diamond necklaces worth a few dollars were in the safe at
the house and I thought she could use them in her line
of work." He smiled a little. "Would you really have
turned Ebony loose on her?"

"Yes," she assured him, and as he continued to look
at her, she asked, "Does she like your new face?"

He stiffened and his nostrils flared. "Yes, she was quite impressed." He stepped closer to her chair. "And you, Kelly? Is it easier for you to look at me now?"

He was getting too close, bothering her breathing, and she stood up to flee toward the table. But as if pulled by some inner force she turned to look at him, considering the question, cataloging the features known so well to her touch before she had ever seen him. "I liked your other face; it had character."

His mouth twitched. "Character?"

She shrugged. "For want of a better word." Kelly put her hands on the back of the chair she now stood behind, half leaning on it for support.

Jonathan's gaze went to her bare left hand. "I took your things to Gary thinking you might want your rings back."

"Why? I don't have a husband, just a man I lived with." She flung the words at him, wanting to hurt him as she was hurting, but if he felt anything at all, he wasn't showing it. That was all right; she hurt enough for two.

He went on as if she hadn't spoken. "Why didn't you use any of the money in your accounts?"

"I was well provided for and didn't need money." Her eyebrows lifted. "Gary didn't understand the paid-up loan and I couldn't explain it to him except I thought you were so glad to be rid of me, it was worth that much to you, plus the sixty thousand you set so much store by. That was quite an expensive proposition but you enjoy reminding me how much I like expensive things."

He reached her in one stride, and his hands were none too gentle as he turned her to face him. "Damn it, Kelly." His mouth came down hard on hers, forcing her head backward. Just as quickly he let her go, supporting her for a moment before he pulled her to the couch and held on to her hands.

"Where do I start, Kelly? Where was I when I made my first wrong move, one among many?" Dark brown eyes bored into her green ones. "It must have been the day you stepped in front of my car and I assumed you were a careless teen-ager daydreaming your way through the world." He studied her face. "From there, I went downhill, thinking I was someone special doing my good deed getting you to a specialist you didn't want or need." He groaned, remembering. "You did more with your cockeyed scheme than I could ever do with money, simply because you put your heart and soul into it." He stood up and moved away from her. "I was the blind one, Kelly, not you."

She sat still and silent, waiting until he turned and came back to stand in front of her. "You can go back to teaching or call Hap and ask for your job back whenever you want to, Kelly. I won't stand in your way, whatever you choose to do." He waited for her to speak and when she didn't, he went on. "I want very much for you to come home with me."

"Why?"

"It isn't the same anymore with you gone. Ebony and Tish wait for you every evening. Selena barely speaks to me. Carl has given his unsolicited opinion of me several times. Jean is ready to exchange her son for a daughter-in-law." He shoved his hands into his jacket pockets. "I'm vastly outnumbered up there."

"And you, Jonathan? Why do you want me back?" She held her breath.

"You're my wife."

"Is that all?" Her heart willed him to give her the right answer. "I settled for less than what I wanted when I married you, Jonathan, but you've changed me into a possessive, greedy woman. I want it all—your money, your ranch, your body, heart, and soul. I'll settle for the last three items but that's the only concession I'll make. If you can't live with that, hire a mistress to satisfy your needs. I have more to offer someone who'll care that I'm a real person, with real feelings." She stopped and they stared at each other, Kelly's breath coming short and hard as she waited.

It seemed an eternity before he took two steps and knelt in front of her, gathering both hands in his. "I'll give you all my love and anything else I have that you care for." He smiled a little. "You're looking at a totally defeated man, Kelly. I surrender: money, ranch, body, heart, and soul, not necessarily in that order." He released her hands and moved to sit beside her on the couch, turning her to him, his hands framing her face.

"I love you, Kelly O'Neil Heath. I've loved you for so long I can't remember how it happened or when it started, perhaps the day I almost ran over you." His fingers touched her lips, lay at the corner of her mouth, as he went on. "It was long ago when I loved Lola. Even before the accident she was restless and I wasn't enough for her. I was old and settled, happy on the ranch as you might say, just being a cowboy." He smiled, his fingers moving from her mouth to push the bright hair back from her cheek. "I didn't mind that Lola had her very successful career; I think women need their careers if they want them, but even that wasn't enough for Lola. She needed other men—other married men—and I objected. We fought over that so many times it finally didn't matter to me and I was glad I was hideous-looking after the accident and she couldn't stand the sight of me."

"Oh, Jonathan." The hurt she felt for him was audible in her soft whisper.

"I was glad when she divorced me." He drew a deep breath. "When I met you, I thought you were young and helpless, and I guess you brought out the paternal instincts in me." He winced. "Until I kissed you."

He was quiet for so long as he looked straight into her eyes that she prompted, "And then?"

He smiled. "My thoughts were anything but paternal and I used your blindness as an excuse to keep you with me. You were such a delight that Selena fell so in love with you on your first visit that she was ready to leave me even then and go stay with you just to take care of you. The same with Jean and Rena." His dark eyes were hidden by the long black lashes and she pushed his chin up to see him better.

He went on. "When I thought you were ashamed to look at my face, I struck out at you to try to hurt you for daring to care what I looked like. Then you had the nerve to ask for an outlandish Christmas present and I was thoroughly confused by my feelings because I suddenly wanted to give you that present. I had known for months how wrong I was—but too stubborn to admit it—so wrong about what you had tried to do for Robbie and others so unfortunate. I wasn't accustomed to people going to such extremes for someone else and I had trouble believing anyone could be so unselfish." His finger touched her chin, rubbing the curve of her jaw, and she smiled for the first time.

"I was like a kid and couldn't wait to give you the Christmas present you wanted so badly. When Lola showed up, all I could remember was the way she looked at me after the accident and the way she looked at me after the operation. I didn't know whether to hate or thank her since it was because of her that I found you." She didn't attempt to break the silence, and after a moment, he went on.

"I sent Lola on her way before Carl came to tell me there was a fire and you were in the stables." He groaned. "You'll never know what I felt, Kelly. Losing you would have—" He stopped, his breath ragged. "Christmas Eve, I wanted to love you so much and you ran away from me. I knew why, but I didn't want to admit it was my fault." Another silence. "I wanted to beg you to give me another chance when you accused me of making love to Lola, but I waited too long and you left me."

She watched in wonder as Jonathan struggled with his own uncertainty. "When Jean learned you had gone, she demanded to know where you were and promised me she'd find you and protect you, that I'd never see you again, which is what she felt I deserved." His laugh was wry. "I'm quite jealous of you and my own mother, did you know that?"

"Redheads are supposed to be the jealous ones."

He shook his head. "Everyone loves you, but I want you all to myself. Kelly?"

"Yes, Jonathan?"

"I want to ask a big favor of you."

Her hands that had remained still on his thighs moved up to frame his face and slowly her fingers traced the features she hadn't touched since forever, over the smoothness of the scar, the unblemished mouth, the rough skin on his throat. She found the buttons of his shirt, and her fingers moved with sure familiarity until they curled into the thick mat of hair. Green eyes lighted as she smiled into his dark ones.

"You can ask," she said softly.

"Can you want to love me again?"

A pulsing happiness trembled through her body as she realized Jonathan was in her arms again, wanting her as she wanted him. "Maybe. With practice."

"How much practice would you need?"

"Starting now?"

"Yes." He kissed her lips lightly and pulled away to look at her. He looked into the brightness of her eyes and whispered, "Kelly." He bent and his lips covered hers, accepting the warmth of her openmouthed kiss, feeling her body tremble as the tip of his tongue probed deep. One hand caressed her thigh; the other glided across her flat stomach and upward to cup her small breast beneath the smooth knit of her shirt.

He lifted his head. "Honey?"

Kelly's eyes opened wide and he stared into a storm of emotion in their depths. Gathering her into his arms, he went through the open bedroom door and stood a moment, looking around the small area, before he placed her on the bed. She watched as he removed her belt and slipped her jeans from her body, taking her pantyhose with them, leaving her exposed to him. Without hesitating, he pulled her up to get the long-sleeved shirt over her head, unfastening and removing her bra at the same time. She lay naked for only an instant until he turned the covers back, picked her up to put her on the sheet, and covered her body, bending to kiss her as he did so.

He undressed and lay beside her, cradling her head on his arm as he brought her body against his, stroking the smooth skin of her hip, going from there to her small breast, teasing the brown tip that hardened between his fingers.

She made a small sound and her breath came quickly. "I—"

He smiled. "Were you going to tell me you love me, Kelly?"

Her hand slid from his hip to his hard thighs and stayed there. He bit his lip, completely at her mercy, waiting for her answer.

Her mouth found his as she put her leg across him and she pushed his teeth away from his lips with her tongue, murmuring, "I love you. I love you, Jonathan." She teased his full lower lip with her teeth and moaned as he took possession of her mouth. With a gentle movement he turned her on her back and trailed kisses down to the dark tip of her breast, teasing it until she quivered. He moved to the other breast, nibbling and kissing until she moaned and her body moved in a sensuous rhythm. His lips skimmed over her belly, hesitating at her hip bone. Fingers tangled in his dark hair, she held his face to her cool skin a moment, then pulled him back within her reach. He was hers completely as she took him inside her, triggering the emotion that lifted them as they cried out in ecstasy.

Slowly their bodies separated but he kept her close to him, unwilling to let even an inch between them. A long time later he asked, "Will you go home with me, Kelly? I want that more than anything in the world."

Dark brown lashes moved a little, then lifted to show the sparkling green of her eyes. She smiled. "Tomorrow?"

He pulled her love-damp body to him, enclosing her in an embrace designed to last the hours till morning.

Chapter Twelve

Coffee cup tilted at a dangerous angle toward her mouth, Kelly sat at the dining room table, staring through the wide window at the swirling snowflakes. She didn't really see them. Instead, she saw the bright curtains in the old-fashioned kitchen at Angela's, wondering if there was still wood left from the two cords Mr. Quantzal delivered more than six weeks ago. It would be mighty cold in that big room without the heat from the wood stove.

Jonathan dropped a kiss on her head and slipped into the chair at the end of the table, reaching to pour himself a cup of coffee from the silver pot on the table. "Been waiting long?"

She shook her head and set the cup down in a safer position. "My first one." She smiled at him, loving the way his mouth curved as he smiled back at her, remembering the tender feel of it on her own.

He took a sip of the steaming liquid and put the cup down, leaning his arms on the table. "Tell me, Kelly. Are Angela Nunez and her 'throwaways' real people?"

Startled, she stared into serious dark eyes that demanded the truth. "Where did you hear about them?"

"You left the papers you're working on out on the desk last night, and I just stopped to look at them out of plain curiosity." He continued to study her face. "They're real, aren't they?"

She looked at her cup, turning it in both hands. "Yes."

The silence lengthened until he said, "You are going to tell me about them, aren't you?"

She took a deep breath and, measuring her words as she spoke, told him about Andy, whose blue eyes reminded her of Robbie, of his brother, Joshua, Tony, Alec, Ed, and pretty Marta, just beginning to blossom into a lovely young woman; about the cold rambling building they lived in with not enough money to heat it.

"That's where you were spending all your time when no one knew where you were?"

"Yes."

"Where did you get the money to pay for all of that, Kelly, if you didn't use any from your accounts?"

"I still had most of the award money from the newspaper articles."

"It must have taken all of it."

She shook her head. "I kept out some to last me till I could find a job when I went to Albuquerque."

Before he could say more, there was noise on the back porch—boots stomping to remove snow—and a moment later Carl came in, his face red with cold.

He grinned at them. "We have four beautiful pups, Kelly."

She rose quickly. "Already? She isn't due yet."

"Just a few days early," he said.

"Ebony's all right?"

He nodded. "A champion right down the line. Al and his boys are with her. We predict two more."

Jonathan's arm went around her. "There'll be a bonus in it for you if your prediction is correct."

"Why's that?" Carl asked.

Kelly's head tilted to look up at her husband and he smiled. "That's what we need, isn't it, sweetheart?"

She nodded, unable to speak, excitement and love for Jonathan all mixed up inside.

He turned her back to the table. "Come have coffee, Carl."

They finished the coffee and Carl left to see how the new additions were and Kelly said, "Let's go see them."

"You'd better put on some warm clothing," Jonathan told her.

She dressed in a hurry, the heaviest pants she had, a sweater under her heavy jacket and boots, all the while whispering a tiny prayer for six healthy pups.

"Come on, slowpoke," Jonathan said from the doorway. She half ran down the hall with him, wrapping her scarf around her head as she went, and caught her breath as the cold wind whipped snow into their faces. He half dragged her through the deep drifts to the warm stable where Ebony lay, tenderly bathing the mouse-sized bits squirming around her.

"Six, Kelly," Carl told her.

"Oh." She knelt beside Ebony and put her hand out. The gentle dark eyes looked her over, then she licked Kelly's hand, thus giving permission for her to touch the precious offspring.

She stood up, leaning against Jonathan. "Don't forget Carl's bonus." She drew a long breath. "A year's a long time but they've waited this long and can bear it, I guess. At least they have hope."

"Why a year, Kelly?" Jonathan's arm went around her.

"The schools usually like for the dog to be a year old before they start training him." She looked up at him and grinned. "Of course, we can invite Chuck Benson out to the ranch for his vacation and he could sort of show the kids how to handle a dog while he's here."

He laughed. "You're a scheming wench."

It was still dark when Kelly awakened and she lay still, her back against Jonathan's, not wanting to wake him. They were taking Ebony's four-week-old pups to Espanola to visit Angela and her children and excitement coursed through her body at the thought. She had written to tell Angela they would be there and that she would have a surprise for the children.

Jonathan turned over and put his arms across her. "What the devil are you awake at this hour for? You're shaking all over."

She shivered and moved her body into the curve of his. "I can't wait to see Andy and the puppies."

"Just Andy? What about the others?" he said.

"Yes, I know, but I mean—" His hand curved over her breast and she put hers over it, rubbing the wiry hairs on the back. She rolled over to face him. "He's so like Robbie, I guess he's my favorite even though I shouldn't admit it."

He kissed her nose. "I won't tell, I promise."

"Jonathan, did I ever tell you that I love you very much?"

He shook his head. "Not recently." He gathered her into his arms and they went back to sleep.

Mid-March winds howled off the mountains, but the day was clear and it was warm in the Cherokee. Kelly glanced over the back of her seat at the big box with Ebony's six puppies lumped in a sleepy pile, heads and feet sticking out at odd angles.

"Ebony wasn't too happy to let us borrow them, was she?" Jonathan asked.

"I don't blame her. We probably look like kidnappers." She squirmed in her seat as he made the turn that led to the sprawling house at the end of the lane.

He stopped at the back gate where she pointed, and smiled at her. "Go on ahead, Kelly. I'll bring the pups."

She was out of the Cherokee and, leaving the gate open for Jonathan, ran to the back door, noticing the two rows of neatly cut logs stacked on the porch. The door opened in answer to her knock and Angela put her hand out to pull Kelly inside and hug her close.

Before they could talk, a chorus of voices rang out. "Hi, Kelly."

"Hi, Marta and fellows," she said, her eyes going around the grinning faces to settle on Andy, blue eyes clear as he looked toward her, unsmiling.

"Jonathan's with me, Angela," she said, breathless, as she turned to open the door for him to enter, carrying the big box, which had squeaking noises coming from it.

"Hello, Angela," he said. "I was instructed to deliver this to you."

"Jonathan." She looked up at the tall man with dark eyes, deeply tanned skin on his face smooth, except for a network of small lines spread down the left cheek as though he had been scratched by a tree branch and the tan didn't quite cover it. She indicated the table where the children sat. "Put it there."

He placed the box on the table, and as Angela introduced the children, his eyes followed her pointing finger. "Andy, Joshua, Alec, Tony, Edward, and Marta."

Six pairs of eyes looked in his direction as they chorused a "Hello," more subdued than Kelly's greeting.

Kelly stepped behind Andy and reached into the box, lifting a wiggling black ball. "Hold out your hands, Andy," she told him.

Small hands opened in front of him and she put the warm furry animal into them. Tiny teeth nibbled at his thumb as he held on.

"A puppy?" Blue eyes swung upward toward Angela. "Mom, it's a puppy!" He giggled as the puppy licked his chin, happily going over his face with a pink tongue.

"They're Ebony's pups," Kelly explained.

The others were still as Andy held on to the squirming animal. Jonathan said quietly, "There's one for each of you."

Faces turned to him, waiting, and he lifted two pups at the time and placed them in reaching hands. The only sound were the yips from the small dogs as they explored chins and ears. As he gave up the last one, Jonathan looked at Kelly, who still waited behind Andy. Instead of the tears he expected, a wide grin showed her even white teeth, the end of her pink tongue caught between them. The green gaze met his and she winked, drawing her shoulders up in an ecstatic shrug. He felt a sudden rush of warm desire for the incorrigible woman-child who was his wife.

Angela invited them to lunch but Jonathan said, "Isn't pizza called for on Saturday? You fellas want to ride with me to get it?"

The boys put down the pups and scrambled for jackets. To everyone's surprise, Andy put the puppy down and went with them. Kelly, watching from the window, saw Jonathan explain the entrance to the vehicle but he didn't touch the boys as he waited for them to get in, except to give Andy a boost upward when his legs didn't reach.

She turned back to see Angela peering into the box. "They're so tiny. Will they be as big as Ebony?"

Kelly laughed. "You bet. You should see their father, Beowulf. He's even bigger than Ebony."

Marta still held a puppy, now sleeping in her arms. "How old are they?" she asked.

"Four weeks. Ebony will start weaning them in a week or so and we'll have to feed them."

"Will you sell them?" The question from Marta held fear.

Kelly looked at Angela. "They'll belong to you once they're trained. I have a friend who trains dogs for the blind and he'll teach you to care for them."

Marta's dark eyes no longer seemed clouded but sparkled at Angela. "Mom?"

"I don't understand, Kelly." She hesitated. "I'm not sure we can take care of them."

"Jonathan has set up a contract with local people here and you'll have supplies and veterinary services furnished as you need them."

Angela sat down by Marta and stared at Kelly, who smiled at her. "I see you ordered more wood. It certainly helps heat this room."

Angela shook her head. "Mr. Quantzal delivered the wood and said it was paid for."

Kelly silently blessed the man. Lots of people had big hearts once they knew there was a need, she decided.

The noise that accompanied one big man and five young ones interrupted them. Jonathan carried three flat boxes that trailed a delightful smell of cheese and spices.

The puppies were removed to a spot near the stove while everyone ate, the young voices arguing over names for the dogs they would acquire.

"I'll call mine Blackie," Josh said.

Kelly laughed. "They're all jet-black, Josh."

"Oh, well." He grinned in her direction. "They'll all come when I call." A general razzing greeted that statement.

"May I be excused?" Andy, sitting near Kelly, asked.

Angela answered. "Yes, Andy. The box with the puppies is to your left near the stove." The small figure slid off the bench and headed straight for the box and, a moment later, sat cross-legged with a puppy nestled close to him.

Jonathan leaned back, wiping his mouth with his napkin. "Angela, I invited the boys to the ranch two weeks from now if you don't mind. You and Marta are to come too, if you like."

Silence reigned as Angela thought about it. "It would be very nice," she said finally.

A collectively held breath was let go and everyone talked at once as Kelly's glance met Jonathan's. She smiled just for him alone.

Clouds sailed from the west skimming low on the mountaintops as they passed Santa Fe, turning toward the ranch.

"Will we be likely to have more snow?" Kelly asked.

"Yes. Even late March is far from tame here, Kelly."

She sighed, dreamy eyes on her husband. "Why didn't you invite the children for next weekend?"

His eyes left the road to meet her gaze. "We'll be on our honeymoon next week."

She sat up straight, no longer half asleep. "Honeymoon? We've been married seven months."

"Does that make a difference?" He flashed her a grin. "We have all the preliminaries taken care of and we can enjoy the island of Kauai, which I hear is something to see."

"What preliminaries?" she persisted.

The look he gave her was no longer teasing. "You belong to me and there's no doubt about it, is there, Kelly?"

She unfastened the seat belt and slid to the console that separated the two seats. "I belong to you, Jonathan." Her hand rested on his thigh. "And you?"

"I'm all yours, Kelly," he answered. He pulled the Cherokee to the shoulder of the road and as he turned to her, she looked straight into the eyes of love.

HARLEQUIN
PREMIERE AUTHOR EDITIONS

6 top Harlequin authors—6 of their best books!

1. JANET DAILEY Giant of Mesabi

2. CHARLOTTE LAMB Dark Master

3. ROBERTA LEIGH Heart of the Lion

4. ANNE MATHER Legacy of the Past

5. ANNE WEALE Stowaway

6. VIOLET WINSPEAR The Burning Sands

Harlequin is proud to offer these 6 exciting romance novels by 6 of our most popular authors. In brand-new beautifully designed covers, each Harlequin Premiere Author Edition is a bestselling love story—a contemporary, compelling and passionate read to remember!

Available in September wherever paperback books are sold, or through Harlequin Reader Service. Simply complete and mail the coupon below.

- -

Enter a uniquely exciting new world with

Harlequin American Romance ™

Harlequin American Romances are the first romances to explore today's love relationships. These compelling novels reach into the hearts and minds of women across America... probing the most intimate moments of romance, love and desire.

You'll follow romantic heroines and irresistible men as they boldly face confusing choices. Career first, love later? Love without marriage? Long-distance relationships? All the experiences that make love real are captured in the tender, loving pages of **Harlequin American Romances**.

What makes American women so different when it comes to love? Find out with **Harlequin American Romance!**

Send for your introductory FREE book now!

Get this book FREE!

Mail to:
Harlequin Reader Service

In the U.S.
2504 West Southern Avenue
Tempe, AZ 85282

In Canada
649 Ontario Street
Stratford, Ontario N5A 6W2

YES! I want to be one of the first to discover **Harlequin American Romance.** Send me FREE and without obligation *Twice in a Lifetime.* If you do not hear from me after I have examined my FREE book, please send me the 4 new **Harlequin American Romances** each month as soon as they come off the presses. I understand that I will be billed only $2.25 for each book (total $9.00). There are no shipping or handling charges. There is no minimum number of books that I have to purchase. In fact, I may cancel this arrangement at any time. *Twice in a Lifetime* is mine to keep as a FREE gift, even if I do not buy any additional books.

Name	(please print)

Address	Apt. no.

City	State/Prov.	Zip/Postal Code

Signature (If under 18, parent or guardian must sign.)

Yours FREE, with a home subscription to SUPERROMANCE™

Now you never have to miss reading the newest **SUPERROMANCES**... because they'll be delivered right to your door.

Start with your **FREE** LOVE BEYOND DESIRE. You'll be enthralled by this powerful love story... from the moment Robin meets the dark, handsome Carlos and finds herself involved in the jealousies, bitterness and secret passions of the Lopez family. Where her own forbidden love threatens to shatter her life.

Your **FREE** LOVE BEYOND DESIRE is only the beginning. A subscription to **SUPERROMANCE** lets you look forward to a long love affair. Month after month, you'll receive four love stories of heroic dimension. Novels that will involve you in spellbinding intrigue, forbidden love and fiery passions.

You'll begin this series of sensuous, exciting contemporary novels... written by some of the top romance novelists of the day... with four every month.

And this big value... each novel, almost 400 pages of compelling reading... is yours for only $2.50 a book. Hours of entertainment every month for so little. Far less than a first-run movie or pay-TV. Newly published novels, with beautifully illustrated covers, filled with page after page of delicious escape into a world of romantic love... delivered right to your home.

Readers rave about Harlequin American Romance!

"...the best series of modern romances
I have read...great, exciting, stupendous,
wonderful."
>   —S.E.,* Coweta, Oklahoma

"...they are absolutely fantastic...going to be
a smash hit and hard to keep on the
bookshelves."
>   —P.D., Easton, Pennsylvania

"The American line is great. I've enjoyed
every one I've read so far."
>   —W.M.K., Lansing, Illinois

"...the best stories I have read in a long
time."
>   —R.H., Northport, New York

*Names available on request.

A Harlequin

ROBERTA LEIGH

Collector's Edition

A specially designed collection of six exciting
love stories by one of the world's favorite
romance writers—Roberta Leigh, author of
more than 60 bestselling novels!

1 **Love in Store**
2 **Night of Love**
3 **Flower of the Desert**

4 **The Savage Aristocrat**
5 **The Facts of Love**
6 **Too Young to Love**

Available in August wherever paperback books are sold, or available
through Harlequin Reader Service. Simply complete and mail the
coupon below.

Harlequin Reader Service

In the U.S.
P.O. Box 52040
Phoenix, AZ 85072-9988

In Canada
649 Ontario Street
Stratford, Ontario N5A 6W2

Please send me the following editions of the Harlequin Roberta Leigh
Collector's Editions. I am enclosing my check or money order for $1.95
for each copy ordered, plus 75¢ to cover postage and handling.

☐ 1   ☐ 2   ☐ 3   ☐ 4   ☐ 5   ☐ 6

Number of books checked_____ @ $1.95 each = $_____

N.Y. state and Ariz. residents add appropriate sales tax $_____

Postage and handling $_____.75_____

                               TOTAL $_____

I enclose_____
(Please send check or money order. We cannot be responsible for cash
sent through the mail.) Price subject to change without notice.

NAME_____
                         (Please Print)

ADDRESS_____ APT. NO._____

CITY_____

STATE/PROV._____ ZIP/POSTAL CODE_____

Offer expires 29 February 1984.   30856000000

RL-A